PRAISE FOR THE AUT*Wedding Favors*

NIKITA BLACK

"The stuff legends are made out of."   —*Midwest Book Review*

ALLYSON JAMES

"Hot! Hot! Hot! . . . If you enjoy stories full of action, both in the bedroom and out, this is one story you will want to read."
                                        —*The Romance Studio*

SHERI WHITEFEATHER

"Sensual, passionate, seductive—lose yourself in the romance of an amazing story."   —Jaci Burton, national bestselling author

Wedding Favors

NIKITA BLACK

ALLYSON JAMES

SHERI WHITEFEATHER

HEAT | NEW YORK

THE BERKLEY PUBLISHING GROUP
Published by the Penguin Group
Penguin Group (USA) Inc.
375 Hudson Street, New York, New York 10014, USA
Penguin Group (Canada), 90 Eglinton Avenue East, Suite 700, Toronto, Ontario M4P 2Y3, Canada
(a division of Pearson Penguin Canada Inc.)
Penguin Books Ltd., 80 Strand, London WC2R 0RL, England
Penguin Group Ireland, 25 St. Stephen's Green, Dublin 2, Ireland (a division of Penguin Books Ltd.)
Penguin Group (Australia), 250 Camberwell Road, Camberwell, Victoria 3124, Australia
(a division of Pearson Australia Group Pty. Ltd.)
Penguin Books India Pvt. Ltd., 11 Community Centre, Panchsheel Park, New Delhi—110 017, India
Penguin Group (NZ), 67 Apollo Drive, Rosedale, North Shore 0632, New Zealand
(a division of Pearson New Zealand Ltd.)
Penguin Books (South Africa) (Pty.) Ltd., 24 Sturdee Avenue, Rosebank, Johannesburg 2196,
South Africa

Penguin Books Ltd., Registered Offices: 80 Strand, London WC2R 0RL, England

This book is an original publication of The Berkley Publishing Group.

This is a work of fiction. Names, characters, places, and incidents either are the product of the authors' imaginations or are used fictitiously, and any resemblance to actual persons, living or dead, business establishments, events, or locales is entirely coincidental. The publisher does not have any control over and does not assume any responsibility for author or third-party websites or their content.

PRINTING HISTORY
Heat trade paperback edition / June 2010

Library of Congress Cataloging-in-Publication Data

Wedding favors / Nikita Black, Allyson James, Sheri Whitefeather. — Heat trade pbk. ed.
    p. cm.
  ISBN 978-0-425-23458-7 (trade pbk.)
  1. Bridesmaids—Fiction.   2. New Orleans—Fiction.   3. Erotic stories, American.
I. Black, Nikita. Binding her heart.   II. James, Allyson. Mortal sensations.   III. Whitefeather,
Sheri. Dungeon dreams.
  PS648.E7W45 2010
  813'.01083538—dc22
                                                                              2010006711

PRINTED IN THE UNITED STATES OF AMERICA

10   9   8   7   6   5   4   3   2   1

Contents

Binding Her Heart

NIKITA BLACK

For Dr. Adrienne Ellis Reeves,
one of the most amazing, inspiring women
I've ever had the privilege of knowing.

Prologue

FRENCH QUARTER, NEW ORLEANS

JAILLISSEMENT DE PLAISIR . . . THE FOUNTAIN OF PLEASURE

Hidden away in a forgotten, overgrown courtyard deep in the heart of the French Quarter, the bubbling marble fountain was aptly named.

If one believed in voodoo . . .

Legend had it that the beautiful, ancient fountain could cast a powerful and erotic lover's spell through a simple wish and the tossing of a coin—whether deliberate or innocently done.

Tout quoi vous voulez, the inscription read. *Everything you wish.*

Was it true? Was the *Jaillissement de Plaisir* magical? Could it weave an unbreakable spell of sensual, carnal pleasure around a couple who'd once met at the dancing feet of its three beguiling muses?

Or was it all just a huge coincidence?

Tessa Kittredge would always wonder . . .

Chapter 1

FRENCH QUARTER, NEW ORLEANS
PRESENT DAY

"*This* is a *brothel*?"

Tessa Kittredge could not be*lieve* she'd let her friend Laura talk her into this . . . this . . . in*sane* idea.

A bachelorette party at a brothel.

"I keep telling you. It's not a brothel, it's a private sex club. Here in the Quarter it's known as a *maison*." Laura—the bride—corrected her choice of nomenclature with a mischievous wink. "Not brothel. *Maison*."

Oh, excuse me. *Maison*. Like there was a difference?

Seriously. Not only was the party to be held at this house of ill repute—however upscale—but the bride had actually arranged for her bridesmaids to become part of the evening's activities—as merchandise!

Oh. My. God.

"Let's see. The guy at the door took my bank information

not just to pay for drinks, but to receive payment for my sexual favors. What part of *that* isn't a brothel?" If Tessa weren't so appalled, she'd have to admit there was a certain cosmic humor to the situation. After all, what was marriage but an elaborate, lifelong contract for sex? Well. At least until one of the partners got tired of the other.

Not that she was cynical or anything.

Still.

"*Possible* sexual favors," Laura corrected again. "Just one option on the menu."

"How do they even get around the law? Last I heard, prostitution was illegal."

"This is a private club, members only, where sexual fantasies are fulfilled. All completely legal. Being paid for sex is just one of the many scenarios you can choose. Though seriously, when was the last time you made a thousand bucks for a few hours' work? Well . . . pleasure."

"Very funny."

"Of course, it's not called that on the invoice. The rooms here are called pleasure chambers, which is technically what the patron pays for, and your remuneration is a consultant's fee."

"Consultant, eh." Tessa tugged at the short skirt of the slinky blue strapless dress Laura had provided for her to wear and glanced nervously around the main floor of the *maison*, Chez Duchesne. Once you got through the strict security check, the bar and reception area appeared completely normal, like those of any other luxurious boutique hotel. Except for the part where some of the guests were walking around wearing nothing but sexy underwear—and some not even *that* much. Along with the golden masks most of the women and some of the men wore to hide their identities.

Which meant they were available. *Available.*

For purchase. Or any number of other sexual diversions.

Oh. My. *God.*

Tessa had been stunned when the other two bridesmaids donned their masks with alacrity and disappeared within seconds of the guard letting them inside.

"This is crazy. Even for you," Tessa murmured to Laura.

Her friend looped arms with her and urged her farther into the sumptuously appointed room. Music pulsed in the background, punctuated by bursts of coy laughter and the tinkle of crystal glasses. The exotic scent of jasmine filled the air. "Darling, *every* woman fantasizes about being a whore at one time or another," Laura said. "Don't tell me you never have, because I know better."

"Fantasies are one thing," Tessa pointed out, her cheeks warming at the candid insight. She had to remember that Laura knew her better than anyone else did. Being college roommates first time away from a repressive home tended to bring out one's most well-kept secrets. "Even schoolgirl fantasies. That doesn't mean I'd actually do it in real life. Especially now that I know better."

Laura smiled meaningfully. "Tell me, how many one-night stands have you had in the past ten years?"

There was no use prevaricating. "One or two," Tessa grudgingly admitted. "But that was different."

"True. Play your cards right, and tonight you'll walk away with a nice fat paycheck instead of shattered illusions."

A thousand dollars for an hour, five grand for the night—which was only half the full charge. Outrageous what men were willing to pay for no strings. Not that she was terribly surprised. Bitter? Hell, not her. It was actually better this way.

More honest. In theory, she had no problem with the arrangement. Just not for her.

"I don't need the money," she said firmly. She had a great job as a landscape architect. Admittedly, not for a thousand dollars an hour.

"After that last nasty breakup, you could use a little fun," Laura pointed out, steering her toward the bar. "A night of unreserved sexual fantasy. Trust me, it'll be amazing."

Easy for *her* to say. Laura had always been the impetuous, spontaneous, wild-child friend. The one that careful, orderly, good-girl Tessa had always envied just a little. Okay, a lot. But she had already spotted the groom among the guests, so she knew very well what fantasy *they* were playing at tonight, and it wasn't sex for money. She, however, had no one waiting in the wings to make the scenario less . . . alarming. Not here. Not back home. Hell, not ever again, if she had anything to say about it.

"You know I'm not into sex with strangers," she said over the pulsing throb of the music. "I'm not eighteen and naïve anymore. Besides, I'm done with men for a while." She was tired of being unfulfilled and then bearing the blame for being too hard to please. Could she help it if the guys she'd met sucked at turning her on?

The men around them were glancing over now, openly interested. The heat in Tessa's cheeks intensified. It made her feel . . . exposed. On display. And surprisingly, a little excited. She couldn't deny the fantasy of selling oneself to a stranger was a powerful one. Heck, doing anything sexual with a complete stranger was, for that matter.

"You don't have to sell yourself," Laura assured her, her eyes flirting openly with one of the lookers. "Not unless you want to. Hell, you could even pay one of these guys to please *you*. No rules, Tessa. No requirements, other than to have a good time."

Yeah, they'd already been through all of this. Outside, in that eerie, overgrown courtyard next door, where she, Laura, and the other two bridesmaids had stopped to make a wish at an unnervingly evocative voodoo fountain. The fountain, called the *Jaillissement de Plaisir*—a more than suggestive name, if her high school French served her—was supposed to bring immense sexual pleasure and everlasting love to all who made an offering to it. After giggling through their wishes and tossing their coins—which Tessa had palmed rather than let fly into the water—they'd sat down on the crumbling fountain wall and Laura had revealed the shocking details of the bachelorette party.

But to be honest, Tessa hadn't been able to concentrate on the explanation. Chills kept running up and down her spine. That deserted courtyard had seemed so strangely, spookily familiar. Like she'd been there before. And the three half-nude muses holding up the fountain all seemed to be dancing just for her, gazing at her with alluring eyes, beckoning her to join them in their wantonness. Not to mention the unnerving feeling that someone had been watching her the whole time. Someone male and hidden from view, with a powerful aura she could almost taste in the sultry night air.

All day she'd been feeling restless, like she was waiting for something to happen. Something that would change her life forever.

Could this be it?

"Come on," Laura said, leading her deeper into the decadence. "Let yourself go. If you don't want to have sex with anyone, don't. Just indulge yourself and enjoy the possibilities. *You* decide how far things go."

"I don't know if I can do this," Tessa murmured, torn between the temptation of the fantasy and fear of the reality.

Laura handed her a golden mask. "Of course you can. Darling, for one night, give yourself permission to become whomever you want, to do whatever you wish." She smiled mysteriously. "Who knows what erotic, sensual spell the *Jaillissement de Plaisir* has already cast upon you? You might just find you like it."

Chapter 2

Treves "Shay" Duchesne strode through the main atrium of the *maison* that bore his family name, heading for the bar. He nodded politely to the many women and even a man or two who turned to flaunt their bodies and smile at him flirtatiously. As on every other night, it was like walking a sexual gauntlet.

"Not tonight, *cher*," he murmured a dozen times without slowing his pace, his own smile firmly affixed to his lips despite his anger and frustration.

Thwarted. *Again.*

Putain de foutre. Fucking hell. This was all that damned fountain's fault.

Jaillissement de Plaisir. Shay snorted derisively. *Not.* More like *Jaillissement de Merde.*

The thing was hexed, all right. But it did *not* grant endless love and pleasure. Not by a long shot. It brought nothing but everlasting trouble.

"Something wrong, boss?" Piron, his friend and Chez Duchesne's majordomo, asked when he went straight to the top shelf and poured himself a shot of twenty-five-year-old bourbon.

Shay tossed it back and poured another. "We've been denied again."

"The permit?"

He nodded. For fifteen years his family had been trying to turn that eyesore fountain courtyard into a beautiful outdoor restaurant—gourmet food, beignets, the whole New Orleans thing. Fifteen years! But each time, the building permit had been turned down. All because he wanted to repair the ancient brick walkways so they wouldn't be a safety hazard. The Historical Society insisted that would be changing the original character of the important landmark. Never mind it was his own great-great-great-*grand-père* who had laid the bricks himself. *Dieu!*

"I own the damn property! Historical *foutu* landmark, *mon cul.*" Jesus. It wasn't like he planned to touch the damn fountain. He'd carefully planned a new intimate gourmet dining area with the *Jaillissement* as its centerpiece. Hell, the fountain would only enhance the restaurant's appeal to the upscale clientele. But not if they tripped and broke their necks on the uneven bricks. "I hope that charlatan Marie Laveau rots in hell for casting her silly love spells at its base for my sadly delusioned ancestor."

The story went, when Shay's great-great-great-*grand-père* came over from France and built Chez Duchesne, he invited the beautiful New Orleans voodoo queen to come and give her blessing to the exotic *maison*, which at the time had been a full-fledged bordello. She'd instantly become enchanted with the *Jaillissement de Plaisir* fountain, and supposedly, the courtyard became one of her favorite gris-gris spots, along with occasionally gracing the *patron de la maison* with her favors. Or so the story went.

Piron shrugged. "A hundred seventy years later, her spells, dey still seem to be working." He gestured to the full house. "Place is packed, everyone enjoying the fruits of her magic."

"Don't *you* start." Shay threw back his second shot with a scowl. "That's due solely to my hard work, and my father's, and his father's before him. Not some witchy curse."

Piron chuckled. "*Mais*, yeah. Goes without saying."

"Stupid superstitions."

Piron slid a key card into Shay's jacket pocket and winked. "Forget about that ol' courtyard tonight. Pick you out a woman, you. Feel better in da morning."

"Not in the mood," he practically growled.

Despite that, Shay's thoughts strayed to the woman he'd seen making a wish at the fountain a little while ago.

Yeah, that was the *other* problem. Of all days to see *her* again—the little vixen who'd sent his life careening down this path of voodoo *merde*. Not that he believed in hexes or spells. Not for a single second. He just needed to find the woman, confront her, and erase her from his memory once and for all. Because two kids tossing coins into some stupid fountain together—*accidentally* yet—had *not* caused his never-ending difficulties with that goddamn courtyard nor his inability to find a lover he was happy with for more than three nights running. The thought was ridiculous, *completement fou*.

This wasn't the first time he'd seen her. Tonight he'd watched the apparition from his past in the falling darkness from his private balcony overlooking the courtyard. And been kicked in the gut by the still-vivid memory of that long auburn hair, the proud, distinctive set to her slim shoulders, the shocked expression in her youthful green eyes as, in his own adolescent cockiness, he'd tried to kiss her. He could still feel the impact of her outraged smack on the cheek . . . just as he had relived in his mind a score of times over the past fifteen years.

Of course, so far it had never actually *been* the woman that sweet *jeune fille* must have grown into by now. But one of these days, it would be her. The *real* her. She would come back. Drawn to that damned fountain by the same insane compulsion that constantly gnawed at his own insides. He felt the certainty of it as surely as he felt the creeping boredom that promised to slowly suffocate him if he didn't find something more to fill his life. Something real. Something like—God knew what.

Merde.

He slammed his empty glass onto the bar in frustration. "Have you seen an auburn-haired woman in a short blue dress?" he demanded of Piron. "She was at the *Jaillissement* earlier. With three other women. They may have come in together a few minutes ago."

Piron's brow arched. "Your pretty obsession again?"

Always a comedian. "Just answer the damn question."

Piron jerked his chin toward the far end of the bar. "You mean dat *fille*, over dere?"

Shay turned to look at the woman his friend had indicated. And froze where he stood. The fine hairs on the back of his neck stood up in shock and amazement.

Le bon Dieu.

It *was* her.

The same beautiful fall of auburn hair. The same proud, slim shoulders. The same lush, tempting lips.

And she was just putting on a golden mask.

Chapter 3

Tessa lifted the featherlight mask to her face, testing the feel of it against her skin. It felt . . . unnervingly good. Cool and satin-smooth. Mysterious and sexy. For a breathless second she actually considered leaving it on.

What would it be like to choose a man and let him explore her body? To let him demand licentious acts of her? To submit to his every sexual whim, and let him pay for the privilege?

A wash of goose bumps spilled down her bare arms. Laura was so right. Tessa *had* fantasized more than once about doing just that. Having amazing, anonymous sex with a hot guy whose only connection to her was a straightforward business arrangement. No games, no future expectations. A night of blissful carnal excess without any of the usual emotional fallout. A man she could totally be herself around without worrying that she didn't measure up to some unachievable standard of perfect feminine behavior. A chance to explore the shadow side of herself she'd never quite dared acknowledge, except in the forbidden dreams she would occasionally wake up from, panting from a mortifyingly intense climax. But this time she'd be awake.

The prospect turned her on. A lot. She felt her body stir with an unfamiliar sexual hunger, urging her to let herself go. Just this once . . .

But no. How could she even consider it? The whole idea was too outrageous. Too risky. Too . . . unlike her. Decisively, she lowered the mask and turned back to Laura. "Honest to God, Laur, I just can't—"

But her friend had vanished.

In her place stood a man. Tall, dark, and exquisitely handsome, he wore an elegant suit that fit him to perfection and a button-down shirt with an open collar that revealed an enticing triangle of tan skin and the barest hint of black chest hair peeking out.

For a split second she faltered. He seemed . . . familiar. Had they met before?

God, only in her most secret fantasies. She definitely would have remembered a man this gorgeous in real life.

He was gazing down at her with an intense regard that instantly kicked her heartbeat into overdrive. "Let me help you put that on," he offered, reaching for the mask. Flavored with a French Creole accent, the words were melodic, hypnotic. *Seductive.*

Her throat went dry instantly. "No. Thank you." She managed not to croak. Too badly. "I'm not—I was just, um, testing how it felt."

He tilted his head. "And?"

She swallowed, knowing what he was really asking. *Was she available?* For sex.

She licked her lips. Oh, Lord. *Was* she? If ever she were to do this crazy thing, now was the time. This man was . . . holy hell . . . pure walking sex.

And *way* out of her league.

"I—" This time her voice did crack. She cleared her throat. "I don't think so."

He smiled, undaunted. "Afraid?"

Was he *kid*ding? "Any rational woman would be," she told him, fighting desperately to gather her quickly flagging wits. And to douse the illicit flames of desire heating her belly.

"*Mais*, a rational woman wouldn't be found in a place like this," he observed. He slipped the mask from her fingers, brushing his hand against hers as he did so. Sparks danced along her skin. *Ho*-boy.

"It's all my friend's doing," she said, her eyes drawn unwillingly as he ran his forefinger slowly and deliberately along the gilded edge of the mask. The gesture was disturbingly sensual . . . as though he were touching *her* instead. Heat flashed down her chest, zinging through her breasts. She jerked her gaze away. "This wasn't my idea."

"And yet, here you are." He took a step closer to her. "All on your own. Not a friend in sight."

His gaze shifted down as her nipples tightened to hard, painful knots. Or maybe it was the low-cut dress that attracted his regard. Or both.

Ho. Boy. She should get out of there. *Now.* Away from this insane situation and this alarmingly sexy man. But her body just wasn't getting the message. It wanted to stay. It wanted to indulge in all of those outrageous fantasies of helpless submission she'd only dreamed of.

Would it be so wicked to give herself to him? To let him use her body for his pleasure? To grant his every wish and fulfill his every sexual demand? And by doing so, fulfill her own fantasy?

Don't do it! her inner good girl cried. *Yes! Dare!* her fantasy self urged.

She stepped back from him. "I should go."

"*Non.*" He lifted the mask once again to her face, capturing her eyes as he adjusted it snugly in place. He placed the elastic around the back of her head. "You should stay." Feathering a lock of her hair between his fingers, he let the strands cascade along the side of the mask. It was all she could do not to press her cheek into his palm. "At least let me buy you a drink," he said, "before you go."

What was *wrong* with her? She wanted to refuse. She *should* refuse! But there was something so powerful about this man's attraction, something so compelling, that her mouth just wouldn't form the words. It was as though he'd cast some kind of sensual spell over her body, filling it with a rush of urgent sexual desire. A *Jaillissement de Plaisir*. Like that mysterious fountain in the courtyard.

She hesitated a shade too long. He offered her his arm with a very gratified male smile, as though the night's end were a forgone conclusion. "*Vien.* Come."

Adrenaline sang through her limbs. *Oh, God.* Did she really want to do this?

Laura's words echoed. *Give yourself permission to become whomever you want, to do whatever you wish.*

And she *did* want to. For once in her life, she wanted to just let herself go. Live the breathless fantasy. *Be* that brave woman who dared the outrageous, the risky. The downright dangerous.

Swallowing her overwhelming qualms, she reached out to take his arm and whispered tremulously, "How long do you want me for?"

His smile turned positively sinful, filled with wicked promise. "*Cher.* How long do you have?"

He led her through the bar area and out through a set of open French doors into a large and beautiful outdoor courtyard. As a landscape architect, Tessa saw at once the careful thought that had gone into the seemingly random and casual plan. Strings of fairy lights lit the way. Next to a winding brick path, round wrought-iron bistro tables sat tucked away in the strategically placed dark recesses among a jungle of verdant blossoming plants and vines. The heavy, sultry night air outside was spiced with soft music and the exotic scents of jasmine, gardenias, and antique roses. Couples sat talking intimately, kissing, touching, lost to the world. It was completely enchanting.

The man pulled her off the path and led her to a hidden niche containing a gurgling water feature. This one was newer than the fountain in the other courtyard next door, depicting a nude, embracing couple who kissed under a cascade of water.

His hand lighted on her bare shoulder. At his discreet but deliberate touch, she straightened and turned to look up at him. His face was shadowed, all olive skin, sculpted angles, and dark bedroom eyes. With a finger he tilted her face up to study it in the moonlight. Her mask shifted slightly, a subtle reminder of her anonymity.

"What shall I call you?" he murmured.

She debated lying and decided against it. "Tessa," she said. He'd probably assume it wasn't her real name, anyway.

"*Enchanté*, Tessa." He bent toward her and brushed his lips over hers, startling her. "I am Shay."

"Hello," she whispered.

Just then, the majordomo appeared carrying a tray with two glasses of champagne. Wordlessly, Shay took them and handed one to her as the waiter disappeared again. "Champagne?"

"Thank you."

He lifted his glass and touched it to hers. "*Tout quoi ti veut.*"

She recognized the sentiment from the inscription around the base of the old fountain next door. *Everything you wish for.* "Everything?" she asked, wondering if this man could deliver what no man before had been able to.

"*Mais*, yeah. And much more," he assured her, and they drank. "The question is, what is it you want?"

"I don't know," she hedged.

"Oh, I think you do," he refuted. He set his glass on the edge of the fountain and stepped behind her. He put his hands on her upper arms and gently steered her around in a circle as he said, "Look carefully. Take it all in. Then tell me what excites you. What fantasy being played out makes you long to change places with the woman?"

Several tables were visible, along with the couples sitting at them. One man was in the process of slowly disrobing his masked companion. Another woman was already nude, the man fondling and kissing her body openly. At a third table, a woman was kneeling in front of the man's chair. Tessa couldn't see what she was doing, but she could imagine.

She licked her lips, a tingle of arousal shimmering through her at the stark displays. "Don't they mind that others are watching?"

He smiled. "I think that's the whole point. Look up."

She did. For the first time she noticed the walls of the buildings around them were punctuated with large windows and French doors with balconies that opened onto the enclosed courtyard. Some had the curtains drawn, but just as many stood wide-open, revealing in more or less detail what was going on in the rooms behind them.

Her lips parted in shock. Several couples were in flagrante, oblivious to the many eyes that followed their graphic exhibitions. Or perhaps, as Shay suggested, that was part of their fantasy—knowing they were being observed.

On one of the balconies, a woman was draped over the ornate wrought iron, being spanked by a tall masked man behind her. Her soft cries echoed through the courtyard.

Tessa gasped softly. He was masked, so she was paying *him* to do that to her. Omigod. Was that—

"Ah," Shay murmured, interrupting her astonishment. "*C'est bon.*"

"What?" Surely, he didn't think— She started to step away from him, to explain that no way was she interested in— But instead of letting her go, he wrapped his hand around her jaw and covered her mouth with his. She let out another gasp of shock. He urged her chin down farther still with his thumb, and his tongue swept in to slick over hers.

He tasted of old bourbon, chicory coffee, and the kind of

man who always got what he wanted. She shivered with unwilling excitement. Because right now, what he wanted was . . . *her*.

His kiss was forceful and bold and toe-curlingly delicious. And oh, Lord, so dangerous. And it got her to thinking—in what little part of her mind that could still function—that she owed Laura an apology. Because maybe this whole fantasy thing wasn't such a bad idea, after all.

Chapter 4

Bon Dieu. For one so unschooled in the ways of the *maison,* the woman kissed like a practiced odalisque.

Shay's heart was slamming in his chest, and his cock waking up with a vengeance from its slumber of ennui. *Not* what he had expected from the little girl who had once clipped him in the jaw rather than kiss him. Perhaps those coins accidentally flung in the fountain all those years ago had worked their magic at last.

Reluctantly, he broke the kiss, giving her lips a final slow lick. But he didn't let her go. *"Vien,"* he said and banded his arm around her shoulders. "Come with me."

Tessa looked as stunned as he felt. *Bon.* Perhaps a bit more. She almost stumbled as he led her back into the *maison's* lobby from the courtyard, past the bar and through toward the grand staircase, to take her upstairs.

"But . . . Shay, wait."

Inside the salon, the heavy beat of the music matched the pounding of his heart. He halted at the foot of the stairs. "What is it, *ma douce?*"

"I—" She swallowed. "I'm not sure—"

Hesitation? Not with the taste of her surrender still sweet on his tongue. He would have her. Of this, there was no doubt.

He regarded her with growing interest. Her resistance told him her sensual skill was instinctive rather than earned. It made him desire her all the more. "But you want me, *non?*"

She blinked. Her cheeks turned red, and she looked down. "Yes," she whispered. "But this is outside my experience. I don't know if I can do it."

He was charmed by her genuine reluctance to give in to her natural desires. It turned him on even more. Her reticence pointed to a guileless innocence that was entirely unique in this place of jaded encounters.

Yet despite her somewhat prim façade, he sensed a wanton lurking behind it, hungering to come out and play. And he was just the man to tempt her. He wondered what would finally push her over the edge. Did she want money? Was that her fantasy?

"I'll double the usual fee if you come with me upstairs," he offered.

Her eyes darted up, widening. She started to shake her head. "I'm not a—"

He leaned down and murmured in her ear, "Admit it, you want to know what it's like to be with a man who craves you so badly he'll pay a small fortune just to be inside you."

Her blush deepened, and he could see her nipples clearly under the silky fabric of her dress, tight and peaked. He knew

it. She wanted him as much as he wanted her. He wasn't the
only one caught in this invisible net of ravenous desire. Almost
as if . . .

Unbidden, a shiver ran down his spine. *Simple lust,* he told
himself. Their raging attraction had nothing to do with spellbound fountains or irrational curses or imaginary voodoo.

"Do you?" she asked. "Do you want me that much?"

In answer, he pulled her into his arms. With a hand to her
backside, he pressed her body into his. Let her feel the thick,
unyielding ridge of his arousal. "Take a wild guess, *cher.*"

Her breath sucked in. He knew he was well-endowed.
Enough so to cause many a maidenly heart to flutter. Tessa was
no exception.

"*Tout quoi ti veut,*" he whispered seductively.

This time, he knew exactly what she craved. And he planned
to give her all of it. Every last naughty wish.

Unable to restrain his eagerness, Shay swept Tessa up into
his arms and mounted the grand staircase before she could
respond. She didn't object. *Merci Dieu.*

He felt the eyes of everyone in the room upon them and
heard more than one feminine sigh. Tonight, as on every other
night in the *maison*, he could have chosen any woman there,
and she'd have willingly spread her thighs for him. Yet he felt
immeasurably triumphant at the impending conquest of the shy
beauty squirming in his arms.

Her dress had ridden up, exposing the delicate white lace of
her panties. "*Arrête!*" he ordered as he carried her up the stairs,
bringing her into his world of carnal indulgence. The squirming
stopped abruptly. "I want you to kiss me. Now."

Her green eyes reflected the glitter of the chandelier above them. A subtle change darkened them. "And if I refuse?"

The corner of his lip curled up. Had the game begun already? Excellent.

"We have an agreement. You are mine for tonight," he reminded her. "My sexual possession, to do with as I please. You must not refuse me anything." His cock thickened in anticipation of all the ways he would persuade her to do his bidding. "Those are my conditions."

A quiver traveled through her body. "What if you ask me to do something I don't want to?"

"Trust me, Tessa. Put yourself in my capable hands," he said. "I promise you won't be disappointed."

After a heartbeat of hesitation, she tightened her arms around his neck and reached her mouth up to his in acquiescence. "All right." Her tongue swept across the crease of his lips, teasing them open. A groan swirled through him, emerging as a low rumble. Their mouths fused, feeding each other in a ravenous kiss. No need to look where they were going; after a lifetime of climbing these stairs to the seraglio of pleasure chambers, his feet knew the way all on their own.

He reached the landing on the second floor. So immersed was he in the kiss that he almost kept going, all the way up to his private rooms on the third floor. He caught himself just in time. Where was his head? He'd never taken a woman to his private rooms. Ever.

He let her feet drop to the plush Oriental carpet and started to back her forcibly down the hallway, kissing her hard, catching her up against him when she snagged her heel walking backward. "Kick them off," he ordered, and she let first one, then the other shoe fall away.

He swiftly unzipped her dress and shoved it down. Before she could protest with more than a breathless gasp, it lay behind them in a receding puddle on the hallway floor. *Mais*, no matter. The observant staff would make sure the clothes found their way back to her by morning. *Dieu*. Her strapless bra and panties were expensive works of art and sexy as hell.

"Better," he murmured and crushed her against him.

Her body was a work of art, too, her curves lush, her waist narrow. Smooth and pale, her skin was even silkier than the dress had been. His hands itched to explore her. He walked them faster, kissing her, fumbling the key card out of his jacket pocket.

He found the right door and powered through it, hauling her up against the wall as he slammed the door shut with a swift kick.

She made a throaty, sensual sound and climbed his body like a wild kitten. The wanton had emerged.

He forced himself to stop before he took her right there against the wall. *Mon Dieu*. They were both breathing hard, their bodies taut with need. But he had no interest in finishing this quickly. He wanted it to last all night.

Taking a steadying breath, he let her kiss him as he marshaled his willpower to slow down. She tasted like heaven itself. And there was a quality to her kisses he'd rarely experienced— complete immersion, no artifice, no self-consciousness at all. Totally there with him in the moment.

"Take off your clothes," she urged him between kisses, and reached for his lapels.

He let her slide off his jacket. She went for his shirt buttons, and he allowed her to pop them open one by one. The brush of her hands on his bare skin sent gooseflesh shimmering down his chest. She started to push the shirt from his shoulders.

"Non," he said and set her down, stepping away from her.

"What's wrong?" She pressed her body back against the wall, palms flat, looking so incredibly sexy and disheveled—and uncertain—that he nearly weakened.

"Nothing's wrong. But *I'm* in charge. You do as *I* say, not the other way around."

"Oh," she said, her expression going even more unsure. "Sorry. I'm, um—"

"A strong woman," he completed for her. "Used to giving orders, not taking them."

She blinked. "Two out of three, anyway," she murmured with a smile.

He smiled back. He liked a strong woman. It made her submission so much sweeter. And she wanted to submit to him. He'd seen it in her eyes as she'd watched the woman on the balcony being disciplined by her lover. That was the scenario that had most captured her attention . . . and heated her passion. "Fight me if you like," he told her. "I enjoy a bit of rough when the woman's into it."

"That's okay," she said, uncomfortable at his invitation to be taken by force. "I'm here because I want to be with you."

"Bon," he said, turned, and walked over to the bed. "I understand. Then let's begin, shall we?"

Chapter 5

Once again, Tessa felt the blood rush to her face. She didn't know whether to be excited beyond belief or terrified at what was about to happen.

"Haven't we started already?" she asked Shay, her heart pounding like a bass drum. She couldn't exactly remember agreeing to this, but here she was, so she must have.

"Hardly," he said and plucked a bottle of champagne from a stand by the bed. He turned and regarded her as he expertly worked the cork out, the bottle dripping melted ice onto the deep Oriental carpet. "Walk over to the French doors," he said, and poured one glass of the amber liquid—just *one* she noted—before slipping off his shoes and climbing onto the high four-poster bed. He settled against the headboard and gazed at her expectantly.

Her legs felt wobbly, leaden, as if any second now she would slide down the wall supporting her, unable to walk.

"Why?" she asked. The curtains at the French doors that led to a narrow wrought-iron faux balcony were wide-open. She thought about the couples she'd seen earlier, making love in full view of the courtyard below. "Surely, you don't mean to . . ." *Oh, God.*

He took a sip of his champagne, leaning back among the pillows like a dissolute sultan surveying a new harem girl. "I haven't decided yet. Would it bother you?"

"Yes!" Her heartbeat took off at a gallop. Her gaze cut to the balcony. She couldn't even imagine being so exposed. It would be . . . *God help her.* She swallowed and looked back at him. She didn't say a word, but he must have read something dark and forbidden in her eyes.

"Shall we try it and see?" His voice was smooth as molasses, and tempting as the Devil's.

"Let's not," she said. But it didn't sound convincing, even to herself.

"Don't forget, you still have your mask on. No one will know it's you."

Again, the balcony drew her gaze. The idea was outrageously wicked . . . and sinfully arousing.

"I want you to walk over and open the doors," he commanded. When she didn't move, he said, "Do it, Tessa."

She took a deep breath. There was no reason to panic. He was right. No one here could recognize her. Except Laura, and her friend already knew her deepest, darkest secret fantasies. Besides, it wasn't as if she was nude or anything. She was still wearing her bra and panties. She pushed off the wall, padded to the French doors, and with trembling hands, opened them wide.

"Turn around and face me." She did. "Now take off the rest of your things. I want to see you naked."

Omigod.

"I can't," she protested, mortified that she'd gotten herself into this position.

"You can," he assured, watching her hungrily. "Don't be shy, *cher*. Live your fantasy. I know you want to."

Illicit excitement purled through her. She felt wicked. And unbearably aroused. Okay, she *did* want to.

Her hands were shaking so badly she could barely get the clasp of her bra undone. The panties were easier. She realized they were wet. So was she. Heat streaked through her.

He smiled and set down his glass. He came to her. Pulled her close and held her tight. His hands slowly glided over her nude body. He still wore his trousers and unbuttoned shirt, and it felt unimaginably erotic to be naked in his arms like that. She wanted to kiss him, but he wouldn't let her. He just held her and caressed her, his hot breath stirring her hair.

Without warning, he turned her in his arms, so her front was facing the courtyard. She gasped. Several people below looked up at the sound to watch them. His hands enveloped her breasts, gathering her nipples between his strong fingers. He pinched them. An electric jolt of desire stabbed through her. She writhed in his embrace, pressing herself back into him, wanting more of the same.

"Do you want me?" he murmured in her ear, as though reading her mind. Or maybe her body.

"Yes," she said. "Please, yes."

To her shock, she felt him reach for his belt buckle and lower his zipper right there. His knees bent, there was a rustle, and seconds later he thrust into her from behind. She was wet and swollen, and his cock went in deep and sure.

She swallowed a cry and struggled to get free. *She couldn't do this in front of other people!* But he held her fast with both arms banded around her middle, not allowing her to move more than a few inches in any direction. She grabbed the top of the wrought-iron balcony. The metal was smooth and cool.

"Shhh," he soothed. "Hold still."

She sucked in a breath. "You can't—"

"I'll decide how far to go. Just be still, for God's sake. I want to make this good for you."

Amazingly, she believed him. Trembling with trepidation, she did as he asked. He was holding her firmly, her legs spread wide, her backside pressed hard up against him. His cock was thick and huge inside her, and she could feel its solid girth throbbing to the beat of their thundering hearts.

"You okay?" he asked.

"No!" She was on the verge of . . . of . . . Oh, God, she didn't know what.

"Tell me what you're feeling."

"Afraid."

"Why?"

"This is dangerous," she said, her voice filled with incipient panic.

"It is," he said. "On so many levels. Possibly the most dangerous moment of your entire life. *Non?*"

"Yes," she breathed.

"Enjoy it," he whispered into her ear. "Life is so dull. So few opportunities to feel truly alive, terrified to lose the comfortable existence you've always known, as you are feeling now."

His words struck an unwilling chord deep within her. *How did he know?*

"Look," he urged. "Look down at the people watching you, and know they are envious of your daring."

She let out a shuddering breath. Daring? *Her?* "I'm anything but," she murmured.

"You're wrong," he said. His hand rubbed down the front of her body and slid between her legs. She tensed. "Watch them," he ordered, and his fingers probed her folds, seeking the aching center of her need.

At his touch, her body arched and she let out a soft cry. The desperate sound drew even more gazes. One strong finger stroked over her clit. She saw stars. His cock pushed in deeper still. His finger circled. She squeezed her eyes shut in an agony of arousal. "Oh, God, Shay," she moaned.

"Shall I stop?" he asked, torturing her. The man was a demon. He knew damn well she didn't want to stop. All along he had known her better than she knew herself, as though he had secret insight into her soul. That for her, doing this was exciting beyond anything she'd ever experienced before or was likely to in the future. And she loved it.

"No. Don't stop," she begged, giving in. *She was so close.*

He pulled out a little, then rammed back into her. His finger pressed harder, circled her clit faster. She felt herself coming fast and gulped down a breath. Just as she was about to climax, he reached up and clamped his other hand over her mouth. "Scream for me," he told her.

Her orgasm crashed over her in a drowning wave of intense pleasure. It robbed her of air and sent her whole body into spasm after spasm of earth-shattering sensation.

She screamed, the sound muffled by the flat of his hand.

And in a sudden flash of total, blissful despair, she knew in her heart that tonight she would do anything this man asked of her. Anything and everything he wanted, without reservation.

And *that* was the most dangerous thing of all.

Chapter 6

The woman was a feast for the senses, a banquet of pleasure for Shay's hungry soul. He made love to Tessa all night, until the rosy fingers of dawn reached into the courtyard, turning the *maison* chamber's white diaphanous curtains a pale shade of pink.

She'd started the evening as a beguiling mix of bashful innocence and willing openness. By dawn she had thrown herself fully into the fantasy of being his *objet de plaisir*. He'd even coaxed off her mask.

"Let me see you," he'd murmured as she rode his lap, their arms wrapped around each other, sitting up on the four-poster bed. "I want to know the face of the woman I'm fucking."

She'd hesitated only a heartbeat, then flung the mask aside. Her cheeks were flushed with the glow of multiple climaxes, her skin dewy from long hours of bed play. Her face was framed by auburn hair in glorious dishevelment, mussed by his own fingers in her slow indoctrination as his personal odalisque. "I guess it's only fair," she returned breathily, "since I can see you."

He'd held her still and studied her until she blushed and pressed her face into the crook of his neck. "Why do you look at me like that?" she whispered.

He kissed her temple. "Like what?"

"Like . . . like you're searching for something in my face."

"Maybe I am," he confessed.

She lifted her head. "What?"

Should he tell her? Ask her if she remembered that long-ago day they'd met?

What the hell. The incident had been haunting him for years. He'd seduced her tonight specifically to purge himself of the absurdly disproportionate lingering effects of that chance meeting with a girl young enough to raise the hairs even on the neck of a sixteen-year-old bad boy.

"You were at the fountain earlier tonight," he said. "The *Jaillissement de Plaisir.*"

Her lips parted, startled. "How do you know that?"

"I was watching you."

A shadow of wariness flitted through her sex-smudged eyes. "From where? Why?"

"From a balcony." He wasn't about to tell her that it was the private balcony of his own suite of rooms upstairs. She didn't know his last name nor the fact that he was the owner of the *maison* Chez Duchesne and heir to the family fortune. He liked the fact that she was ignorant of his wealth and his reputation. It made her honest, a rare commodity in his experience with

women. He winked. "I heard four beautiful women laughing in
the abandoned courtyard. Who could resist a peek? By the time
I looked, the others had left. Then I saw it was you . . ." He let
his words trail off, coaxing an acknowledgment, a sign that she
shared his powerful memory.

Her brows drew together. "What do you mean, it was me?"

"You've been there before, at the *Jaillissement*, *non*?" he
prodded.

She started to shake her head, then all at once she halted,
looking astonished. "I'd almost forgotten, but yes, I have! When
I was young, visiting the French Quarter with my parents." She
gasped. "My God. It was *that* fountain? *That's* why the old
courtyard looked so familiar!" Her wide eyes met his. "How on
earth did you know?"

He tamped down a flare of disappointment. "You really
don't remember me?"

"You?"

As she struggled to dredge the memory of him from the
murky depths of forgotten experiences, he shifted and drove
his cock farther up into her. A reminder to himself that the
past didn't matter. All that mattered was that he had her now,
here, tonight. "Do you recall anything else that happened that
day . . . ?" he prompted, despite an overwhelming irritation
with himself for giving a *foutu* damn. What did it matter if
she'd forgotten him?

It was her turn to study his face. But his cock play was dis-
tracting her. She closed her eyes when he rammed up into her
again. "My God, the boy!" she breathed. "In the courtyard.
The one who tried to kiss me. It was *you*!"

He rubbed his cheek with a thumb. "*Merci Dieu*, you did
not have the same reaction tonight as you did back then."

She made an embarrassed noise. "Oh, damn. I slapped you, didn't I?"

"More like sucker-punched. You've a wicked right hook, you." His lips curved as he grasped her jaw in his palm and held her for a thorough, drowning kiss. "I may just have to punish you for that."

Her consternation melted to an undulating whole-body purr. "Promise?"

They'd been fucking like minks since closing the French doors earlier; explosive but fairly conventional stuff. He'd been gradually initiating her into the role of his submissive, and she'd been a quick study, more than willing to please him.

"*Mais*, yeah," he promised.

Excitement spurted through him. His gaze sought the array of restraints and other equipment hanging next to the headboard, standard equipment in all the *maison*'s pleasure chambers. Because of her relative inexperience, he'd been holding back from what he really wanted to do to her.

Time to raise the stakes.

He lifted her up off his cock and ordered, "Turn around." They untangled their legs, and she obliged with her back. "Raise your arms." She did, and he grasped her wrists, bent her forward, and quickly manacled her low to the headboard.

She gave a little cry and met his eyes in the large mirror hanging behind the bed. "What's going on?" Her bottom was in the air, enticingly displayed.

"What do you think?" he drawled.

"But I don't . . ." She swallowed, pulling at her bonds. "What are you going to do to me?"

Pleased that she hadn't stopped his actions, only questioned them, he ran his hands down the sides of her torso and over her backside. Instead of answering, he asked, "Do you know the legend of the *Jaillissement de Plaisir*?"

"What does that have to do with tying me up?"

He drew back his hand and gave her ass a sharp smack.

"Ow!" She tried to jerk up, but the fur-lined cuffs prevented it. "What the—!"

He smacked the other side.

"*Ouch!*"

He rubbed over her plump flesh, feeling the heat of the sting and her growing arousal, drawing it into his hands. "When I ask you a question, you must answer me."

"That—"

He raised his hand again, along with a brow.

"Okay!" she rushed to say. "I'll answer! Um, what was the question again?"

"The legend."

"Right. Yes. I've heard that throwing a coin in it and making a wish is supposed to grant the supplicant endless sexual pleasure. If you do it with your true love, you'll be forever fulfilled and in love."

He watched her reflection carefully in the mirror. "Is that what you were doing there earlier? Hoping for a magic spell?"

"I suppose."

You believe in voodoo, then?"

"God, no. I told you, all this was my friend's idea. I didn't make a wish, anyway."

He pursed his lips. "Not this time," he murmured.

"Not—" Suddenly her eyes widened in consternation. "Oh, my God. You and I . . . back then, we threw coins!" she said on a rush of breath. "I remember. They landed in the fountain!"

"A complete accident. And we didn't throw them," he refuted. "I was running to buy an ice cream for my little sister. When you and I collided, the coins merely flew from my hand."

"I was about to make a wish with mine," she said, her gaze turning dreamy as she dipped into the past again. "I wanted a kitten for my birthday."

He moved forward, took her hips between his hands, and spread her knees wide apart with his. "*Et voilà*. Nothing to do with us. Or love. Or this attraction we feel. The fountain nonsense, it's just a silly superstition."

Her gaze came back into focus. "Of course it's not real."

"There's no such thing as voodoo. Or endless pleasure," he stated unequivocally and thrust into her.

"Or someone loving you forever," she gasped as he withdrew and thrust in harder.

"*Complètement fou.*"

Craziness.

That's what he told himself as he hammered into her over and over, drawing moans and gasps of pleasure from both of them until they exploded in a mind-bending climax. Crazy that he'd been thinking of her all these years.

Crazy, he told himself as he spent the rest of the night exploring her body, teaching her to touch him in ways that drove him mad with desire. Crazier still, he told himself as he gently introduced her to the many pleasures of submitting to a man's will, that he'd even think about blaming his troubles with the building permits and his unfulfilling love life on some absurd voodoo magic. Craziest of all, he told himself firmly as he now stared at the dimming shadows creeping across the ceiling as pink sunlight peeked into the room, that he'd thought fucking this woman for a single night would exorcise her from his dreams, along with the winds of discontent that had blown through his life for the past fifteen years.

Putain de merde. He knew damn well *voudoun* wasn't real . . . but it sure as hell felt like he'd been caught in some kind of black magic spell that refused to relinquish him. How could he possibly have thought having sex with her would break him free?

"Shay?" she whispered. She'd been dozing in his arms for the past hour, the two of them sprawled across the pillow-strewn, sheet-tangled bed, emotionally replete and sexually sated. For now . . .

"Yeah, *cher.*"

"So, about that kiss at the fountain . . ."

Dieu. Was she a mind reader as well as an erotic sorceress? "Mm-hmm?"

"What made you do it?" she asked. "Why would a boy like you"—she turned in his arms and peered up at him—"try to kiss an awkward, gangly girl like me?"

He avoided the pitfall. "You were far from gangly, *cher.* And a boy like me? What's that supposed to mean?"

She smiled. "Older. Cute as hell. Probably a bit of a bad boy, too, I wager."

He cringed. "Cute? *Merde.*" He grinned. "But I'll give you bad. Yeah, definitely bad."

"So, why?"

"Ah, Tessa. You were young and sweet and on the verge of blossoming into a real beauty. Even a clueless boy like me could see that. When I ran smack into you and those coins went flying, you looked so damn upset that I'd spoiled your little wishing ritual . . . I couldn't resist giving you something else to remember instead."

Amusement danced in her eyes. "No ego there or anything."

He chuckled. "I've always wanted to apologize. It was just an impulse. Honestly, I didn't mean to frighten you."

"You didn't. I was just surprised. I've always regretted smacking you. After you'd gone, I wanted to kick myself." She nestled closer to his body, extended her tongue, and licked at his nipple.

He fought a moan and, amazingly, his body stirred. They'd indulged in nonstop, down-and-dirty fuck-me sex all night, and still he craved more. He couldn't get enough of the woman or her body. It was insane how much he wanted her.

In a well-practiced motion, he rolled on top of her, gathered her wrists in his hands, and pinned them above her head again. He'd learned through delightful experience how much she enjoyed being restrained. And he liked nothing more than being in total control. Especially of a beautiful woman.

"Did you wish you'd let me kiss you?" he crooned. He pressed a kiss into her hair, then her temple and her cheek, breathing in the feminine scent of her. The smell of his own sex spiced her lips as he kissed them. It aroused him even more. "Do you wish you'd given your very first kiss to an unknown boy in a deserted courtyard? A stranger?"

"Yes," she admitted softly. "I wanted you to come back and make me kiss you."

His cock went hard. "Do you wish you'd let me push you down on the grass and touch your soft, virginal body? Awaken you to the pleasures of young love? Is that what you wanted, *cher*?"

She looked up at him, and he knew it was true. His heart crowed.

"Yes," she whispered. "God, how I wanted you to come back and touch me."

"I was sixteen, and you hadn't even begun to be a woman, but I dreamed of you," he admitted, the years of frustration rushing back through him as he reached for another condom. "For years I watched that courtyard, waiting for you to return." He slid into her. She pressed her thighs around his hips.

"When I learned to pleasure myself," she confessed, "it was always you I imagined doing it to me. I may not have recognized you right away tonight, but I've never forgotten your face as it was back then." She gazed at his features, stalling on his mouth. "So handsome, so temptingly sexual. You *did* awaken me to the pleasures of my body, Shay," she whispered.

Back then, he couldn't understand why he'd felt those things for a girl so young. He blamed his obsession on that *foutu* voodoo tale and the gentle teasing of those who believed in it. Not that he ever did. Raging teenage hormones. That's all it had been.

But now they were both very grown-up. *Merci Dieu.*

"Show me," he urged, pulling out of her and lifting her up against the pillows. He spread her knees wide and held them apart. "How did you touch yourself?"

She blinked, her cheeks coloring. "Really?"

"I want to see."

Her lips parted a fraction. Hesitantly, her hand went to her pussy. Her fingers spread her folds, exposing her clit. His mouth watered as the fingers of her other hand sought out the glistening nub. She sucked in a breath as she made intimate contact. His cock lengthened in an aching lurch.

Not letting go of her knees, he scooted down and lay between her legs, putting his face close enough to lick her. "Don't stop," he admonished when her fingers faltered. Tentatively, they started up again.

He drank in the sight and the scent and the bloom of her desire for him. Watched her clit swell and weep as she coaxed it to stiff arousal. Finally he couldn't take it any longer. He extended his tongue and joined her fingers with it. She moaned low, and he tasted the spurt of passion clear to his balls. He dragged his tongue down along her valley and filled her wet passage with it. Her back arched. She was close, he could tell.

So was he. His taut, quickened body reminded him painfully of how much he'd wanted her all through the years. Desperation surged through him. Doing this was *not* going to banish his need for her! But what could he do?

He couldn't ask her to stay. It was nearly morning. And as much as he wanted to, he could not linger in bed with her for much longer. He had somewhere to be today. Somewhere important.

But somehow, he had to find a way break this erotic spell she had him under.

Suddenly, he had an idea. That damned fountain had started his misery, this whole *foutu* curse. Surely, it could end it, too. Did you have to believe in the magic for it to work?

He put his hands over her fingers, stopping their movement.

"Shay, what are you doing?" she gasped, trying to pull them free.

"We need to finish what we started," he told her.

"That's what I'm trying to do," she said, her voice strangled.

"No. I mean at the *Jaillissement*." He raised up to his knees, grabbed her hand, and pulled her along as he rolled off the bed. "*Vien*. Come with me. It's time to end this accursed nonsense!"

Chapter 7

"*Wait*. What?" Alarm filled Tessa as Shay hustled her toward the chamber door.

"We need to get this voodoo bullshit out of our systems once and for all," he said. "Show ourselves that there is nothing to it. Just a foolish legend."

Her body throbbed with unsated lust. God, not *again*! Why did men insist on leaving a woman unfulfilled? "But, Shay, I already know it's foolishness! Can't we just—"

"Indulge me," he said and paused to lean down and kiss her. "Please. You've indulged every other whim I've had tonight. Grant me this last one, too."

"But—" Oh, hell. She had a terrible feeling she knew what he had in mind. The courtyard where the *Jaillissement de Plaisir* stood was secluded and long-deserted. But a dozen or more of the *maison*'s balconies overlooked it. Even this early—or late, depending on one's perspective—someone might be awake and see them. She wrapped her arms around her middle. "How will wishing on that same fountain prove there's nothing to the legend?"

He uttered an oath. "It won't. But I need to break the damned curse it has over me," he said. "This is the only way I can think of."

"But can't it wait a few minutes, until we—"

"*Non!*"

Okay, then.

Aching with frustration, she let him lead her down a back staircase that smelled dusty with disuse, their bare feet silent on the worn oak. A weathered door at the bottom creaked and groaned when he unlocked it and shoved it open. The morning air whooshed over them in a solid wave of sultry warmth. What was he *doing*?

His words came back to her. *Nothing to do with us. Or love. Or this attraction we feel. The fountain nonsense, it's just a silly superstition.*

"But doesn't doing this mean you actually *believe* in the magic?"

His olive skin glowed golden in the wash of predawn light that hit him. His erection jutted thick and tall as he turned and gave her an undecipherable look. "Hell, no."

It made no sense. But if making a wish would get him back inside her . . .

He tugged her out into the courtyard and down an overgrown brick path into the feral tangle of blossoming vines and shrubs. She felt like Eve in the Garden of Eden. Flowers were just opening with the dawning light, and the perfume filling the air was exotic and spicy. Birds were awakening, singing the end of nighttime. Even a pair of beautiful butterflies flitted past. He led her into the clearing where the fountain gurgled and turned to her. A light spray of water hit her naked body. She glanced around. Was someone watching them?

A spill of illicit excitement sifted through her. She couldn't be*lieve* she was doing this.

Suddenly, she remembered. "We forgot to bring any coins!" she lamented softly.

He slanted her a dark look. "I guess we'll just have to think of something else to offer the muses of the *Jaillissement*."

"Oh?"

He took up a wide stance in front of the fountain, facing it, and with his hands on her shoulders he urged her down to her knees before him. "Something extra special to end their accursed reign over us."

There was no time to ponder what he meant by that, if not a belief in the enchantment of the muses. *"Oh!"*

Oh, God.

He fisted his hand in her hair, bringing her lips whisper-close to his rampant cock. She didn't need to ask what he wanted to sacrifice. Scandalized, she nevertheless felt her unsated desire flare back to life with a vengeance.

"Open for me, *cher*," he commanded in a low growl.

What could she do but obey?

He slowly fed her his engorged member. She moaned in surrender to the man, to the act, to the bewitching spell of the magical fountain. Her senses filled with the musky male taste of him. She laved his satin head with her tongue, cradling his balls in her fingers, working his iron-velvet shaft with her hand. He was big and hard and thrillingly responsive. To every touch and every lick came an answering jerk or moan or masculine growl of pleasure. She forgot where she was, her reservations falling away in the sheer eroticism of what she was doing. Arousal shimmered through her clit, bringing her to the brink of coming. She increased her pace and felt his climax start.

Abruptly, he withdrew. "For this to work, it must be both of us," he ground out.

Again, frustration swept through her like wildfire. "Please," she begged, reaching for him.

"No, like this," he said, and swiftly lowered her to the dew-laden grass. Shivering at the drench of coolness against her back, she spread her legs for him, unmindful of prying eyes. She didn't care anymore. She was too needy, wanted him too badly.

To her shock, he didn't mount her in the usual way. He sixty-nined her, lowering himself onto her and thrusting his cock back into her mouth. His own mouth latched on to her, his tongue stroking over her so powerfully she nearly came in a rush. Her muffled cry vibrated through his rigid flesh, and his body jerked in response. His teeth bit down and his tongue ravaged her clit, sending shock waves of pleasure through her, enough to raise them both from the ground. She squeezed her eyes shut, starting to catapult over the edge.

"Make the wish!" he commanded hoarsely. "Now!"

Orgasm slammed into her. He followed close behind, spurting his essence deep into her throat as her whole body shook with double satisfaction. She tried to hang on and do as he asked. Wish for the spell on him to be broken. And for the erotic magic between them to end when they parted this morning, so she wouldn't be under *his* commanding spell for the rest of her life.

But for some reason she couldn't conjure the right words in her head. Every time she started to ask the three dancing muses to lift their sensual bewitchment, the plea came out the same. And not what either of them wanted.

Please, Jaillissement de Plaisir, *let the pleasure go on forever!*

Luckily, the muses did not listen.

Instantly, it seemed, the enchantment of the night was shattered.

After lying in the grass for several gasping minutes catching their breath and retrieving their wits, Tessa and Shay quickly scrambled up and ascended the stairs back to their chamber, then spent several awkward minutes getting their clothes on as quickly as they could.

"I'll call you a taxi," he said and lifted the phone.

She ducked into the bathroom, and when she came out, he was waiting by the door.

He slid his hands in his trouser pockets. "Thank you for tonight, Tessa," he said as she scooped up her purse. "I had a good time."

"Yes, so did I," she admitted, suddenly acutely embarrassed. This man had seen more of her, learned more of her secret sexual desires, than any other person on earth, and she didn't even know his full name. "It was . . . an interesting experience." She opened her mouth to ask his name . . . and maybe to see him again. But he beat her to the punch.

"Your consulting fee will be credited to the bank account you provided when you registered," he said, reminding her of their true relationship. "Double, as promised."

She stared at him, feeling as though he'd smacked her. "You obviously misunderstood. I don't want your damn money," she stated, hurt and anger clenching her stomach. What had she been *thinking*? That there had been more to their lovemaking than . . . Oh, hell, she didn't know what she'd thought. Obviously he didn't agree. He only wanted to be rid of her, now that he'd gotten what he came for.

There was a shock. It always seemed to come down to that. Men wanted, and women gave.

"I'll walk you downstairs," he said.

"No!" She took a breath to steady her reeling heart. "That's not necessary. I can find my own way."

He frowned. "I insist."

"Fine." She didn't want to fight. She only wanted to get away from him.

They descended the grand staircase, Shay nodding to the few staff members who were about at this early hour, as though he did it every morning.

He held the outer door open for her. Her cab was waiting at the curb.

"Will you come back tonight?" he asked, his eyes capturing hers.

Only in her dreams. "The wish at the fountain, it was to be free of our attraction for each other, right? There's no reason for me to come back."

"*Bon,*" he conceded. But there was something dark lurking in his expression. "Will you at least tell me your real name?" he asked.

"No," she said. "That was the agreement," she added, more to remind herself than him. "No names. No rules. No future expectations." He'd been an incredible lover, but the last thing she needed was another one-sided relationship. God. *Relationship?* Who was she kidding?

"*Bon,*" he echoed, opening the taxi's door for her. "Very well."

"Good-bye, then." She extended her hand.

He looked at it incredulously, then slid his fingers into her hair and pulled her mouth to his. He tasted like sin and excitement and profound regret, all rolled up in an exquisitely sexual kiss. Despite everything, one last agonizing flare of desire burst through her. *Damn,* the man could turn her on.

"Good-bye, *cher,*" he murmured, then let her go, leaving her feeling cold and empty and wanting to stamp her feet in disappointed aggravation. Disappointment at herself for wanting more. Would she never learn? Well, at least he'd been a powerful, masterful lover, tapping into her secret fantasies of being completely and utterly possessed. The night had not been a total loss in that sense. Far from it.

She climbed into the taxi, gave the driver her hotel's address, and let out a long, shuddering breath as it pulled away from the *maison* Chez Duchesne. Thank *God* she'd escaped in one piece! *And with your heart intact,* a little voice added in her head before she could squelch it.

Her *heart*? Wow.

It was true, last night was exhilarating, at times shocking, an amazing once-in-a-lifetime experience she was lucky to have stumbled into. And Shay? As he'd promised, Shay was everything she'd ever fantasized about in a lover, and more. *Much* more. He'd taken her body in every way possible and left her yearning for a chance to do it all over again. And again. And again.

Okay, fine. She'd be a fool not to want him as a steady lover.

But her heart?

God, no. Not even a factor.

Seriously.

She'd be an even bigger fool to involve her heart in any way, shape, or form with a man like Shay.

And she hadn't.

Honestly.

The taxi cruised past the hidden courtyard, and she couldn't help stealing a final reluctant peek at the spellbound fountain. And she swore she saw the dancing muses wave to her, laughing merrily as she sat back in her seat, groaned, and muttered, "*Damn* that man, anyway."

Chapter 8

"*Piron!*" Shay bellowed into the bustling kitchen for his majordomo. A damn *miracle* had just happened.

"*Quoi?*" came the answer from the walk-in refrigerator. Piron ambled out. "Dere a fire somewhere, boss?"

Shay raised the papers in his hand and shook them. "You will not believe what this is. We got the building permit."

Piron's brows shot up. "For the courtyard? *C'est vrai?* Since when?"

"Since this morning. It was just couriered from building commission."

Piron grinned. "Damn! What made dem change their mind?"

"The Historical Society has relented on the old brick path repair issue. Apparently the city promised to split our restaurant licensing fees with them. Money speaks. I'm shocked." He put the papers in Piron's hands. "Call the construction company. I want them here next week. Pay them whatever you have to. I want this done before the commission changes its mind again."

"Hell, yeah! This calls for a celebration." Piron headed for the cooler. "Champagne all around!"

"Sorry, not for me. Gotta go, or I'll be late." Shay reached up to fix his bow tie, glancing at his watch. It was just after one. "Etienne's wedding, remember?"

Etienne Gardet was the youngest son of another prominent New Orleans family. He and Shay, along with two other wealthy scions, had grown up sharing honors as the youthful holy terrors of social gatherings, holiday balls, and charity events all across the city, then turning into the nightmare of every Louisiana debutante's mama when they went off to college. Despite now having just nudged into their thirties, Etienne was the first of the four to get married. Naturally, Shay was a groomsman.

The nuptials started at two, and he was not about to be late. He was most definitely in the mood to celebrate. On more than one count.

The sacrifice this morning had worked! He was finally quit that absurd curse! The permit coming through so unexpectedly *proved* it. At last his luck was changing.

Shame that auburn-haired spitfire wouldn't be coming back to the *maison* tonight. He'd like to commemorate this momentous turning point in his life by tying her to his bed and giving her the hardest, fastest fuck of her lifetime. And then do it all over again.

"See you later," Shay said with a wave to his majordomo. "Hell, maybe tomorrow if I get lucky." Yeah, after the warm-up with Tessa last night, he was craving a bit of kink. Surely there'd be an accommodating bridesmaid or wedding guest he could avail himself of.

Though he *really* wished he'd asked Tessa to the wedding as his date. Even if the spell between them was now shattered, *merci Dieu*, she was still the most enticing and appealing woman he'd met in years. Possibly ever. He didn't know what it was about her . . . she wasn't the most beautiful woman he'd ever seen, wasn't the most adventurous by far—though she had been very open to learning new things—nor did she seem particularly impressed by him, this morning especially, for some reason. But he just couldn't shake her from his mind. Or the cravings of his body. Just thinking about her was making him hard. Obviously it wasn't the fountain's influence, since that was gone. But his attraction to her had in no way diminished. If anything, it had grown with these few hours' separation. Why hadn't he *demanded* she return to him?

"Watch out for that pretty obsession of yours, boss," Piron admonished with a wink.

It was really irritating how everyone on the planet had suddenly become a goddamn mind reader.

"I have no plans to see her again," he returned.

"Why am I not surprised?" Piron said with a wry glint in his eyes. "You moon after dis one for years like some ol' love-starved hound dog, an' when you finally find her, you kick her to the curb jus' like all dem other women you fuck an' leave. Whatsa matter, Shay? She don' like your cock or somethin'?"

"I did *not*— You know what?" Shay said, cold water dashed on his prior good mood. "You're fired! Collect your pay and get the hell out of my *maison*."

Piron just guffawed and strolled off, back to the kitchen. *Le connard.* "You have fun at dat weddin', hear?" he called over his shoulder, not in the least concerned, since Shay fired his arrogant right-hand man at least once a month.

"She liked my cock just fine!" Shay shot back, to the amusement of the rest of the kitchen staff. At least she sure seemed to. Right up until those last few minutes, after the curse had been reversed.

Not that he fucking believed in curses, he reminded himself firmly.

Bordel de merde.

He slung his tux jacket over his shoulder and stalked to the garage for his car. He should probably take a taxi, but on an impulse he decided to head out to the plantation after the reception. Spend a couple of days up there, thinking about his life and the future.

Being with Tessa last night, a woman he could actually picture a life with, and having his luck turn so abruptly this morning had triggered something inside him. A certain knowledge that things could not go on the way they'd been going for much of his life.

Something had to change. He'd known it for years, but suddenly it felt more urgent. As though if he didn't put his life in order right now, the chance would vanish, and he'd be condemned to live this way forever, as his father and his grandfather had before him. There was nothing wrong with being the owner of the most exclusive private sex club in New Orleans. But he no longer wanted it to define him as a man, as it had until now. He'd worked hard at getting the establishment to the point of the quasi respectability the club enjoyed now.

Tout quoi vous voulez, the *Jaillissement*'s inscription promised. Anything he could ever desire. Endless pleasure. But Shay already had all that. You couldn't be the rich, good-looking owner of a club like Chez Duchesne and not have an embarrassing wealth of sensual pleasures thrown at you every night of the week. Could that really be all there was to his life?

Impossible.

He wanted more. He was ready for a new challenge. Something different.

Had that been what that totally out-of-character ritual fuck this morning at the foot of that accursed fountain was all about? A cry in the darkness to a magic he didn't believe in, a desperate attempt to bring about the change he so wanted but had no idea how to accomplish?

Non, he thought as he drove to the church and the wedding that symbolized all he longed for. Wishes and voodoo would not fulfill his greatest desire.

What he really wanted was to find someone special to share his life. To love and cherish and grow old with. *That* would change everything, make all his efforts with the club worthwhile . . . because he could leave it in Piron's capable hands and turn to more important, fulfilling things. Like raising a family of his own.

At which point, his thoughts returned to Tessa. Lovely, seductive Tessa.

Sa belle obsession . . .

Was she the one he was seeking? Why had he let her go? He should have kept her! Taken her upstairs to his suite and handcuffed her to his bed so she couldn't leave.

Hell, at least invited her to the damn wedding.

Anything but let her walk out of his life again. What kind of an idiot was he to let her slip through his fingers? For the *second*

time. The first woman in years who had stirred his body and
fired his imagination. The perfect combination of beauty and
intelligence, strength and submissiveness.

He wanted her back.

Foutre de merde, he wanted her back!

He got to the church, a small but stately stone affair on the
edge of the Garden District, parked, and hunted down the back
dressing room that had been reserved for the groomsmen.

After a round of backslapping greetings, Shay produced
the generous flask of bourbon he'd tucked into his tux pocket
and poured a round in four conical paper cups from the water
cooler.

"To the future Mrs. Gardet," the four best friends toasted.

"Speaking of whom . . . You two have fun at the *maison* last
night?" Shay asked Etienne with a grin. He and his adventurous fiancée were regular guests at Chez Duchesne, enjoying the
openly sexual atmosphere and sophisticated fantasy play on
offer there. Although Shay hadn't seen them, he knew they'd
planned to spend their last night as singles indulging in decadent behavior at the *maison*.

"Oh, yeah," his friend answered with an even bigger grin.
"As always. But what's this I hear about you and a certain lady
in blue?"

"Tessa," he said, and threw back a second shot, filled with
regret. "Do not even go there, *mon ami*."

Etienne's expression went sly. "What's this? Has the mighty
Treves Duchesne fallen at last? Stay tuned, my good friends.
This afternoon should prove interesting!"

What he meant by that, Shay had no idea.

The others oohed and made a few bawdy comments, but
before Shay could correct their mistaken assumption that she

would be with him, the organ music swelled inside the church. That was their cue. Taking a deep breath, Shay stowed the sizable spike of annoyance at the reminder of his lost opportunity and filed into the nave with the other men, lining up below the chancel alongside the groom.

He really was happy for Etienne. It was obvious the man was head over heels. And Shay was determined to have a good time at this wedding with his friends and forget about the woman he'd let get away.

Hell, there were plenty of other women here. Pretty women.

Just look at the gorgeous bridesmaid gliding down the center aisle looking demure and virginal. Okay, so she was blond, and he wasn't really into blondes today. No matter. There was a brunette stepping out after her, and she was just as pretty. Though he wasn't particularly feeling the brunette either. What he really wanted was a tall, shapely, auburn-haired beauty with soft eyes and a sharp, very clever tongue.

Kind of like the one following the brunette down the aisle.

Shay did a double take at the last bridesmaid, and his jaw dropped in surprise. Their eyes collided, and hers went wide as saucers.

Slowly he began to smile.

Mais, yeah.

Exactly like her.

Chapter 9

Tessa almost tripped over her feet and landed on her face in the middle of the aisle. She caught herself just in time.

Oh. My. *God.*

She could not be*lieve* what she was seeing.

That man standing calmly at the front of the church, smiling like a fallen angel, one of Etienne's groomsmen, *it was him!* Shay!

Shay of the huge cock, commanding whisper, and dark bedroom eyes. The man she'd spent the entire night—

God, she didn't even want to *think* about what she'd spent the entire night doing with him!

What the *hell* was he doing *here?*

She bared her teeth at him behind a plastered-on smile, barely resisting hurling her bouquet at the devil. This was injury to insult. *He must have known all along who she was.* Laura frequented the *maison* often, she'd said, and Shay had obviously known his way around the place, too. And just as obviously was great friends with the groom. Had her friend set her up? God, surely she hadn't *hired* Shay to entertain her? If so, she'd kill Laura. *And* Shay.

The nerve of the man! Seducing her, doing all those . . . *things* . . . to her, then offering to *pay* her for her services, knowing all along she'd have to face him today. *And* be his partner in the ceremony. Lord. That's what Tessa got for missing the rehearsal due to a delayed flight.

Jesus help her.

She refused to look at him again, the cad. But she could feel his gaze on her the whole time. Hot. Tempting. Powerful.

When the ceremony was over, she was forced to walk back down the aisle on his arm. And smile like her insides weren't careening around in somersaults and her panties weren't getting wetter by the second.

She was mortified by her body's reaction to him. Like she was expecting him to throw her down on the vestibule floor and take her in front of God and everyone. As he'd done this morning. *And* last night. She was getting turned on just thinking about it.

Oh, God. She was *so* going to hell.

"Let me go," she gritted out under her breath, trying to jerk her arm free. But he'd put his hand over her wrist and was holding on like a dog with a bone.

"No way." He smiled. "We've got photos. And the receiving line."

"If you think I'm going to—"

Without loosening his grip, he slung his arm around her shoulders, pulled her close, and kissed her. And *not* an innocent groomsman to bridesmaid thank-you kiss, either. It was deep and hot and involved his tongue, and it took her totally by surprise.

"There," he said when he let up. "That should put a stop to the designs every other man here is having on you."

"How dare you!" she began.

"Another? My pleasure." He kissed her again, this time pulling her body up against his.

It was all she could do not to surrender to it and climb the man like a favorite tree to get to the sweet, sweet fruit. *Mercy.* The man kissed like a freaking god. Okay. He did *every*thing like a god. That was the whole problem. When he touched her, her brain simply ceased to function.

He raised his head and smiled down at her, putting his thumb to her lip as though he were fixing a spot on her lipstick. An intimate gesture that did not fail to have everyone in the entire vestibule staring at them. The women, all with envy. The men? Who knew? She could only see one man in the whole freaking place. The one preventing her from sliding to the floor because her knees had suddenly stopped working.

"What do you think you're doing?" she quietly demanded, trying to pull away subtly, so as not to attract any more attention. And not end up on her butt.

"Just claiming what's mine," he said matter-of-factly and walked her toward the place where the wedding party was gathering for photos.

"I am *not* yours."

"That's not what you said last night," he reminded her, the beast. "I believe your exact words were—"

"Stop it," she hissed. "You made it very clear this morning what our relationship was based on. So just stop pretending—"

He halted and looked down at her. "Is that what the frost was all about? Because I said I'd pay you? That was our agreement, *cher*. And I'm nothing if not a man of my word."

"I told you I didn't want your damned money. And another thing—" But she wasn't able to ask about Laura's role in their encounter because the photographer beckoned them, and fifteen minutes of staged photos ensued.

To her irritation, he insisted on muscling his arm around her in every single picture.

Okay, maybe she wasn't irritated as much as . . . All right, fine. She liked it. To be honest, regardless of how they'd met, it *thrilled* her to have a man as ridiculously attractive as Shay keep his arm firmly around her, willing to show the world that he wanted her so much that he'd go down through posterity in Laura and Etienne's wedding album coupled with her.

Not even Laura's worried glances and concerned whispered, "What have you gotten yourself into, girl? We need to talk," could make her come to her senses—though it seemed to answer the question of her friend's involvement.

Still, there was no way she'd let *him* know his actions were making her cream her panties. She knew a player when she saw one. *Hello*, they'd met in a bordello! Oh, excuse me, a *maison*.

Thank God he'd made that unthinking remark about money this morning and reminded her that their relationship—and she used the term very loosely—had zero future. And *there* was her problem with men in a nutshell. She was far too quick to involve her heart, when almost always the man's only interest was in a short-term good time. She wanted more than that. She wanted a dress and a ring and a happily ever after, the whole nine yards. She wanted a man to sweep her off her feet and take command of her in bed and treat her like a lady out of it. Yeah, she wanted a man to look at her the way Etienne was now gazing at his new bride. But all she ever found were men who were only interested in having fun. *Their* fun.

When would she *ever* learn?

She'd tried last night. Really, she'd had every intention of using Shay as he was obviously using her. As a temporary sex object and nothing more.

But then he'd been so . . . compelling. Gently leading her to do things she'd never in a million years believe she'd do. Subtly urging her, little by little, to submit and surrender to his powerful will. And she had. Willingly. Eagerly. No wonder she'd begun to surrender her heart to him, as well. The man had a voodoo all his own.

The one time she'd met a man who knew how to take command of her and sweep her off her feet in every possible way, he'd turned out like all the rest. *Damn.*

"Shall we dance, *cher*?" he murmured in her ear.

Though, to be fair, he *was* thrillingly persistent.

He'd driven her the few blocks to the reception in his—get this—*Lamborghini*, and she hadn't trusted herself to say a word to him. They were now standing silently at the side of the dance floor watching the bridal couple take one last spin before inviting the rest of the crowd to join them. Shay was directly behind her, his body pressed intimately into hers, his arms looped casually around her middle. She was about to disintegrate from confusion.

"What do you want from me, Shay?" she asked. "I'm *not* going to sell myself to you today—or ever—if that's what you're after."

"Hell, no. I won't make that mistake again."

She ground her teeth.

"What I meant was," he backpedaled, apparently feeling her back stiffen, "I won't make the mistake of trying to *buy* your favors."

Good save. But . . . "Nice try. Except you distanced yourself from me even before the money was mentioned." It had been her first clue to his perspective on their affair.

His arms tightened slightly around her. "Yeah. And I'm sorry if that made you uncomfortable." He glanced at the dance floor. *"Vien."*

He led her out among the dancers, and she didn't have the strength to protest. Naturally, it was a slow number. She went reluctantly into his arms, doing her best to ignore how incredibly right it felt to be there. She really had it bad.

"I'll admit," he continued as they began to move, "I was pretty freaked out by the whole fountain incident. Not sure what happened there. I kinda lost it for a few minutes."

In spite of herself, she gave him a faint smile. "You think?" To be honest, he hadn't been the only one.

"I don't believe in voodoo. I honestly don't," he assured her.

"Then what was that virgin sacrifice all about?" she asked dryly.

He pulled back and grinned. "Hardly a virgin by that time, *cher.*"

"Ha-ha."

He led her in a twirl. "Anyway. As I said, I sort of lost track of myself. Definitely *not* something that's in my normal repertoire. But whatever that sacrifice was all about, it seems to have worked."

"Oh?" A tingle of foreboding spilled through her.

"This morning I received some good news about a project

my family has been trying to get off the ground for fifteen years. A courtyard restaurant next door to the *maison*. Fifteen years of rejections and stalling by the Historical Society, and suddenly, just hours after we made our wish, or broke that damn curse, or whatever the hell we did, I get the green light. A weird coincidence, *non?*"

Oh, dear. Was there such a thing as a coincidence?

She felt her ears going warm as her own wish echoed through her mind. *Please, let the pleasure go on forever!*

She was so screwed.

She choked on her bad choice of inner laments.

"What?" he asked at her pained expression.

"Yes, I agree," she recovered. "Very strange. But that has nothing to do with you and me. I'm still not interested in repeating last night."

He captured her eyes as he pulled her closer. "Liar," he said, then bent to nuzzle his nose against her neck. "I can smell it on your skin—your desire for me." He traced a path upward, to her ear, and whispered, "If I slid my hand into your panties, they'd be drenched, wouldn't they?"

She didn't dare deny it. He'd probably just insist on proving he was right.

Thank God the song ended, and she almost flew backward out of his arms. She backed straight into Laura, who cheerfully looped her arm through hers and said to Shay, "Is it okay if I borrow my bridesmaid for a moment, sugar?" She winked at him with a grin. "Bouquet strategy."

He sketched a graceful bow, though Tessa didn't miss the flash of impatience in his eyes. "By all means."

As soon as they were out of earshot, Laura drew her close and hurried her toward the powder room. "Omigod, girl, what are you *doing* with that man? Do you have any *idea* the kind of things Treves Duchesne is into?"

"Wait. Who?" Tessa asked, momentarily distracted from confirming that Laura hadn't set her up.

Her friend glanced at her incredulously. "Shay! Please, don't say you don't know who he is? He didn't *tell* you?"

"He's . . ." Tessa faltered, growing alarmed at Laura's obvious agitation. "Well, no, actually. We never exchanged last names. Who is he?"

Her friend shoved her into the powder room and plunked closed the toilet lid, pushed her down on it, and locked the door with a rustle of silk and a pouf of petticoats. "Oh. My. God. Tessa! That's Treves Duchesne!" When she didn't react, Laura explained, "As in Chez Duchesne. The owner of the *maison!*"

Shock rendered Tessa speechless. The *owner*?

Laura paced back and forth in the tiny confines of the powder room. "When I saw you go upstairs with him last night, I was stunned to say the least." *So much for being set up*. Laura gestured widely. "But okay, he can be charming, and despite his reputation for enjoying, um . . . bondage and domination . . . I know he's not into actual pain, so I figured you were safe enough." She turned to Tessa, eyes wide as dinner plates. "But Jesus, girl! You can't possibly be interested in him? As in *interested*?"

"I, u-um—" Tessa stammered.

"Don't get me wrong, he's a great guy and a good friend to Etienne," Laura blurted out. "But obviously, he's the worst kind of womanizer going. There's no *way* you'll last more than a night or two in his bed, no matter what kinky stuff you let him do to you or how good it feels. You know that, right?"

No kidding. Tessa wasn't particularly surprised at either

revelation. She'd figured out that much all on her own. "I appreciate the warning," she found herself saying. "And I promise you, if I do get involved with him"—*What?* she exclaimed inside her head—"I'll be careful not to put emotions into the equation."

"Wow," Laura said, visibly taken aback. *Join the freaking club!* "When you decide to let yourself indulge in a fantasy, you really go whole hog."

Tessa smiled shakily and stood up. "I guess I do. Who'd have thought, huh?"

Laura chuckled, totally fooled by Tessa's hard-won and very fake bravado. "Ho-kay, then," her friend relented. "You realize you'll be the envy of every woman here, including me? Shay Duchesne is considered *the* lay of New Orleans."

Why did that not surprise her? "Yeah?"

"His reputation as a cockswain is pretty damn impressive. But he's very choosy about who gets to see him naked. And lately, there hasn't been more than a handful of women who've succeeded in tempting him." Laura kissed Tessa's cheek then unlocked the powder room door. "So, you go, girl. Just promise me you'll be very, very careful."

"I will. I swear," she said. And she meant it. She would *not* mistake a fling for anything more than it was.

Laura went to join her new husband, leaving her with a parting shot. "I'm serious, Tessa. No matter what he says, do *not* give that man your heart."

Chapter 10

Tessa returned from her little tête-à-tête with the bride and walked straight to a clutch of satin-clad bridesmaids, grabbed a flute of champagne off a tray, and proceeded to deliberately ignore him. Shay couldn't decide whether to be aggravated or impressed.

Clearly, his cover was blown. He was only sorry because he'd wanted to tell her himself that he was Treves Duchesne, of the infamous New Orleans Duchesnes, owner of the *maison* and heir to a fortune. Lord knew what lurid tales Laura had spun for her. He *should* have told Tessa in the car. But he hadn't been thinking of anything but how to finesse her out of that slinky pink bridesmaid outfit. Obviously, Tessa'd decided to let him twist in the wind. And just as obviously, she did not know him very well if she thought that would deter him from his pursuit.

He'd never been concerned for reputation, and he certainly wasn't afraid of a bunch of satin-clad women. But he had to admit, it was refreshing that the woman in question was not impressed by his outward credentials and wealth. It gave him hope that she was different. Special.

He strolled over and joined them. He kissed Tessa on the cheek. "Miss me, *cher*?" He smiled broadly when she gave him a death-ray glare. Oh, she was different, all right.

"No."

There she went, lying through her teeth again.

The other women giggled nervously. As usual, his notorious reputation preceded him. So what was new? "I understand you ladies were guests at Chez Duchesne last night. I hope you enjoyed the *maison*'s unique hospitality?"

One of them blanched, the other's cheeks went scarlet.

"Ah," he said with his most charming smile. "I see you did. Excellent. Now, if you'll excuse us, I have some business to discuss with Miss Kittredge." Mais, *yeah*, he told her with his eyes as he took her arm, *I now know exactly who* you *are, too.*

"I'm getting a little tired of being hauled around by everyone like a sack of potatoes," she said as he led her away.

"Not my fault your friend felt compelled to warn you about me." He spoke pleasantly but didn't let up on his grip or his pace. He was heading to his car. "Bouquet strategy? Really, now."

"Yeah," she said. "How to *avoid* catching it."

"Now, that's just plain hurtful," he returned evenly. "If you don't want to marry me, just say so."

She just glared at his attempt at humor. "Where do you think you're taking me?" she asked, digging in her high heels when they reached the path to the parking lot.

"My place."

"Shay, we've already been through this. I have no intention of going back to your house of ill—"

"My plantation," he corrected her. "Up by Bayou Lafourche."

She blinked, nonplussed. "Your . . . Why?"

He lifted a shoulder. "I was planning on going up after the reception anyway. Check on things. Maybe spend a day or two. I like to do that every few weeks. Make sure the old place is still standing. I could use some company. To hold my hand when the ghosts start rattling their chains."

Not that there were any ghosts. That he knew of, anyway. And the only chains were the ones he'd fasten around her limbs just before he fucked her to within an inch of her life.

"What do you say?" he asked, getting warm under the collar of his tux shirt just thinking about the assortment of toys awaiting them.

He could see he'd piqued her interest. An old Southern plantation was irresistible to women. Usually involving some fantasy about mint juleps and Rhett Butler. Hell, he could do Rhett Butler. But *his* movie would definitely be X-rated.

She licked her lips. Always a good sign. He waited patiently.

"It sounds intriguing," she finally said. "But I'm afraid I can't. My flight home is tomorrow."

"Flights can be changed," he said. "I'm sure there'll be another on the day after, or in three days. Or a week."

Her brows rose. "I was told I wouldn't last more than two nights in your bed."

"You shouldn't listen to gossip, *cher*. It's almost always wrong."

"And in this case?"

"Wrong." He swept her into a tight embrace and covered her mouth with his. He teased open her lips with his tongue and sank into the kiss with a silent moan. *Mon Dieu*, she was fine. He held her and kissed her until she stopped wriggling to get away. "Dead wrong," he murmured when he finally let her up.

"Shay—"

"Please? Let me change your flight for you." When she would object, he cut her off. "It's not paying for your services, it's being a gentleman. Since it's my fault you have to reschedule. I'll even upgrade your ticket to first class."

"It already is first class," she said tartly, and he grinned, wanting her even more.

"*Vien avec moi, 'tite chatte,*" he pleaded softly, his smile slowly fading. "Let me tie you up in velvet bonds and make you come in ways you've only dreamed of."

He felt a quiver travel through her body. He lowered his hand to her backside and pressed her into him, center to center. There was no possible way she could miss his massive hard-on.

"Don't make this more complicated than it needs to be," he told her. Except now *he* was the one lying. Because it *was* complicated. And getting more so by the minute. He realized if she didn't say yes soon, odds were he'd just lift her into his arms and carry her off anyway.

Dieu. He'd never felt this much like a caveman over *any* woman before. It was downright terrifying.

But that wasn't going to stop him.

"All right." She relented. "I'll come with you," and he let out the breath he'd been holding, probably since the first second he'd seen her at the *maison* bar last night. Hell, since the first second he'd seen her, a skinny little angel gazing up at the *Jaillissement*, fifteen years ago.

What was *happening* to him?

She scraped his hand off her ass and started toward the parking lot, her curvy bottom twitching back and forth enticingly as she walked. "Better hurry. Before I come to my senses."

Chapter 11

It was official.

She'd lost her mind. This was a huge mistake.

Tessa looked at Shay, then back at the imposing plantation house he'd parked the Lamborghini in front of. Like everything else about him, it was impressive. It was also very spooky.

Three stories of columned, antebellum elegance were tucked in shabby dissolution among the massive tangle of vegetation and forest of hardwoods and palmettos that covered the twenty or so acres of the surrounding estate. Vines crept over the mansion's gabled roofline, petals of heavily scented yellow jessamine flowers dripped from its covered galleries. Spanish moss hung in ghostly strands from the magnificent oaks that towered over it and cast the entire structure into shadowed gloom. Oh, what she could do with a landscape canvas like this!

As magnificent and striking a picture as it was, the place looked like there should be a serial killer living in it.

"It's, um . . ."

"Creepy?" Shay helpfully supplied along with a sardonic smile.

"Yeah," she admitted, feeling a trickle of nervousness despite her professional objectivity about the out-of-control garden. "Very."

"Don't worry," he said. "I was kidding about the ghosts."

She darted him a glance to see if he was teasing. He grinned. She made a face. "You can't tell me you don't have the money to fix this place up. Hire a landscape architect."

"I do," he said, unlocking the front door. "And I've tried. But as soon as I have it cleaned it up, the plantation house decides it doesn't like being presentable, and within weeks it's back to looking like this. I've given up, and we've declared a truce. As long as it doesn't start dropping roof tiles on my head, I leave it alone."

Wow. And this was the man who didn't believe in voodoo? "Maybe it just needs a woman's touch," she murmured without thinking.

"Maybe it does." He swung the door open for her. "If you want the job, it's yours."

She might just take him up on that. "Or maybe it doesn't," she breathed, her jaw dropping in astonished awe as she walked into the foyer. "It's absolutely gorgeous, Shay." He led her into the great room, and she turned in a full circle, taking it all in, then looked at him with a whole new respect. "I guess the house doesn't mind looking nice on the inside."

"A fickle thing, admittedly. Would you like to see the rest?"

"Yes, please."

Each room was more beautiful than the last. Not new and shiny, but glowing with venerable age and impeccable taste; even the slight fraying at the edges lent an air of worldly contentedness.

On the third floor, he pushed open a set of carved wooden doors and walked in. He turned back to her and spread his hands. "My rooms," he said simply.

Even if he hadn't said it, she would have known. She stepped into a luxurious sitting room furnished in rich, masculine leathers and blues and greens. The rugs were deep Orientals, as at the *maison*. There was a fireplace, bookshelves, and beautiful paintings of local unique landscapes.

She walked up to one. It was a moody painting of an outdoor maze. The hedges that made up the living puzzle were verdant green and clipped in a wild, unkempt style that belied the exact precision of the intricate pathways. In the middle, a woman in a flowing white gown waited for her lover, who was in the midst of the tangle of paths, hopelessly lost.

"Wow," she said. "This is beautiful. And very . . ."

"Disturbing?"

She smiled at him. "Yeah. Kind of. But the maze is, well, amazing. I love it. Is it a real place?" She'd told him on the drive up that she was a landscape architect. He had also surprised the hell out of her by opening up about his life and his hopes and even some of his most personal aspirations. Treves Duchesne was a complicated, thoughtful man.

"I've always wanted to do one." She made a face. "Not a lot of demand for them, unfortunately. Mazes are a particular interest of mine, professionally, I mean."

"Hell, you definitely have the job, then."

"What do you mean?"

"Look," he said and led her over to the French doors.

The mullioned glass door led to a covered gallery overlooking a vast, sloping meadow that ended at the reedy shore of a shallow bayou. "That was once a thriving branch of the Mississippi," he said at the direction of her gaze. "When the water disappeared, my family wasn't affected, but the planters who depended on the river for their livelihoods were bankrupted."

"What happened?"

His smile wasn't pretty. "Politics happened. What else?"

For some reason, she felt compelled to go to him. She put her arms around his neck. "Thank goodness for Chez Duchesne."

He smiled down at her, skimming his fingers down the slippery fabric of her bridesmaid dress, shaping her waist and hips with his palms. "Yeah," he said, his black eyes darkening. "But this is what I really wanted to show you." He pointed to an area of dense shrubs growing to the side of the meadow, bearing the faint, ghostly outlines of what obviously used to be a maze.

"It's the maze in the painting!" she exclaimed.

"Yeah," he said, putting his arms around her again. "The couple in the painting, that was my *grand-père et grand-mère*. She's the one who designed the maze, as a kind of living symbolism of their convoluted love story. You see, *Grand-mère*'s parents, they didn't approve of *Grand-père*. She came from one of those *Mayflower* type Northern families. In those days, Chez Duchesne was still a real bordello, and his reputation wasn't any better than it had to be, if you know what I mean."

"Sort of like you?" Tessa murmured with a smile.

"Very funny, *fille*. If I'm so bad, what are you doing here with me?"

She brushed a kiss over his lips. "Oh, I'm here *because* you're so bad."

"Is that so?" His hands traveled slowly down her sides. "You like your men bad, do you?"

"I like *you* bad," she whispered.

"In that case," he said, "I have more to show you."

"More?"

"Rooms in the house."

"Hmm. Let me take a wild guess." They both knew what was about to happen. There was no reason to be coy. She pressed closer. "Your bedroom?"

"For instance. Shall we take a look?"

Through an open side door she caught a glimpse of an antique wrought-iron bed. It looked high and wide and very sturdy, with ironwork rising from each of the four corners to form a sort of canopy box, but without the canopy fabric itself. "Is that where you keep the velvet bonds?" she asked, her pulse starting to pick up speed. Her boldness was so out of character, she hardly recognized herself.

His lips curved. "Would you like to try them?"

She swallowed heavily. *This was it.* This was something she'd been fantasizing about since Shay had taken charge so thoroughly last night. She hadn't had the guts to bring it up then. But today, ever since Laura had mentioned his predilections . . . well, she hadn't been able to get the idea out of her mind . . . or her body. "Shay . . ."

"Yeah, *cher*?"

Her knees started to tremble. "Laura told me you're into bondage and domination?"

His eyes narrowed, a shade warily. "I got the impression you are, too."

"I . . ." Nervously, she slipped her hands under his tux jacket, brushing them over his white silk shirt. She could feel his compact nipples harden at her touch. It gave her the courage she needed to say, her voice almost a whisper, "I want you to dominate me."

He regarded her cautiously. "What exactly do you mean by that, *cher*?"

"I don't know," she quietly confessed, feeling her face heat with mortification. Both at her request, and at her naïveté. "I'm not even sure what it involves."

His fingers tightened on her hips. "You want to find out? Is that what you're saying?"

She pillowed her aching breasts against his chest. "Last night you called me your sexual possession. That's what I want to be. Yours, to do anything and everything you want to. No limits. Nothing forbidden."

His black eyes swirled with dark, glittering excitement. "Are you sure?" he asked.

"Yes," she whispered. "I'm sure. Take me, Shay. Make me your odalisque."

Chapter 12

For a second Shay's heart stopped in his chest, then surged to life, pounding fast and hard in exhilaration.

Tessa's tremulous request thrilled him to the marrow.

This was *exactly* what he needed.

"And you're willing to do anything I ask of you?" he wanted to know. "You're not afraid?"

"Terrified." The shaking of her voice confirmed it, but she said, "I trust you, Shay. I know you won't hurt me."

Her blind trust humbled him, filling him with a fierce surge of protectiveness. "I am not into pain," he assured her. "Strictly a pleasure man."

"I'm glad to hear that." She smiled uncertainly, as though she'd never considered that risk. *Dieu*, she was an innocent.

"*Donc*, if at any time you wish to stop, just say"—he thought for a moment—"coffee break."

She seemed to understand. "Okay. But I won't."

"Best to be safe." He smiled back. "This way you can scream *no* all you like."

She paled, but in a good way.

Last night he had toyed with her will, coaxing her submission in their light forays into public exposure; he had also bound her wrists during their love play. He'd sensed instinctively she'd enjoyed both experiences. She was a natural submissive with daring tastes . . . yet another thing that had fascinated him about her. The adventuress inside versus the conservative exterior—an intriguing combination.

What submissions should he choose for her tonight? The possibilities were endless. It would take a lifetime to explore all the facets of bondage and domination they could enjoy together. Suddenly, he wished they had a lifetime to do so . . .

Tessa, she just may be the special woman he'd been looking for.

Wordlessly, he took her through the open door to his bedroom. He watched as she absorbed the room and its decor. His grandfather had been a collector of erotic art, and much of it was on display here. Little-known paintings by well-known artists, a few Art Deco sculptures, an amusingly suggestive wall clock, and an abundance of gilded mirrors—including a large one above the iron bed—all set the mood for decadence. But the bed was the centerpiece. Specially commissioned in France by *Grand-père*, the hand-wrought masterpiece was large enough for an orgy, yet hid secrets in its iron lace, perfect for the intimate initiation of a novice by her new master.

"I don't usually sleep in here," he told her. "Unless I have company."

"Do you have company often?" she asked, a jealous bite to her tone.

He smiled. Jealousy was a good thing between lovers. "Not nearly often enough. In fact, hardly ever anymore. I've been waiting for . . . someone special to bring."

A look of uncertain hope mollified her expression. But she didn't comment.

"Your dress goes remarkably well with the room," he said, bringing her further into it. Calf-length and elegantly cut, reminiscent of what his nude Art Deco figurines might have worn had they been dressed, the hem of her slim-fitting pale pink satin gown slashed down dramatically on one side, nearly touching the side of her sexy pink high heel. The draped neckline exposed the slopes of her breasts to perfection.

She glanced down, smoothing her hands over the slick fabric. "Laura has wonderful taste."

"Mmm. Too bad you won't be wearing it much longer."

"No?" She nibbled her lower lip, looking like a schoolgirl about to be punished by the older teacher she had a crush on. The thought was more than appealing.

"You have been a very naughty bridesmaid," he announced in low tones. "And as your groomsman, I feel it is my duty to discipline you."

Her throat worked. "But I *haven't* been naughty," she demurred, catching on at once to the fantasy.

His lip curled in alacrity. "Haven't you? Tessa, what were you doing at dawn this morning?"

Her cheeks reddened. "I . . . I was giving a man a blow job."

He frowned at her. "And where were you doing this?"

"Outside," she confessed reluctantly. "In a courtyard. It was deserted," she hastened to add.

"But in full view of a dozen windows and balconies?"

"Yes."

"Who was this man? Your boyfriend?"

"I— No, I met him . . . last night."

"A stranger, Tessa?"

"Yes."

"You had a strange man's cock in your mouth, with any number of people watching? And you don't consider that naughty?"

"I guess it was," she whispered. "I am naughty. Very naughty."

"*Bon,*" he said. "Then you must be punished, *non*?"

"Yes, Shay."

"Call me sir," he ordered.

"Sir," she obeyed, though her feet shifted. A sign of defiance? He'd see about that.

He took a step backward and lifted his hands away from his sides. "Take my jacket off for me."

After a heartbeat's hesitation, she came to him and slid it from his shoulders, her hands caressing the muscles of his biceps as she drew it off. She leaned in and placed a kiss on the side of his throat.

"Did I say you could kiss me?"

"No, sir," she murmured breathily. "I couldn't help myself. I want you so much."

He'd been aroused since they got to the plantation, but at her sweet declaration, his cock went thick and hard. "I'll decide when you can touch me," he said. "Now take off my tie and unbutton my shirt."

Her fingers fumbled with the knot, but she managed to slide the bow tie from around his neck. She started with his top button, struggling to pop it free. *Bon Dieu*, she was driving him mad!

It finally gave, and she glanced up at him briefly in relief, then went to work on the next one. He stood his ground, burning with splendid impatience. When she'd gotten halfway through the buttons, he couldn't wait.

"Lick my nipples," he commanded.

Her eyes darted to the V of exposed skin. She drew the shirt to one side and put her tongue to the disc of his nipple, flicking around the nub like a butterfly. He wanted to groan but didn't allow the sound to escape.

"The other," he said, and she obeyed. "Bite it," he commanded, his voice betraying his barely suppressed rapacious need. "Gently."

Her teeth nipped him just right. Light enough not to hurt— too much—and hard enough to send a streak of arousal straight to his balls. She did the same for the other one, ending with a firm suck. *Merde.*

He grasped her arms and set her away. "That's enough. Now take off your dress." He strode to a wing chair and sat down to watch her disrobe. He steepled his fingers in front of him. "Slowly."

She obliged, in a shy display of excruciating sensuality. "You should do this for a living," he growled, shifting against his ever-thickening erection. "You'd make a fortune."

She smiled coyly. "I only want *you* to see my body. Sir."

Once again, her lingerie was exquisite. Wisps of palest pink barely covered her breasts and mound. She wore pink thigh-high stockings with her sky-high I'm-a-bridesmaid fuck-me heels. She was a vision, enough to make any man's cock weep with desire. His was already sticking to his boxer briefs.

"Now your bra." As pretty as it was, he wanted it gone.

She slipped it off. Her full, beautiful breasts spilled out, making his hard-on practically leap from his pants. By now he was pretty sure *he* was the one being punished, not her. Not that he was objecting.

He liked her like this, in a half state of undress, and he decided to keep her that way for a while longer. "Go to the wall over there," he directed, pointing.

She walked to the other side of the room, opposite the floor-to-ceiling windows that overlooked the gallery and the woods beyond. There were heavy velvet curtains, but he never bothered to close them. The nearest neighbor was fifteen miles away.

She looked at him expectantly, standing by the wood-paneled wall.

His pulse quickened with anticipation. "Grasp the handle, there, and slide the panels open."

As she did so, her gasp of shock was fuel to the fire between his thighs. It was his toy cabinet, a wall-to-wall array of every sexual implement imaginable, all hidden discreetly in a deep recess behind the sliding doors of the false paneling, brought to light only when he was in the mood for something . . . out of the ordinary. And Tessa certainly was that.

She jumped backward and scanned the assemblage in horrified fascination. She shuddered out a breathy, "Oh, my God."

"Change your mind?" he asked, not sure if he'd let her, even if she wanted to.

"God, no," came her husky reply.

Merci Dieu.

"Go ahead, then. Pick your punishment."

"Just one?" she asked, and he blessed the day he was born with a penis.

"Hell, *cher*, I've got all night. All week." *A long, lonely life-time.* "You go for it, you."

She walked to the beginning of the collection. She moved like a racehorse, her naked back straight, her legs miles long in her high heels, her mane of auburn hair tumbling over her shoulders. *Salleau prie,* she was stunning.

Slowly, she examined his toys, implements, and bondage equipment. "I don't know what half of this stuff is for," she murmured. "And the other half I'm only guessing." She fingered a thin, clear glass dildo with raised red hearts scattered along the shaft.

"Go ahead and grab that one," he told her. "Whatever I end up doing to you, it *will* involve a dildo or two."

She turned to look at him anxiously. *"Two?"*

He just smiled. Surely, she hadn't thought she could avoid getting something put up her ass?

Apparently she had. Her eyes went round. To her credit, she moistened her lips, turned back, and slid the dildo from its rack, holding it gingerly in one hand as she continued her study.

She touched many of the things as she moved along the cabinet. More dildos, a multi-stranded leather flogger, a particularly inventive cock ring, several of the two dozen or so tethers and restraints hanging by their straps and chains. She was also fascinated by the spanking bench and the spreader bars.

Foutre de merde, he was getting voraciously horny just watching her look. His nipples were still zinging from her tongue, and he couldn't wait to return the favor.

"Enough," he said, rising from the chair. "Choose, or I will." He went to stand behind her when she hesitated.

Sensing his determination, she reached out and picked up the leather flogger, then returned to the dildos, and selected a large, realistic one. She turned to him and rested it against her lips, giving the tip a little lick. "This one reminds me of you, sir," she said innocently.

He swallowed, remembering all too well how amazing those lips felt wrapped around his cock. "Excellent choice." He took it from her, along with the flogger and the glass dildo. "Restraints?" he asked, brow raised.

She glanced over the selection.

"You choose," she said at length. "I want to please you, Shay." She looked up at him. "Show me how."

He searched her eyes and saw she truly meant it. How could he resist such an eloquent plea to be used in the most wicked and enticing ways?

He set her three items on the bed and went to the cabinet to make his choice of restraints for her. He decided on a set of long, heavy chains with fur-lined manacles. The effect would be more psychological than physically restraining, the sound and weight of the metal reminding her every second that she was in irons. He could also attach them in creative ways to the sturdy framework of the bed, holding her body open for him, for hours if he wished.

Her breath sucked in when he pulled the chains from their storage hooks. "Worried?" he asked as he let them spill noisily onto the bed, joining the other things.

"Yes," she whispered hoarsely. But that only seemed to increase her arousal. A stain of blush lay on her upper chest and throat, and her nipples stood at rigid attention.

Which reminded him . . . He went back and fetched a set of light nipple clamps. "You need to be punished for pleasuring mine," he said, holding them up.

"But you told me to!" she protested breathlessly. "Sir."

"Are you arguing with me?" he asked evenly.

"No!" She blinked at the bright red aluminum clamps, joined by a strand of red crystal beads, then returned her gaze to him defiantly. "I mean, yes. It's not fair."

If he weren't so painfully aroused he would have allowed himself a moment of amusement. Damn, she was a quick study. And so fucking perfect it made him dizzy.

"Pull down your panties, woman. Just to your thighs," he admonished when she would have taken them off completely. Again, for psychological effect. Somehow it was far more wanton to have one's knickers partway down that to be totally naked.

"You are a bad little bridesmaid," he said reprovingly as he strolled slowly in a circle around her, looking at her lower body. "Showing yourself to one of the groomsmen like this. Why do you do such naughty things?" Her neatly trimmed pussy was glistening wet, her ass round and plump as a juicy mango, beckoning to him.

"I let you see me because you're handsome and sexy," she said timidly. "And I've heard things about you . . . bad things."

He put his hand on her bottom, and she jumped a little. "What kind of bad things?"

She breathed in. "That you have a huge cock, and you know how to use it."

From behind her, he slid his fingers between her legs, gliding them along her wet slit, eliciting a low moan, gathering some of her juices. Then he slid them up to her back opening. She gasped softly as he rubbed her there with his slick fingers, hinting at things to come. Her cheeks turned bright red.

"Have you ever taken a man here before, Tessa?" he murmured, continuing to toy with her.

"N-no."

"Hmm," he hummed speculatively. "I see." He pressed his finger gently against the tight circle. It gave a little. He pressed harder. With his other hand he grasped one of her nipples and squeezed it hard, just as his fingertip slipped inside her.

"*Oh!*" She grabbed his arm and clung to him.

"Do you like how it feels?" he asked, wiggling his fingertip slightly.

She made a noise. "Yes," she said in barely a whisper. "Sir."

"Good," he said and withdrew, stepping over to the nightstand. He availed himself of a box of baby wipes, then brought out a box of condoms from the drawer. "Then we'll get along just fine."

She swallowed heavily. Her green eyes were the shade of a midnight forest by now, following his every move while he fetched one of the metal spreader bars she'd been looking at in the cabinet, and unbuckled the leather cuffs at either end of the three-foot rod. He could see her knees shaking as he fastened her wrists into the cuffs, which held her arms stretched wide apart.

He slid her panties off.

Leading her over to the bed, he reached up and swung out a sturdy metal rod attached to the upper rail of the iron canopy frame. The room's ceilings were twelve feet high, and the curlicue bed frame reached nearly eight. He attached Tessa's spreader bar to a chain that hung from the rod and raised the bar and her arms along with it. When it was high above her head, he locked down the chain so it wouldn't move.

"You're my prisoner, Tessa," he said. "Mine to do with as I wish. There will be no escape for you. Not until I allow it."

"Please, Shay," she said, twisting her wrists fretfully. Her breasts rose and fell, her breath coming in little anxious pants. "What are you going to do to me?"

"Sir," he corrected, with no small satisfaction at having total power over his beautiful captive. "Now, *ma chérie*, your punishment begins."

Chapter 13

Tessa's heart was hammering so fast and loud she thought it might just pound through her chest.

She watched in titillated terror, gasping as Shay squeezed a nipple clamp onto the pebbled tip of first one breast, then the other. The string of beads suspended between the two pulled the clamps downward in addition to the pinching sensation on her nipples. She squirmed as streaks of pleasure coiled through her breasts and tugged fiercely at her center.

"Bon?" he asked. "Feel good?"

"God, yes," she squeaked, squirming with the unfamiliar pleasure. She pulled at her bonds, wanting to touch her nipples, to make it go away, or maybe to make it pinch harder.

He smiled and unzipped his fly, pulling his engorged cock out so it jutted from his trousers like some kind of fertility god statue. "There, that's better."

She looked at it and felt her pussy unfurl.

"You want it?" he asked.

"Yes. Please. Sir."

He stepped up to her and brushed it across her belly, leaving a wet trail behind on her skin. "It wants you, too." He drew a finger through the wetness and brought it to her lips. She sucked the finger into her mouth, tasting his essence. He jerked lightly on the strand of beads hanging from her breasts, making her nipples sing with pleasure-pain.

She cried out, and he took back his finger. "But first . . ." He picked up the realistic dildo from the bed and sheathed it with a condom. "Spread your legs."

She hesitated. She'd never used a dildo before.

He gave her bottom a hard smack. "I said spread your legs."

"Ow!" she cried, but did as he asked. God, he was serious. Last night he had been playful, but tonight he seemed . . . different. Like he meant business. Like if she didn't do as he commanded, he really would get angry and punish her for real.

Alarm buzzed through her just as the dildo slid up into her. She gasped as the hard silicon stretched and filled her. It felt . . . amazing. "It feels like you," she said, and suddenly it started to vibrate. A low, steady hum that she felt clear to her toes. She tilted her head back and moaned in pure bliss. Oh. Mygod. *So much for punishment.*

The vibrations snapped off.

Her eyes shot open. Shay held up a small remote control and gave her a devilish smile. "Close your legs and don't let it slide out," he told her, "and I might turn it on again."

"You're evil," she murmured in frustration.

"You have no idea," he murmured back. He reached up and pulled a lever. The chain fastened to the stretcher bar above her head started to glide along the crossrail toward the center of the bed. When she was stretched taut, bent at the waist over the mattress, her feet on the floor and knees bumping the side, he pulled the lever again. It stopped, and she was held fast in that position, breasts grazing the silk coverlet, her bottom pushed out on display for him.

The vibrator turned on again.

And something tickled her ass. The thin leather strands of the flogger dragged over her skin, raising a rash of goose bumps.

"Oh, God," she whispered and squeezed her eyes shut.

He brushed the strands up and over her back, causing a flurry of shivers up and down her spine. "Don't lose the dildo," he warned, and she clamped her legs together tighter. The low vibrations were edging her closer to orgasm. She didn't want them to stop.

The first stroke of the flogger took her by surprise. It felt like a handful of snow granules hitting her backside. Sharp little stings that shocked her flesh to life. She cried out, not sure if it was pain or pleasure. He flogged her again, a sharp, light swat. And again. She gasped his name.

"I believe you like it," he murmured. "That won't do. This is supposed to be *punishment*."

She heard him take something from the cabinet. She didn't dare look. Her nipples were dancing with fire from the clamps, her pussy heavy with the dildo, her clit twitching from the effects of the vibrator, and her ass stinging from the leather. She didn't think she could take much more.

"Please," she begged. "Fuck me, Shay. Just fuck me."

"Oh, I plan to, *cher*. You can count on that. Just not quite yet." Something cool and wet landed between her bottom cheeks. "And you really must learn to call me *sir*."

She sucked in a breath as the tip of something round and smooth caressed her back opening, spreading the lubricant generously over her. The memory of his finger in her earlier flashed through her body like an electrical charge. "What are you—?"

"Shhh," he told her. "Just relax and enjoy it."

The toy was a curved glass dildo, made up of a series of graduated spheres. Her instincts said to panic, but it was hard to stay tense with the other dildo vibrating deliciously between her legs. She felt Shay's hand on her ass, kneading and caressing, helping her muscles let go. The glass head suddenly breached her opening and slid into her. It was slick and good, and Shay's hand kept a steady pressure on the thing, popping it slowly into her. One bead after another breached her with an accompanying staccato gasp, until the biggest sphere was lodged deep inside her. She gave a desperate moan at the heavy, strange sensation, struggling against her bonds to get free.

But it was no use.

"Shay," she pleaded, her voice guttural with need.

The flogger stroked over her ass. "Have you been punished enough?" he asked.

"Yes! No." She swallowed her frustration, her body a bundle of explosives desperately searching for a detonator. "I don't know. Please Shay, make me come," she begged.

The sting of leather burst over her ass, and she cried out. She felt the cool brush of his lips on the sting. He kissed her flesh, then bit her lightly. She felt the first tingle of orgasm. She stiffened. And the vibrator shut off.

"No!" she moaned. She felt the buckles of her bonds fall away.

"Crawl up on the bed," he ordered, and helped her up. "Lie on your back."

She did so in trembling anticipation, aching to come, spreading herself open for him. Wanting him so bad she could taste it.

She'd forgotten about the chains. But he hadn't. As soon as her wrists were rid of one form of restraint, he clamped on another. Still, the fur lining of the manacles felt luxurious after the leather of the stretcher bar. He locked them around her wrists, and this time also placed a pair just below her knees, fastening the chains to the bed so her arms were flat on the mattress above her head, but her knees were raised high in the air and bent, her legs spread wide apart. She was still impaled by both dildos.

She'd never felt so exposed.

Or so alive.

He watched her watching him undress as she lay there waiting for him to come to her. He peeled off his shirt and trousers, running his hands over his magnificent body. God, how she wanted him! *Please, please, please.*

"Hurry!" she urged him. Her clit screamed for completion.

Her heart begged for even more. *It* had never felt so exposed, either.

Or so alive.

What was it about this man that made her want him so badly? He was sinfully handsome, smart as a fox, rich as Croesus, and bad enough to keep her body begging for a lifetime of his special brand of decadent sex. But it wasn't just those obvious things that drew her to him. It was the way he always satisfied her needs before his and the consideration he always showed her, even as he did things to her that rightly should terrify her. That . . . and the way he looked at her. Like she was the only woman for him and he wouldn't have it any other way. An illusion, she knew, but it felt oh, so good.

"Please, Shay, please," she begged.

"I'm here, *cher*."

He crawled between her legs, gliding his hands down her inner thighs. He kissed the crease of her leg. Then found the remote and started the vibrator again. Instantly she felt the first shimmer of her elusive climax return. This time he didn't stop it. He put his mouth on her clit and sucked. She cried his name. He added his tongue to the mix, bringing her up off the bed. "Come for me, *cher*," he commanded, and she came apart. He started to tug the beaded dildo out of her backside, one intense bump at a time, and, with a scream, she catapulted into the most intense orgasm she'd ever had in her life. It hit her like a hurricane, rushing through her senses, pounding her with wave after wave of insane pleasure, sweeping away her past in a single screaming vortex of conscious realization: This experience, this man, had changed her profoundly. Irrevocably. Her life would never be the same again.

She would never be the same.

But he . . . he would move on, no doubt, and find other amusements. He would never know how intensely being with him had affected her.

Afterward, breathing hard, her blood rushing back to its normal places, she lay there, physically spent, mentally stunned, and emotionally numb.

Oh, my God.

She was in *love* with the man!

Unbidden, Laura's warning tripped through her mind. *No matter what he says, do not give that man your heart.*

He released her from her bonds, kissing her wrists as he unbuckled each of the restraints. Then he climbed on top of her and looked down at her with half-lidded, unreadable eyes.

The moment dragged out until she wondered if there was something wrong. If he could somehow see into her mind and read her guilty secret. That she loved him to distraction.

"What is it, Shay?" she asked.

"I've decided I want you to stay with me," he finally said.

Shocking her to the core.

For a second, hope raced a path through her heart. Had he gotten a similar flash of momentous insight as hers?

But, no. She must have misunderstood.

"Stay? You mean for a visit?" she asked, looking up at him.

"No," he said. "Longer."

Was this part of their fantasy game maybe?

It didn't feel like a game. He seemed serious. But that wasn't possible. Shay Duchesne was a self-admitted, confirmed player. He didn't do relationships longer than three nights. Everyone had told her that.

"For how long?" she asked, knowing full well that to spend one more night with him would be her undoing. Both literally and emotionally.

She felt him take the fake penis out of her. And suddenly his real one was there in its place. He felt hot and alive inside her, pulsing with need. She moaned softly.

"Forever," he said. "I want you to stay with me forever."

She wrapped her arms and legs around him, not trusting what she was hearing. But hoping like crazy anyway. "You can't possibly mean that. We've only known each other two days."

"*Non, cher.* I've known you for fifteen years. Dreamed of you. Waited for you. Thrown aside every woman in New Orleans because she wasn't you. You may as well say you'll stay, Tessa, because now that I've found you again, I'm not about to let you go. Even if I have to chain you to my bed to keep you from leaving."

A shiver spilled through her at the dark possessiveness reflected in his eyes as he said the words that turned her world upside down. How could she doubt his sincerity?

"I love you, Shay. And I do want to stay, but . . . This isn't about the fountain, is it? Marie Laveau's curse, or love spell, or whatever it was that you were trying to break this morning?"

"God, no." He kissed her then. A kiss filled with longing and with promise. And yes, a bit of magic, too.

Then he smiled down at her and said, "Call it fate, call it enchantment or love at first sight. You're the woman I want to be with. I love you, Tessa. Marry me, and I'll prove it for the rest of my life."

Epilogue

They say the three muses danced at the wedding.

The bride looked radiantly beautiful as she walked down the aisle of ancient brick to meet her handsome groom at the foot of the *Jaillissement de Plaisir*. The short ceremony was intimate and festive, and the best part was where the guests, led by the new Mr. and Mrs. Treves Duchesne, all tossed coins into the fabled fountain en masse and made a wish.

The reception that followed in the newly and gorgeously renovated courtyard turned rather wild, living up to the inscription's promise.

Tout quoi vous voulez, indeed.

But then the strangest thing happened. Every couple that attended the wedding together ended up married themselves by the end of the year.

But of course, *that* was a complete coincidence.

Because, after all, there's no such thing as voodoo . . .

Mortal Sensations

ALLYSON JAMES

*This story is dedicated to the amazing,
supportive, wonderful readers of Allyson James's
red-hot erotic romances.
Thank you!*

Chapter 1

Thomas Dupree looked like every woman's wet dream in a tux.

He stood at the end of the line of groomsmen, his rich brown eyes trained on his eldest brother, Leon, who was taking his vows. Madison Rainey had a fine view of Thomas from where she stood with the peach satin and tulle–clad bridesmaids sweating in the sultry New Orleans afternoon.

A drop of perspiration trickled down Madison's cleavage, and she had the brief, hot fantasy of Thomas, still in his tux but with black tie dangling, chasing the trickle with his tongue. As she shifted in her stilt heels, clenching her bridesmaid's bouquet, Thomas's eyes flicked to her. Their gazes caught and tangled, and Thomas gave her a hint of a smile.

Her blood heated, felt thick. Thomas had a square, hard face, hair so dark brown it was nearly black, and eyes the color of coffee. Rich black coffee, not a wimpy latte. When he looked at her, he truly *looked* at her, no evasive eye contact or pretending he didn't take in all of her. He studied her and damned anyone who caught him doing it.

Madison had been having hot fantasies about Thomas Dupree for nine years, ever since high school in Fontaine, where she'd shamelessly chased him. He'd teased her, she'd written about him in her diary; she'd drawn hearts with *MR + TD* in them on picnic tables. She'd even bought him an ID bracelet, a gold-plated one with the name Thomas engraved on it in fine script, and slid it into his locker. One day she'd caught him wearing it, and that day he'd finally asked her out.

The date had been a complete disaster, but she'd spent one golden week in giddy anticipation.

They'd lost touch after Madison moved in with her grandmother in New Orleans before her senior year, after she lost her parents in a car accident. She'd seen Thomas from time to time over the years as he'd changed from cute teenager to a hot, tasty man, but they'd never reconnected. These days, whenever Madison had a sex fantasy or an erotic dream, Thomas Dupree was its star. She imagined him pouring champagne into tall glasses while slowly removing his tie, or he'd pick her up in a red-hot sports car and drive her somewhere they could be absolutely alone, or he'd take her out in a limo and make slow, sweet love to her in the backseat.

Seeing him in person today made her nipples perk and her peach satin panties grow damp. Thomas in the flesh was tall and broad-shouldered, with a dangerous air of take-no-shit she'd always liked. Would real-life sex with him be slow and sensual as in her dreams, or wild and wicked and no-holds-barred?

Madison had heard a few unnerving whispers about Thomas. How he and his brother had begun a courier business, but Thomas seemed to leave town a lot, returning looking like he'd been living in the wild for weeks. No one knew exactly where he went, and his brother wasn't saying. Thomas might only be taking extended fishing trips, but looking at him, Madison didn't think so. No one who made the air crackle like that was sitting in a swamp fishing.

Madison realized with another frisson of pleasure that Thomas was assessing her, even if he didn't do anything so crude as run his gaze down her body while they were standing in a church with a priest between them. Still, he looked as though he knew every thought going on behind her eyes and every wicked fantasy she'd ever had about him. And knew he could make them come true.

If only.

The ceremony was long because they had a sermon and Communion, the whole works. But at last the recessional played and it was time to hurry down the aisle to photos, champagne, and a catered dinner in the beautiful old hotel down the street.

"Maddie." Thomas Dupree extended his arm. A nice arm, thick with muscle under his coat.

Madison put her fingers through the crook of his elbow, trying not to shiver at the raw strength of him. He moved with a quiet confidence and even more animal-like grace than when she'd known him nine long years ago.

"Haven't seen you in a while," Thomas was saying. "What you been up to, *cher*?"

His bayou accent wrapped its warmth around her; his voice had grown deeper and fuller.

"You know. Life." *Trying to keep everything from being ripped out from under me, trying to put off frightening decisions.*

"Yeah, I know." Thomas's smile fanned the spark that his *cher* had ignited. Heat curled down her spine to park between her buttocks.

They'd almost reached the door. The guests surged around them, pushing their way to the bride and groom, who stood on the steps. Thomas leaned to Madison, dark head bent.

"Maddie, I need to talk to you. Can we meet up later?"

The heat inside became a river of fire. She was acutely aware of his fingers on her arm, the way his head tilted, the way his dark eyes held hers as he waited for her answer. Madison caught his scent, warm, masculine, coupled with whatever musky cologne he'd dabbed on.

"Sure, if you want." Lord, she sounded so nonchalant. As though men as blatantly sexual as Thomas asked to speak with her all the time. As though her knees weren't bending, ready to let her slide her face down that tight, gorgeous tux to the nice bump between his legs.

"I need to ask you a couple of questions about your grandmother's house," Thomas said.

Madison's warmth died to ice.

The house. Of course. Everyone wanted to talk about the damned house. It had been in her family for two hundred years, and everyone from the historical society to developers wanted to get their hands on the property. So did predators like the prick Keith Girard, who wanted to marry socialite Madison so he could live in the famous house and move up the New Orleans food chain.

She was sick to death of everyone asking about her house,

sicker because both she and the property were in such bad
financial straits that she might have to sell it. And that she determined never, ever to do. It was her *home*, damn it. The place
she'd been happiest, the memories of family built up year after
year like layers of paint.

She gave Thomas a cool look. "Sorry. I think I'll be busy
later."

Madison released his arm and flowed away into the crowd,
but not before she caught his frown and the flash of anger in his
coffee-brown eyes.

Thomas watched Madison's slim form as she moved down
the church steps to hug Val and Leon in congratulations. She
looked like a flower in the peach satin and tulle, her dark hair
in a French braid that revealed her regal neck and the proud set
of her head.

What the hell had he said? Thomas had been saying the
wrong thing to Madison for years, ever since their one awful
date. He still squirmed when he remembered that date, and he
knew Maddie did too.

Lord, she got more beautiful every time he saw her. Madison
was twenty-five now, elegant and gorgeous. Those wide, dark
eyes looked as though they could see straight into his soul.

He needed to be with her, to talk to her. Thomas needed
to find out why the parasite Keith Girard was fighting so hard
to get his hands on Madison and her grandmother's house.
Girard was at the wedding today, invited by Thomas's mother,
because Girard's family owned half of Fontaine. There he was
now, ogling Madison and not bothering to hide it. Thomas had
never paid much attention to Keith Girard, until rumors began

to fly around that he was courting Madison Rainey and that an engagement would be announced soon.

Thomas's goal in life since then had been to find out all he could about Girard. He had decided it would be best to take Madison out after the reception, to a bar, maybe, where she could sip a clear martini, her lips lingering on the rim of her glass. He'd ask how she felt about Girard. He had to know.

He hadn't spoken to Madison in years, but he'd been aware of her, had seen her picture in newspapers and magazines. Madison the Crazy Hat Lady, they called her. Even in high school she'd created unusual and elegant hats, and now her hats were sold in upscale shops all over New Orleans. Everyone from celebrities to the social queens of New Orleans wore them, couldn't get enough of them. Madison wore them herself, smiling her big, charming smile under their brims.

Thomas hadn't spoken to her in months, and somehow he'd managed to piss her off in under two minutes. He'd pissed her off all those years ago, too, and he'd regretted it ever since.

No, it was safe to say he'd changed his life because of what had happened that night.

"Your eyes are about to fall out of your head, bro." His brother, Jean-Marc, another of the groomsmen, had come up behind him on the church steps. Marc was closest to Thomas in age, only a year younger, and the two had always been tight. "Close your mouth before you drool on your expensive tux."

"I don't drool over beautiful women," Thomas said. "I get dry-mouth, instead."

"Hey, didn't you have the hots for Madison in high school?"

"That was a long time ago. Another life."

"You're not that old," Marc said. "Neither is she."

Thomas shook his head. "Wrong time and place."

Marc grinned, his looks so close to Thomas's that many people were surprised they weren't twins. "Bullshit. Ask her to dance at the reception and see where life takes you."

Thomas wanted to. He'd love to cup his hands around her waist and pull her against him while they floated around the dance floor.

Madison had moved off with the other bridesmaids and the bride for the photo session. Val, Leon's bride, wasn't from Louisiana, or even the States. Val knew no one here, so Thomas's mother had recruited the daughters of the Duprees' old friends to be Val's bridesmaids. Madison had been happy to help out. But Madison was like that, always welcoming, always friendly.

Leon kept smiling at his new wife, Val, slim in the white dress that hugged her body. Another man was watching Val, a friend they'd brought home with them from their travels, a Greek called Demitri. Thomas's youngest brother Remy, who'd been with Leon out in Egypt, had told Thomas the incredible detail that Demitri joined Val and Leon in bed.

A ménage à trois. Thomas never would have believed it of Leon, the dutiful oldest Dupree son, who walked the straight and narrow. Thomas and Marc had embraced an adventurous sexual life, and even belonged to a club, but Leon had never been wild. Now, Leon looked happier than he ever had in his life.

Thomas was called to join the photo shoot, which went on and on. Shots of the bride; the bride with the groom; the bride and groom with Mom; the groom with his three brothers; the groom with the bride, the three brothers, and Remy's wife. Leon with his best friend, Demitri, and a shot of Val, Leon, and Demitri together.

A threesome. Hmm. *You go, bro.*

"Go for a run later if you don't get lucky?" Marc asked Thomas as they walked to the hotel for the reception.

Thomas nodded. He knew what Marc meant—a run in the swamps around Fontaine in some form other than human. Thomas and his brothers could shape-shift into any animal they wanted, provided they'd touched that animal at least once. Another barrier between himself and Madison. Shape-shifters weren't thick on the ground. How could he explain to the woman of his dreams that he sometimes liked to run around as a jaguar?

It probably wouldn't matter anyway, because Thomas couldn't even get close to Madison at the reception. Thomas ate the banquet food and raised his glass in the many toasts to Leon and Val, wishing he were sitting next to Madison instead of between Marc and Remy at the other end of the table.

Finally the lights went down, and the newlyweds had their first dance. Thomas watched Leon gaze into Val's eyes and her wicked smile flash in return. Val coiled her fingers around Leon's neck, her body in the sleek wedding gown sliding against Leon's. She certainly loved him. Their friend Demitri stood on the edge of the dance floor, watching with an intense dark gaze.

The music stopped, and the rest of the guests were invited to dance. Thomas looked for Madison, spotted her talking and laughing with girlfriends, her smile piercing his heart. Her scent, like orange blossoms, had filled him when he'd taken her arm, and it seemed to cling to him still.

He imagined hooking his forefingers into the off-the-shoulder dress and pulling down until he discovered whether she wore a little strapless bra underneath, a slash of lace on skin, or nothing at all. He'd teach her what he'd learned since their truncated relationship nine years ago—how to articulate her deepest needs and then beg for Thomas to fulfill them.

Everything you desire, deep in your heart. I will make it come true.

Someone blocked his view of her. Keith Girard, stopping to talk to Madison. *Damn.*

Madison was obviously uncomfortable with him. She stepped back on one heel as he curved over her, but Keith kept leaning in, talking fast.

Thomas was across the room before his brain registered that his feet had moved. He slammed his drink to an empty table and reached Madison and Girard in time to hear Girard say, "You know you want to, Maddie."

"Keith, not now," Madison said.

Girard grabbed Madison's arm. She glared at him, and Thomas's animal rage roared to the surface. He shoved himself directly between them, breaking Keith's contact with Madison.

Keith's face flashed anger. "What the fuck are you doing, Dupree?"

"The lady, she don't want to dance with you," Thomas answered, his Cajun accent flowing out with his fury. "You leave her be."

Girard sneered. "Can't you talk right, Cajun boy?"

"I'll talk better when you leave her alone."

"Don't make a habit of butting in to what you don't understand, Dupree. I can make life hell for you."

The man was an idiot. "I can make it a hotter hell for you, Girard."

Madison had stepped to Thomas's side, her wide eyes filled with anger. "Stop it, both of you. You're like a pair of . . . rutting goats."

"Maybe you should take this outside, gentlemen." Marc had moved to them and stood between Girard and Thomas now, speaking in a quiet voice. "Don't fuck up Leon's wedding."

He was right. Thomas stepped back. "Marc has a point. This isn't the place." He held out his hand. "Will you dance with me, Maddie?"

She glared. "No, I will not."

Damn it. "Madison."

"Don't 'Madison' me, Thomas Dupree. You ignored me for nine years, and now you push people around and want to dance with me so you can poke me for information about my house. Well, forget it."

"I don't think that's the only way he wants to poke you," Girard said. "You'd better watch him, Maddie."

"I think she'd better keep an eye on *you*," Thomas said. "I am."

Girard's gaze flickered at that, but he kept up the smile. "This isn't the swamps, boy, where you act like animals."

The trouble was, Thomas had animal in him, or at least an animal spirit, passed down from a shaman ancestor. Sometimes it did his thinking for him, and he had to shift and run, hunt, to let off steam.

"Both of you. *Grow up.*" Madison whirled, her tulle skirt floating. "I need some air."

Girard took a step after her, but Marc was there, hemming him in with Thomas, and Madison strode out of the ballroom unimpeded.

Girard's sneer remained as he straightened his cuffs. Thomas smelled fear on him. One Dupree brother Girard thought he could handle. He knew he wasn't up to handling two.

"You're not worth it." Girard brushed off his coat, then deliberately turned his back and walked away.

Thomas let him go. As satisfying as punching the man in the mouth might be, he had more important things to take care of.

He started for the door. "I gotta run, bro."

"Let me know what you find out," Marc said behind him. He added, just loud enough for Thomas to hear. "Good luck."

Tomas exited the ballroom of the old French hotel and hurried through the echoing tiled halls. The valet looked up inquiringly when he emerged from the front door, but Thomas didn't need his car. He needed Madison. Needed her so much his body berated him for not simply taking her out of there when he'd had the chance.

The valet said he'd seen Madison walking away, up the block to the right. Thomas quickened his pace. His gaze darted everywhere as he walked one block, then another, but nowhere did he see a woman in a peach dress with a fluffy meringue skirt. Madison was gone.

Chapter 2

"*Stupid* men." Madison stomped down the sidewalk, her spike heels catching in the cracks.

She hated Keith Girard, who assumed he was God's gift to women, and who also assumed he could paw at Madison whenever they met. Keith was the kind of person who tried to bully others with his money and power, and he'd made it clear that he wanted to get his hands on the Lefevre mansion as well as Madison, last scion of the Lefevre family.

Tonight Thomas Dupree had smiled at her, made her skin heat and her nipples peak, made her remember she was a woman. Until he'd started prying about the house and had made that little macho scene with Keith.

Well, screw them. She'd live in her old house until she was too elderly for anyone to care about her, and she'd liven things up by getting herself a boy toy. A sleek Cajun male called Raoul or something, who would lounge around in a thong all day and slather massage oil on her whenever she wanted.

Except that boy toys liked rich women, and Madison was up to her ears in debt. Even her exclusive hat designs couldn't cover both the loans and her day-to-day expenses, not to mention fixing the house that was crumbling around her.

Screw all men anyway.

The streets teemed with people, the French Quarter becoming one big party during the weekends. No one gave Madison a second glance in her frothy tulle and tight bodice, still carrying her bridesmaid bouquet.

Madison wanted peace and quiet. To go home. But her ride was Mrs. Dupree, and everyone in the wedding party would be spending the night in the hotel.

So she'd walk around, calm down, and head back. She'd sneak up to the room she was sharing with the other bridesmaids, take off her dress, and go to bed. Except the other two had planned to party on after the reception, and they'd probably drag Madison out on the town with them. Maybe she could pretend she was sick. She just wanted to be left alone.

A gate on the street stood half open, beckoning her into a narrow lane and a quiet, dark garden. The garden stood next to a hotel and looked to belong to it, but it also looked inviting and deserted.

Madison ducked inside, breathing a sigh of relief as the street noises died behind her. The air felt cooler in here, the humidity receding and a fresh breeze touching her skin. Someone had lit hanging lanterns around the place, the soft glow soothing.

She heard the trickle of a fountain, likely why the air felt nice. She followed a path through the overgrown garden, moonlight picking out lush green leaves and colorful flowers, the scent of night-blooming jasmine in the air. Her heels sank into the earth between the stepping-stones, everything damp.

Madison found the fountain in the middle of the garden. The bowl was round marble, old, streaked with age. The pedestal in its center held the curvaceous figures of three women. As old as it was, water still trickled through the fountain, the sound relaxing.

An inscription ran along the lip of the bowl. Madison walked slowly around the fountain, reading the simple line: *Tout quoi vous voulez.* She didn't speak French as well as her grandmother had, but she thought she understood the gist: "All that you wish."

She felt her limbs grow heavy and warm as she circled the fountain a second time. Tension drained from her, though somewhere in the back of her mind, anger wound on.

The story of my life thus far. Only granddaughter and last surviving relation of Felice Bouvier, the famous beauty. Felice had descended from a Creole family who'd been living in New Orleans long before the 1803 purchase brought in the upstart Americans. Rumor had it that a Bouvier ancestor had been a friend of Jean Lafitte, that perhaps Madison's great-great-ever-so-great-grandmother had once been his mistress.

Rumor also whispered that Madison's grandmother, Felice, one-quarter black, was a voodoo witch. How else had she landed Pierre Lefevre as a husband? Felice had married Pierre, himself of mixed American and Creole ancestry. Pierre had inherited a grand old house in the Garden District, and the two of them had moved in. Already the place had been falling apart, the Lefevre fortunes having dwindled. But because the two were so popular and came from two of the oldest families in New

Orleans, they'd thrown the wildest parties in town, knew all the stars of early Hollywood and the wealthy and the great.

Photos of Madison's grandmother as a young woman showed her in flapper garb, with large, dark eyes and a short bob of black hair. The photos did not disguise the wicked sense of humor that had never left her, even into old age. Madison's fondest memories of childhood were the summers she'd spent in the house with her grandmother.

Before her grandmother had died last year, she'd told Madison that the rumors were true—Felice did have magic and *her* own grandmother had been one of the most powerful voodoo practitioners in the bayous. Felice had infused the house with magic and inferred that the magic would make sure Madison would always be safe and well.

Madison, inheriting not only the house but its tax liens and unpaid second mortgages, hadn't seen where magic had helped her much.

The Lefevre money was all gone now, so the investors and bankers told Madison. Madison's parents had died suddenly the summer before Madison's last year in high school, killed on the road between Fontaine and New Orleans during a bad storm. There had been nothing for Madison to do but move in with her grandmother.

When Madison's grandmother died, loneliness had descended on her. She'd had a few boyfriends during and since college, but no relationship that lasted. She assuaged any horniness with fantasies of Thomas Dupree. Even now, as annoyed as she was with him, she wanted him there to peel off her dress and lick his way down to her clit, which was swelling at the thought. She wanted him to drink her, and she wanted to unzip his pants, to go down on her knees and explore every facet of his penis with her lips and tongue.

He'd be big and luscious, long and dark. She wanted to learn his taste, smell his skin, know the feel of his head gliding into her mouth.

Her nerves tightened, her nipples pulling as though they anticipated the nip of his teeth. He'd say her name in his deep, Southern voice, the Cajun lilt rippling over her senses. *Madison. Cher.*

All that you wish. The fountain seemed to beckon to her.

Madison fished in the little purse that dangled from her arm and pulled out a quarter. She took a deep breath and thought a minute, trying to find the right words.

"I wish for one night of over-the-top sexual ecstasy that reminds me why I love being a woman. With the hot-bodied Thomas Dupree. And no talk about my house. Just one night, that's all I ask."

She tossed the coin. The quarter made a soft plop in the dark water, the sound spreading through the quiet.

Her words died off into a sigh. The garden was still, the breeze barely moving the leaves. If she expected magic, she had to be crazy. She'd finish the wedding weekend, go home, and be lonely, horny, and worried.

Anger surged through her. She was sick of worry, sick of watching other people's happiness while she fought to keep body and soul together, sick of people trying to use her, thinking they could manipulate her because she was desperate.

She slammed her small bouquet into the fountain's bowl. The petals broke apart, floating on the water like sparkles of light.

"No, wait, I wish for a sex god to come down and teach me all there is to know about sex. There. How do you like that, fountain? I want sex, sex, and more sex. Pleasure so pure it makes me scream."

The fountain gurgled, and Madison drew a long breath, relaxing into a laugh. "Hey, if you're going to wish, why not go for it?"

Her anger slightly sated by her absurdity, she walked back out of the garden and glided into the street. A bar called Les Bon Temps beckoned her from across the street, and she crossed to it with a surge of people, a drink suddenly sounding wonderful.

In the garden behind her, a male figure stepped out of the shadows. Moonlight gleamed on what might be horns on his head, or it might be a trick of the light. His name was Alexi, and he was the son of Eros, the god of love and sexual joy. The desperate plea pulled at his heart, and he thought that maybe, just maybe, he'd at last found the means to his own redemption.

Thomas finally spotted Madison, her tulle skirt swirling as she strode into Les Bon Temps. The bar overflowed with people, laughter and music spilling out into the street. Thomas's heart beat faster at the thought of her in there alone, with drunk males eyeballing her in her off-the-shoulder satin that vividly showed the poke of her nipples.

He growled.

He pushed his way into the bar, searching for Madison through the dark and the crowd. So many people were out tonight, the weather nice, the weekend in full swing. Girls in low-rise jeans that revealed bits of thong sashayed in front of their men, their cropped tops baring belly buttons with navel studs. Men in jeans and boots, beers in hand, talked with friends or flirted with the ladies.

He saw Madison at the corner of the bar, standing out in her peach froth. She leaned on the bar and toyed with an olive in her drink. As he watched, she lifted the olive to her lips, curled her tongue around it, and drew it into her mouth.

Thomas stopped dead, his cock responding. He watched her lips close around the cocktail stick where the olive had been, mouth pursed as she sucked.

Damn.

The man standing next to Madison noticed, too. The large, fleshy goon gave Madison a leer and moved closer.

No. Mine.

The predator in Thomas got him across the floor in record time. He slid himself between the goon and Madison and leaned against the bar, facing her.

"Hey, *cher.*"

She gave him a wary look, but her rage seemed to have dissipated. "Hey, Thomas."

Thomas gestured to the bartender and asked for a bottle of beer. The bartender nodded and thunked an open bottle to the bar. The goon who'd been ogling Madison looked Thomas up and down and decided to move off in search of easier pickings. Thomas slid out a twenty and told the bartender he'd pay for Madison's drink as well.

"You didn't have to do that," Madison said.

Thomas shrugged, upended the beer, and poured some down his throat. "You all right?" he asked after he swallowed.

"Yes, why wouldn't I be?"

"I'm sorry if I made you mad back at the reception," Thomas said. "You seemed pretty upset at Girard, and I wanted to help. If he's harassing you, tell me. I'll do something about it."

"Oh, yes? Are you my guard dog now?"

"Girard's a creep. Steer clear of him."

"He's one of the richest men in New Orleans," she pointed out. "Not to mention Fontaine."

"That's true, but trust me, you don't want to get involved with him."

"Thomas, I *really* don't want to talk about Keith Girard."

"Fine by me, *cher*. Let's grab a table."

"There aren't any. It's too crowded."

Thomas took her elbow and guided her away from the bar. Just as he knew it would, a corner table emptied as he walked toward it—it was strange how humans responded to his dominant and predatory stare.

A cocktail waitress who looked run off her feet but still smiled cheerfully gave the table a quick wipe-down, and Thomas assisted Madison onto the tall chair. "I need to talk to you, Maddie."

Madison took a sip of her martini and set down the glass. "Not about my house."

"All right." But if she didn't want to talk about Keith or the house, he didn't have an opening. "So what do you want to talk about?"

"You." Madison moved the cocktail stick around the glass, her brown eyes fixed on him. "Tell me about this business you started with your brother."

Thomas shrugged, but he picked his words carefully. "Not much to tell. It's a courier business. We deliver things."

"By slow ship? You're gone for weeks at a time."

The fact that she'd noticed made his heart go thumpety-thump. "We do deliveries around the world." Thomas gave her the cautious line he gave to the curious. He and Marc did do deliveries, domestic and foreign, but they were documents or packages that needed to be guarded at all costs. Sometimes they delivered human beings—escorted wanted men back to the States for trial or helped hostages escape to safety. They did their good deeds and got paid, but they couldn't step into the limelight for it. That had always been fine with Thomas.

"Interesting," Madison said. "I've always wanted to travel."

"So why don't you?"

"I'm broke, that's why. Plus I have the fall and spring seasons to design for every year, and the charity dinners grandmother always gave that all of New Orleans expects me to continue. You know, real life."

She was prickly tonight, but it only increased Thomas's libido. He wanted to lift her into his arms, carry her off to some exotic island, make love to her in the moonlight. He didn't want simple, romantic sex either. He wanted sexual play that would set his body on fire, and hers. He wanted to give this woman pleasure. He craved to do so.

Thomas moved his hand to where hers rested on the wooden tabletop. He touched the backs of her fingers, finding them too cold. He wanted to envelop her small hand in his, warm it.

Her gaze went to their joined hands, and her chest rose against the satin décolletage.

"I want to apologize," Thomas said to her.

"For what? The reception? You just did."

"No, for our date nine years ago."

As he'd hoped, she gave him a sudden Madison smile. She'd broken his heart with that smile. The one night he'd tried to impress her he'd succeeded in making a complete idiot of himself, but Thomas had grown up a since that night. He wanted to show her how much.

"You mean the cramped front seat of your pickup?" Madison asked, wrinkling her nose. "The gearshift in my ear that nearly knocked me out?"

"That's the one. I was clueless, and you deserved so much better."

"For my first time?" Her smile could light a room. "I was sixteen and also clueless."

"You were pretty pissed at me, I remember."

"I was embarrassed. And pissed at myself."

She didn't move her hand from under his touch. She lifted her fingers slightly and twined them through his.

Waves of heat ripped through his body, and Thomas's hard-on gave a throb. "We should get out of here," he said. He could smell the scent of orange blossom again, even more so. He wondered if she'd taste of oranges if he lifted her hand to his lips.

"We could go to my house."

Thomas looked at her in surprise. "Your house?"

"You want to talk about it so bad, we might as well go there."

"I thought you were staying at the hotel, like everyone else."

"I'll call my roomies and leave a message not to worry about me." She withdrew her hand and took another long drink of her martini. "Besides, I want to get out of this damned dress."

Thomas's heartbeat felt thick as he imagined her unzipping the bodice, sliding the dress from her shoulders while he watched. Yep, leaving was a good idea before anyone else saw his cock rise up out of his pants.

Thomas held his arm out for her as he had when they walked down the aisle in the church. As before, she slipped her hand through the crook of it, leaning a little on him. He liked the feel of her pressed all along his side as they made their way through the crowd.

Near the door, they passed a dark-haired man he recognized from the wedding. A friend of Demitri's, he remembered. A man of dark good looks who'd kept to the background, a little mysterious. He wore a tux but had loosened the tie. Alexi, Thomas remembered his name was.

The man was giving Madison the once-over. Dark eyes traveled down her body to her legs that were lusciously sexy in her high heels. It was a longing look, a covetous look.

Sorry, son. The lady is mine.

Thomas tightened his hold on Madison's arm and led her from the bar.

Behind them, Alexi watched them go, his body tight with need. After they exited, he rose to his feet, poured the last of his drink down his throat, and followed.

Chapter 3

Madison's house was in the Garden District, a stand-alone that hadn't been turned into high-priced condos or a bed-and-breakfast. The façade was pink stucco with black wrought-iron railings on the front porch and second-floor balcony. Shutters lined the tall windows. Despite the fact that the house needed much work, Madison tried to keep it nice-looking on the outside, sacrificing her weekends to painting and keeping the yard trimmed.

She said nothing as Thomas helped her out of the taxi and paid the driver himself. She felt so cheap letting him pay that plus the eleven-dollar martini she'd ordered on stupid impulse, but she hadn't lied when she said she was broke. She barely had enough left over for toothpaste.

She walked up onto the porch that had been the scene of so many childhood play days, Thomas's tread heavy on the stairs behind her. Madison fished in her little purse for her key, her hands clumsy. Thomas took the purse, plucked out the key, and unlocked and opened the door.

The double scent of beeswax and sandalwood met them. Madison kept the inside of the old place as clean and sweet-smelling as she could. Thomas looked around in appreciation at the soaring hall, the twisting staircase with its wrought-iron railing, the big open double doors leading to the parlor on the left, the dining room and kitchen behind it.

"You could bowl in here," Thomas said, looking down the length of the hall. The house ran a long way back into the property, like a shotgun house, with rooms on one side of the main corridor.

"My grandmother would have a conniption," Madison said, dropping her purse on a table. She winced as she pried the pumps from her feet. "Don't think I didn't try it."

"It's beautiful."

"It's old and falling down. Do you want a tour? Or to try to talk me into selling? You can tell me how stupid I am to try to keep it from being sucked up by developers, and then offer me a lowball figure that you think I'll be desperate enough to take."

Thomas folded his arms and leaned against the open doorframe to the parlor. "People are really shitting on you, aren't they?"

"They say Felice Lefevre was a crazy old woman. She sat on this gem until it was too run-down to be worth anything." She sighed. "Maybe she was. My grandmother was always saying that the house would take care of me, but I don't know what she meant. And now I'm following in her eccentric footsteps."

"I don't want to buy your house, Madison."

"Well, that's a relief." Her sarcasm bled through. "Then why are you so interested?"

"I want to know why Girard wants to buy it."

Madison shrugged. "Hell if I know. I think he wants to be a man-about-town, lord of the manor, married to the Lefevre heir, that kind of thing. My grandmother always regarded the Girards as white trash that got above themselves."

"Your grandmother was right. But I'm white trash from the swamps, so I can't really talk too much."

Madison shook her head. "Grandma always said the Duprees had a bit of class. Good people, she said."

A smile touched Thomas's mouth. Damn, didn't he look good leaning there in his tux, with his tie loose? Like a male escort getting ready to make sure he fulfilled all his required duties.

"You know, *cher*," he said slowly, "there's another reason I brought up our date nine years ago."

Madison's heart tripped at his sexy tone. "Our only date. We were still using pimple cream. It hardly matters now."

"I made you unhappy that night. I didn't fulfill you, and that's what I've wanted to do from the beginning."

Warmth snaked through her. "I still liked kissing you," she said, voice soft.

"Your unhappiness made me want to remedy my skills." Thomas switched his hands to his pockets, his rumpled suit and his dark eyes making him look like a sex god. "So I did remedy them. Marc and me, we joined a club."

Madison tried a grin. "A club for survivors of disastrous virginity taking?"

"I've learned a lot about pleasure over the years, Maddie. About discovering what a lady wants, even when she doesn't understand herself. And then giving it to her. Pure pleasure. A lady puts herself into my hands, and I give her what she most desires."

A dark feeling spread from her heart. "Is that what you want me to do? Put myself into your hands?"

"I do. If you wish it."

"To make up for one bad date nine years ago?"

Thomas shrugged, a nonchalant gesture that rippled muscles under his suit. "Why not?"

"I'm not really into casual sex." To be honest, she rarely had the chance for it, hence the wish at the fountain.

Thomas lifted himself from the doorframe. "Let me give you this pleasure as a gift."

She held up her hands. "When you say 'club' . . . I'm not really into S&M kink, either."

For answer, Thomas gave her a slow smile. "Neither am I. It's not what you think, Maddie. It's trust and pleasure. I want to give that to you."

"Why?"

"So many reasons."

Madison went silent, feeling the cool floorboards through her stocking feet. She wasn't sure she truly knew this Thomas Dupree. The Cajun kid Thomas, yes. The sexy businessman with the orgasm-inducing smile, not so much. She didn't know much about bondage except what she heard in jokes, and she never watched porn. Why spend time watching people getting what she couldn't have?

Her imagination put a riding crop into Thomas's hands as he

stood there in her hall, looking so good. He'd tap it against his palm, smooth the shaft between his fingers. Ask her, *Madison, have you been naughty?*

"I'm not sure," she heard herself say.

"That's all right. It's trust, not force."

Thomas's throat was dry, and it was all he could do to stand quietly and wait for her answer. She still had her hands raised defensively, her eyes challenging him. In his usual encounters, the lady would have already been begging for him to do what he liked. He'd gotten cocky with his sexual prowess, used to every woman wanting a chance to be with him. Madison was another story.

"I do want to give you this gift," he said. "Maybe I should ask what you would like. Anything you desire, and I'll give it to you."

Madison wet her lips, making him remember her red tongue curling around the olive at the bar. "Anything?"

"Anything. I'm yours tonight, *cher.*"

She tilted her head to one side, and Thomas held his breath. He'd never offered this to a lady before—always he was in control, telling her what they would do, when they would begin, when they would finish. But he didn't want to rush Madison, the woman he cared for. She was like a precious gem in his hand, to be treasured, not tossed around like a worthless pebble.

"What I'd like," Madison announced in a slow, sensual voice, "is to see your cock."

Thomas hid his jump of surprise. He'd expected her to want to be stroked, to be brought to orgasm, to be put to bed relaxed and warm. She wanted to see *him*? If he dropped his pants now, she'd see a cock that was swollen so hard it was almost painful, a cock that was dying for her.

"You did say whatever I wanted," Madison said as he hesitated. "Are you going to run out now and proclaim to the world that Madison Rainey is a slut?"

Sweet gods, what kind of asshole men did she know? "What is between me and my lady is always private, never food for gossip. And you aren't a slut."

"I didn't think I was. But I've heard about locker-room talk."

"In the locker room, *cher*, I only remind my brother how I kicked his ass at racquetball. Or basketball or whatever it was we just finished playing."

Madison folded her arms, pushing her breasts against her bodice. "Does Marc ever kick *your* ass?"

"He does. And he reminds *me* about it."

She tapped her finely formed foot in its sheer stocking. "It's getting late. Are you going to show me? Or are you too shy?"

For answer, Thomas shed his jacket and draped it over the nearest chair. His tie followed, then the restraining cummerbund. He clicked off his cuff links and rolled up his sleeves, and finally popped open the catch on his pants. He let the slacks fall and pool around his ankles, and he followed those with his black satin boxers.

No fear that she wouldn't be able to see his cock. It jutted out, thick and long, visible in the brilliant light of the overhead chandelier. Madison's gaze went to it, her tongue playing on her lips again.

Thomas's balls were so tight they ached. He wanted to shove the pretty tulle skirt out of the way, part her thighs, and take her in a good, hard fuck. He wanted to turn her over and work on her sweet, petite little ass until it opened for him, and then he wanted to fuck her there. He wanted her to scream in pleasure until she couldn't scream anymore, and then he wanted her to smile at him in gratitude for giving her the pleasure.

After that he wanted to kiss her lips, curl up with her in bed, and protect her from any other man who wanted to do the same.

She put one hand on her hip, rocking her heel as she touched fingertips to her lips. "It's not bad," she said.

Not bad? "Glad you like it."

"What I really want to do is suck it."

Look at her, all challenging, thinking she wants to dominate. Thomas never let his subs touch him until they understood that the play was all about their pleasure, that he got his pleasure from mastering and fulfilling their desires.

Now he was getting his rocks off watching Madison trace her lips with one fingertip and gaze longingly at his cock.

He swallowed. "Come here, then."

Madison crossed the hall slowly, her skirt rustling like leaves in the wind. She stopped when she stood face-to-face with him, only the length of his cock keeping them apart. The tulle touched his tip, the scratchy fabric incredibly erotic.

Thomas had never seen her beautiful face this close. On their best-forgotten date, it had been pitch-black out when they'd started kissing and groping in the front seat of his pickup. He'd never looked at Madison from inches away, allowing himself to gaze into her soul-dark eyes.

"How do you like to do it?" he asked her.

Madison blinked. "The usual way, I guess."

Thomas's breath caught. She was still an innocent. Any man she'd gone down on had probably only wanted cock in mouth, quick come, finished.

"I'll teach you a new way," Thomas said. "You'll have to keep my cock sated, or I'll just want to fuck your mouth and come fast. You need to lick it, touch it, get to know it. Then you suck it, slow and sweet."

Madison listened, her eyes darkening. She gave him a nod.

Thomas caught her before she could descend to her knees. He cupped the back of her neck, pulled her up to him, and kissed her.

He tasted the bite of cocktail she'd drunk at the bar, the sweet taste of Madison behind it. Her lips were soft, pliant, warm on his. She melted closer to him, his cock lost in the froth of her skirt. His mouth took hers, tongue moving gently, not mastering.

He needed this kiss. He needed to taste her, to feel her tongue in his mouth. She arched up to him, her hands curling around his back, pressing her lips harder and harder against his. She wanted to be kissed as much as he wanted to kiss her.

Thomas wound his arm around her, feeling the curve of her waist through warm satin. He rarely kissed and held a woman—he pleasured them and he let them go, never completing the emotional connection. But he wanted to kiss Madison. To kiss her and hold her and sleep with her and wake up with her in the morning. He didn't do that with women either. Thomas never wanted to be vulnerable.

Madison eased back from him and touched his face, tracing the line of his cheek. More things not allowed. And Thomas stood there and took it.

"Are you ready?" she asked him.

Was he ready? His cock was trying to poke its way through her skirts to find the warm nest of her pussy, ready to press his way home. He tried not to laugh. He was so hard he was pounding, and he thought he'd burst or die before she started. Imagining his come all over her face didn't help.

He dragged in a raw breath. "You go for it, sweetheart," he said.

Chapter 4

Madison held his hands to steady herself as she sank to the floor. She pooled the skirt under her to cushion her knees, then she put her hands on his hips and observed the penis in front of her.

Her heart raced behind her boned bodice, her blood so hot she thought she'd scald from the inside out. Thomas's cock jutted out to her from a dark thatch of hair, the staff long and dark. It moved a little with his pulse, as though anticipating her mouth. Thomas's hands were on his hips, fingers tight on his skin, the knuckles whitening as he waited.

Madison liked his salty, warm smell, his body heat enticing her to come closer, closer. She leaned into him, inhaling.

When she put out her tongue to lick the tight skin, Thomas flinched. Madison wanted to laugh. The gorgeous Thomas Dupree, who talked so confidently about mastering Madison's desires, gasped when she touched him. She nipped his tip, and he flinched again, sucking a breath between his teeth.

"You keep doin' that, you'll regret it." His voice dropped to a growl, commanding, no longer gentle.

"Will I?" She nipped him again.

"Madison." The word held a warning.

"Tell me what you want," she whispered.

"Lick it. Get it wet. Then take it in your mouth."

Madison studied the cock, running her tongue over her lips. He was big, and she wondered whether he would fit.

"Do it, Madison."

Madison had a wild impulse to obey, so compelling was his voice. But she took her time, touching the crown with her tongue, tasting the hot darkness of his skin. He smelled so good. She wanted to rub her face against his penis and balls, smelling him, tasting him.

She ran her tongue underneath the tip and circled the head again, wondering if he knew she'd been fantasizing about doing this when she sucked the olive off her cocktail stick. Her wish at the fountain had opened her mind to deeper, darker fantasies.

She widened her mouth, curled her tongue around him, and then took him between her lips.

Thomas let out a groan. He threaded fingers through her hair, imbibing sensation after sensation. The softness of her hair, the wet heat of her mouth, the flick of her skilled tongue ran together in his brain in a cloud of erotic ecstasy. He looked down, watching her lips pucker around his shaft, her dark lashes resting against her skin. She clutched his hips as though she feared he'd run away, but there was no reason to fear that.

Madison's tongue rubbed the underside of his cock, and heat

glided to Thomas's anus, then down his legs to his toes curling inside his shoes. God, she was beautiful, this proud, lovely
lady. She needed help and didn't want to need anyone; she stood
straight and strong but was so vulnerable at the same time.

And damn, wasn't she good with her mouth? Thomas let his
head rest against the doorframe as her tongue did its work. He
resisted rocking into her mouth, not wanting to hurt her. Let her
get used to him. His cock was so rock-hard it screamed at him,
his balls tightening with each suckle. He wanted to fuck her
lips, to lay her down and drive into her sweet pussy; he wanted
to do so many things with her.

He wouldn't come in her mouth, though. Thomas was always
safe, and though he knew he was clean, he'd do her the courtesy
of not worrying her. Her well-being was his responsibility, and
he took it seriously.

Madison continued to suck, her mouth working, her fingers
sliding around to his ass. *Oh, yes, cher.* Wouldn't it be lovely
if she learned how to touch him there, how to slide a butt plug
into him while she sucked him off? The imagined pleasure of
that heightened the pleasure of what she did right now.

He felt the pulses that meant he was about to come. He
didn't want to stop, didn't want to pull out. But he would. He'd
not rush her.

Madison felt Thomas deliberately remove his hands from her
hair, clench his fists, try to step back. He wanted to stop. From
his ragged breath, the swaying movement he couldn't stop, the
tension in his body, she knew he was about to come. He was
trying to pull away before he did it all over her.

Well, too bad. As Thomas stepped back, Madison sank her
fingers into his buttocks and pulled him onto her again. Thomas
swore, his body jerked, and he groaned her name. At the same

time, sweet liquid poured into her mouth, the seed of the man she'd been longing to taste for nine years.

Alexi watched from the landing above as Thomas threw his head back, fists clenched, and cried Madison's name. Alexi's own cock stood up hard and tight as he imagined Madison's sweet tongue on it and the pleasure that Thomas must be feeling.

These two belonged together. Alexi knew it, and deep down inside, they knew it, too. But there was a wall between them; Alexi could almost see the barrier shimmering between their bodies despite the most intimate act they were sharing.

Madison feared that no man would love her for herself, wasn't certain any man could. Thomas feared exposing himself, being vulnerable. Ironic that a man who'd become a Dom worried that he wasn't good enough for the beautiful woman on her knees before him.

It was through these two people that Alexi would make up for his sins and be allowed to return home, where he belonged. Exile was bitter, and Alexi had had enough of it.

That didn't mean—he thought with a chuckle as he watched Madison dreamily swallow all the come that Thomas could pour into her—that he didn't get to have any fun.

"I want to know everything about Keith Girard," Thomas said when he walked into the office on Monday morning. "What kind of money he has and where, what he's up to, what he's done in the past, anything dirty on him. The dirtier, the better."

Marc looked up in surprise from his computer, and their secretary, Angela, who sat in the chair to the right of Marc's desk, raised her elegant brows. "A new case?" she asked. She gave Marc a disapproving look. "You never told me about a new case. I don't have a file started."

"It's not a case," Marc said. "It's my brother's new obsession."

"I want to know why Girard is so hot to get his hands on the Lefevre mansion," Thomas said. "What about that house has got his attention?"

"Maybe the lovely woman inside it?" Marc grinned. "She certainly got your attention at the wedding. Everyone saw you go after her when she stormed out of the reception. And then she calls our mother and says she won't be returning to the hotel." Marc waggled his brows. "I hope you had a good time."

"I didn't spend the night with her, if that's what your leering look means."

"No? Huh. How disappointing."

"Since when has my personal life been discussed at the office?"

Marc's smile didn't leave his face. "Since you started wanting to rake up dirt on the guy who's giving Madison a hard time."

"She's an old friend. I want to help her."

"Sure, bro." Marc returned to his computer. "Don't worry, we'll figure out what Girard is up to."

Angela's smile echoed Marc's. They both thought Thomas had fallen for Madison, and they were patronizing him.

They weren't far from wrong. Leaving Madison Saturday night had been one of the hardest things Thomas had ever done. When he'd withdrawn from her mouth to see her lips red and wet with his come, he'd re-hardened instantly. Her smile had held triumph.

Holding her afterward, his arms wrapped around her while they stood silently together in the hall, had been one of the best experiences of his life.

She hadn't asked him to stay, hadn't asked him to pleasure her in return. In fact, she'd seemed kind of in a hurry for him to go. She'd walked him to the door, pausing in the foyer for another long, deeply satisfying kiss.

"I've had my eye on Girard for a while," Thomas said, breaking the silence that had stretched too long. "He's too squeaky clean. That always arouses my suspicion."

"And when you found out he was hitting on Madison Rainey, you became even more . . . aroused," Marc said.

"If he's so rich and successful, why does he want a house that will suck out a ton of money to pay off its debts and fix up?"

"Like I said, it comes with one hell of a pretty lady," Marc said.

Thomas shook his head. "Girard doesn't strike me as a man head over heels in love. In lust maybe, but not adoration. I don't want Maddie marrying anyone who doesn't fall down and worship her."

Marc winked at Angela. "He has it bad, doesn't he?"

Angela gave them both a wise smile. "I'll start a file on Keith Girard."

"You're a peach, Angela," Thomas said.

"Flattery will get you everywhere." Angela disappeared back into the front office.

"Seriously, Thomas, what's up?" Marc asked after Angela had closed the door. "This has you bothered. I haven't seen you this uncertain about a lady in . . . well, ever. I take it that Madison's not someone you'd invite to the club."

"She isn't into the lifestyle. And that's fine with me."

"I see." Marc gave him a long look. "Don't let yourself get your heart broken, bro. A weeping Dom isn't what the ladies have in mind."

"I'm not going to get my heart broken," Thomas growled.

Sure. He'd held a secret yen for Madison for years, and touching her and kissing her on Saturday night had only fanned the fire. She was already wrapped around his heart, but if she didn't want him, he'd at least make sure she was all right. Starting with keeping the irritating Girard away from her.

Thomas went back to his desk, frowning, while Marc openly laughed.

"*I'm* so extremely busy, it isn't funny," Madison said to Keith Girard.

Girard wouldn't get off the porch. He'd waltzed up and knocked on the door, leaving his sleek gray Jaguar at the curb in a no-parking zone. Madison wasn't more busy than usual— she had a lunch date with her liaison at the couture house about designs for next spring, but that was several hours from now. Still, she had no intention of wiling away the time with Keith. After her evening with Thomas, she'd decided hell would freeze over before she considered marrying Keith Girard to save her house. She'd find another way, any way.

"Sit out here a minute with me, Maddie. It's a nice day, and I need to show you something."

"Really, Keith. Busy."

"You're going to want to see these." Keith took a manila envelope from a pocket of his laptop bag. He opened it and slid out a picture just far enough for Madison to see herself in vivid color, on the floor of her own hallway, her face pressed to Thomas Dupree's crotch.

Madison's mouth went dry. "What the hell?"

Keith dropped the photo back inside the envelope and seated himself on an Adirondack chair on her porch. He set down his laptop bag, crossed his ankles, and let the manila envelope rest on his stomach. "We need to talk, Maddie. How about some tea? It's warm out here."

"No way in hell am I fixing you tea." Madison folded her arms, clenching her fingers so he wouldn't see them tremble. She perched on the end of the porch swing, bracing her sandaled feet against the worn floor. "Give me that picture and get out."

Keith fanned himself with the envelope. "There's more than one. You're a naughty girl, Madison Rainey."

"And you are a Peeping Tom. What I do in my own house is my own business."

Keith opened the envelope again and drew out the glossy photos. He must have taken them through the side window, the curtains of which had been open. That meant he'd climbed the fence into the yard, stood on something, and used a zoom lens. What kind of person did that?

Someone who wanted something from her.

Keith studied each photo before passing it to her—Madison and Thomas kissing, Thomas dropping his pants, Madison on her knees, Thomas's head thrown back, eyes screwed shut in pleasure while her hands cupped his smooth ass.

It occurred to Madison that Thomas could be compromised by these pictures more than she could. Neither of them were married, they hadn't been doing anything many adults didn't do, and they'd been in a private house. But while Madison worked in the fashion design world, where sexual adventurousness wasn't that unusual, Thomas had a business to run, clients to reassure with his reliability. What if these photos came up on an Internet search of "Dupree Courier Service, New Orleans"?

In anger, Madison tore the photos into shreds and let the pieces drop to the porch.

"I printed those off my computer," Keith said. "I can send them anywhere I want to with the click of a mouse."

"What do you want?" Madison asked in a hard voice.

"Sell me your house, Maddie. I'll make you a good offer. I'll call my real estate agent right now, and we can start the paperwork. Then I'll delete the photos."

Sure he would. Madison's gaze went to the laptop bag. He followed her speculative look and smiled.

"I saved them on a server. Even if you steal my laptop, I can still get to them."

Madison scowled. "My grandmother would roll in her grave before she let a Girard live in her house."

"So you want the world to see that Madison Rainey, the Lefevre heiress, likes to suck cock?"

Madison felt a chill out here on this hot porch, but his words enraged her. "You're sick."

"It wasn't me with my mouth full of come. Tell you what, do that to me, and I might erase half of the pictures."

"You do know that extortion is a crime, right? That you can go to prison for it?"

"Yes, but these photos would have to be submitted as evidence at my trial. So many people would see them."

"You're an asshole," Madison snapped.

"All you have to do is give me the house. I know you're in

debt to two big loans on it, and the tax men haven't been nice to you. What else are you going to do?"

"I'll think of something," Madison said through tight lips.

"You're desperate, and you know it. Here's what I'll do—you agree to marry me and deed me the house, and you can live here the rest of your life. For that I'll delete the pictures."

"Go screw yourself."

Keith's smile faded, and his eyes went hard. "I know things about Thomas Dupree that he wouldn't want getting out. I know things about you, too, Madison. I want this house, and I want you. And Keith Girard doesn't stop until he gets what he wants."

Madison sprang to her feet, the shreds of photos falling like spent petals. "Keith Girard can get the hell off my property."

"Don't be stupid. I can humiliate you. And Dupree. Ruin you both."

Madison's heart beat swiftly. He could hurt Thomas, and she couldn't deny that she'd be embarrassed as hell if those pictures got passed around. Would Thomas be angry at her for not doing something as simple as closing the drapes? But the yard was fenced. How could she have anticipated that Keith—or maybe someone he'd hired—would snoop around like that?

"Damn you." Her words sounded feeble, but she didn't know what else she could do. Hack into Keith's network and delete the photos herself? Fat chance. She'd never figure out how to do that. Madison and computers didn't mix beyond simple e-mail.

"Shall I call my real estate agent?" Keith got to his feet and took out his cell phone.

Damn it, why had Madison given in to temptation and invited Thomas to come home with her? And let him seduce her in the hallway? She could at least have taken him upstairs to her bedroom, where the back windows and balcony were screened by honeysuckle vines.

Her fountain wish hadn't even come true. Thomas hadn't stayed, and she'd not been ravished by a sex god. But maybe that was a good thing, because Keith would have only taken pictures.

Madison's skin crawled. She couldn't let Keith get away with it, but at the moment, she had no clue what to do.

"Is this gentleman bothering you?" a smooth male voice asked.

Madison jerked around. A tall, broad-shouldered man with black hair and dark eyes had come up the steps. He wore a business suit, like Keith, except he'd taken off his jacket, and his tie was loose against his dark blue silk shirt, as though he'd been walking home from work. But he didn't live around here, Madison knew. She'd not have forgotten a hunk of man like him in the neighborhood.

He did look familiar, though, as though she'd met him recently. Ah, that was it. He'd been at Val and Leon's wedding. He was a friend of Demitri's.

"Butt out," was Keith's gracious reply.

"Yes, he is bothering me," Madison said. "I was just trying to get him to leave."

Chapter 5

The tall man gave Keith a look that would have made a more intelligent man run away. Keith nonchalantly picked up his laptop case and settled the strap over his shoulder.

The stranger gave the bag a scrutinizing glance. Madison swore that just for a moment the man's eyes blazed white-hot, but then he blinked, and his eyes looked normal again.

"I'll be in touch," Keith was saying to Madison. "I'll give you until tomorrow to think about it. Then I do what I have to."

Madison didn't answer. She folded her arms and ground her teeth, waiting in silence while Keith made his way down the porch steps and out to his car. Too bad a cop hadn't driven by and given him a ticket.

"What was he saying to you?" the tall man asked. "You look unhappy, sweetheart." His voice was deep and wine-dark, slurred by a faint accent she couldn't place.

Madison had been raised to be hospitable to strangers and visitors, but Keith had sapped whatever was left of her patience. "I met you at Leon's wedding, I know, but I've forgotten your name. Why are you here?"

"I sensed you were in trouble." He smiled, his eyes warm and dark. "My name is Alexi. I am a friend of Demitri, who is the third in the ménage with Leon and Val."

Madison's eyes widened. She started to blurt her surprise, then she lowered her voice, mindful of her neighbors. "A ménage? Leon and Val?"

"Leon and Val and Demitri are lovers together," Alexi said, as though he were announcing nothing more alarming than that he'd had potatoes at dinner last night. "Did you not know this?"

"No. It's not something you discuss, is it?"

"Not among your kind."

Her kind? What did he mean, *her kind*? "Do you want to come in?" she asked, her curiosity getting the better of her. "It's hot out here. I have a pitcher of sweet tea brewed. Do you like sweet tea? It's kind of a Southern specialty."

"I have acquired a taste for sweet tea, yes." He smiled again, and Madison thought that if she hadn't already been far gone on Thomas, she'd be attracted to this man. He was Greek, she thought, like his friend Demitri.

She led the way into the house, shutting the heavy front door behind them. Damned if she'd let Keith and his camera take pictures through the screen.

Alexi followed her to the back of the house to the sunny kitchen, which was Madison's favorite room. As a child, she'd spent days perched on a stool watching Myrtle, her grandmother's Creole cook, create miracles with food. The room was large, with a counter dividing it from the breakfast room, which was a glassed-in back porch. French windows led from it to a shaded courtyard behind the house.

Madison took the pitcher of tea from the refrigerator, filled up two tall glasses, added ice, and sliced a lime to garnish.

Alexi accepted the tea with thanks and took a long swallow. He wore his black hair pulled back into a ponytail, and he looked like nothing more than a handsome-faced, athletic male model.

"I didn't realize that Leon was in a ménage," Madison said. "You probably shouldn't have told me."

Alexi took another drink of tea, set the glass carefully on the counter, and draped his coat over the back of a chair. "Neither Demitri nor I see shame in such things."

"Maybe you don't, but the town of Fontaine would have a fit. Don't go spreading that around."

"I have told no one but you. The man Thomas Dupree is interested in you. Thomas is the brother of Leon, who is the lover of my friend Demitri. Therefore, I can tell the secrets to you."

Madison lost track of his reasoning and took a hearty swig of tea. "I do appreciate you chasing off Keith." She knew it was only a temporary respite. Keith would either make good on his threat or return to coerce her further. Her heart sank, but at the same time, she was so angry she wanted to scream.

"I saw him showing you pictures," Alexi said. "What were they?"

Madison hesitated. Alexi might think she was one he could tell secrets to, but Madison was unsure of who she could trust. "Nothing important."

Alexi came to her and turned her to face him. He brushed

one finger under her chin and looked into her eyes. "Tell me your pain."

Madison's tongue loosened, though she wasn't certain why. "He saw me with Thomas. Keith, damn him, took pictures."

"Of you giving Thomas Dupree fellatio?"

Madison jerked away. "Shit, don't tell me you took pictures, too. I'm surrounded by creeps and perverts."

"I saw." Alexi's eyes darkened. "It was beautiful, what you and Thomas did. I loved watching it. But I would never harm you with this knowledge."

"I don't believe this. Where were you, outside the living room? While Keith was outside the hallway? Did the two of you plan it?"

"I was unaware of Keith Girard's presence, or I would have put a stop to it. I stood on your upstairs landing, looking down over the railings."

Fear and anger clawed at her at the same time. "You were in the *house*? Son of a bitch." She swung around, reaching for the phone, ready to call the cops and get this guy out of here.

She found Alexi between her and her phone, when she swore he'd been on the other side of the room a second ago. He took her hand between his warm ones.

"I'm sorry I frightened you, Madison. I know that humans can regard such things as a violation, but I meant you no harm. I want to help you and Thomas Dupree."

"Help us? By spying on us?"

"By making sure one such as this Keith person can't hurt you. Did you destroy the photos he brought?"

"I tore them up, but that doesn't matter. He has the originals saved on his computer."

"Have no fear about that. I wiped all the data from the machine in his shoulder bag."

"You did? When?"

"When we stood on the porch. Do you believe in magic, Madison Rainey?"

No. "My grandmother did."

"She was skilled at it. I am much more skilled, but then, I am the son of a god. I can go where I like when I like, which is how I got into your house Saturday without you knowing. I watched over this house while you slept alone that night, when you cried out in your sleep in longing. And I wiped the data from Keith Girard's laptop computer."

Madison wasn't certain she could or would believe that. "It doesn't matter about his laptop. He's got the pictures on a network, on a server, which means he stored them somewhere remote and can access them from anywhere he wants to as long as he has the password."

"I will discover where he's put them and erase those, too."

"You're nice to want to help me, Alexi." Madison didn't believe for a moment that the man was firing on all cylinders, but she preferred his sultry smile to Keith's obvious leers.

"I help you to help myself. It's entirely self-serving." He held Madison's gaze. "Then there is the matter of your wish at the fountain."

Madison froze. "How do you know about that?"

"I happened to be in the garden when you voiced your wishes."

Her face went hot. "Oh, hell."

"The *Jaillissement de Plaisir.* Do you know the legend of the fountain?"

"There's a legend? I made a wish, because that's what you do at fountains. Plus it had an inscription about wishing."

"It's the fountain of luck in pleasure. If you make a wish to it, you find your wishes for the greatest pleasure coming true. In other words, it helps you release your inhibitions and find the joy that has been eluding you."

"Oh." Madison's embarrassment flared. She wasn't certain she believed in magic like Alexi seemed to, but maybe wishing at the fountain had created a self-fulfilling prophecy. She'd made a wish for something she'd wanted deep in her heart, and in giving voice to the wish, she found herself more able to take steps to grant it. "In other words, that's why I . . ."

"Invited Thomas Dupree to your house and gave him fellatio. It's something you've always wanted to do."

Oh, yeah. Gorgeous, hard-bodied Thomas. He'd looked so good with his tux half falling off him, his eyes closing as he felt what she did to him. His eyes could suck her in, remind her that she wasn't just crazy Maddie in her rambling, falling-down house, make her feel beautiful. Thomas had always been able to melt her heart.

"You want more with him," Alexi said.

"Of course I do. But it's not that simple. I haven't seen him in years. We're different people now."

Alexi touched her cheek. "That is what your head tells your heart, to keep the heart from hurting. You convince yourself that nothing can grow between you because it is not logical. But love isn't logical. The heart makes its choice, and the head must catch up to it."

His words didn't make things any easier. "I've always had a thing for Thomas," Madison said. "But he has a life, which doesn't include the madwoman who won't sell her tumbledown house because it's special to her."

"There is also magic in this place," Alexi said. He looked around at the high ceiling, the polished dark beams against whitewashed walls. "This house has stood for two hundred years, through war and hardship, disaster and pain. And yet it's still a haven for those within it. I can feel the magic in its bones."

"Can you also feel the corroded plumbing? How about the woodworm?"

He smiled. "That, too. But place your trust in me. I will help you find your heart's desire, and when you have that, all your troubles will float away."

Madison laughed, suddenly liking him. "Sure. What kind of magic are you going to conjure up?"

"The simplest kind." Alexi leaned against the counter and lifted his tea to his lips, once more looking like the best gigolo ever born. "Call Thomas Dupree and invite him over here Saturday evening. Give him dinner—men like to be fed. Leave the rest to me."

"That easy, is it?"

Madison's skin tingled pleasantly at the thought of seeing Thomas again. He wouldn't be wearing a tux, of course, but he was equally hot in a casual business suit or in jeans and a plain shirt. She remembered the warm taste of him in her mouth, and the tingle grew into a spike of erotic pleasure. She'd comb through the recipes Myrtle had left and cook her heart out if dinner could lead to more of that. If she couldn't have Thomas in her life, maybe she could at least have him once in her bed. She'd cook all day for that.

Alexi was watching her, his dark blue shirt enhancing his

brown skin and black eyes. "Exactly, sweetheart. You call him, and I'll take care of everything else."

Madison's voice poured over Thomas like water into a thirsty man's mouth. He held his cell phone to his ear and sank into his office chair to enjoy it.

"What's up, Maddie?" How he managed to sound so casual, he had no idea.

Thomas tried to ignore Marc's smirk and bathed in Madison's cool tones as she spoke. That is, until she told him about Keith Girard and his dirty photos of them.

Thomas sat up straight. "I'll kill him. I'll fucking kill him."

Marc was alert now, eyes on Thomas.

"Alexi said he took care of the pictures," Madison said. "I'm not sure if I believe him."

"Alexi? Who's Alexi?"

"Demitri's friend. Remember? You met him at the wedding. Anyway, he said not to worry about the pictures, but I'm still worried. Can we talk?"

Thomas's head spun. He now remembered meeting the Alexi guy before the wedding and then seeing him again in the bar, right before Thomas took Madison home.

Shit. Were *two* guys stalking her?

"Talk," he said. "Yes. I want to."

"How about Saturday night? I'll make you dinner. I can cook." She laughed, and Thomas's libido tore through his anger.

"Saturday?" It was only Monday—how the hell was he going to get through the rest of the week? "Sounds great."

"Good. Be here at seven. Thanks, Thomas."

She hung up. Thomas sat staring at his cell phone, wondering if he'd just dreamed that Madison Rainey had asked him on a date.

In spite of his rage at Girard, he was suffused with excitement, like a teenager with a crush. But damn it, when hadn't he been crazed as far as Madison was concerned? Hell, he'd been living his entire life for her.

Madison was different from any woman he'd ever known. Elegant, beautiful, old-world, untouchable. And she'd happily gone down on him in her hallway this weekend.

Keith Girard had taken pictures of that beautiful moment.

"He's going down," Thomas said. "Girard threatened Madison, and he'll live to regret it." He told Marc what Madison had told him, and Marc gave a grim nod. Keith Girard was toast.

On Saturday night, after a week of pure hell, Thomas showed up on Madison's doorstep with a bottle of wine in one hand and flowers in the other.

Thomas's heart turned over when Madison gave him a big smile and took the flowers. "Thank you. You're so sweet," she said. "Come with me to the kitchen, and you can pour that."

She walked away from him, her lithe form swaying in her light blue sleeveless sheath dress and high-heeled sandals. Classic elegance, that was Madison.

Thomas's breath caught as his gaze roved from her trim ankles up her sexy legs and then over her round backside, nipped waist, and soft shoulders. Her hair was in the French braid again, baring her neck for his love bites. She was no sub, but Thomas couldn't help picturing her in a tiny leather skirt, her breasts free, with her hands bound behind her. His already hard cock flared. He'd kill himself thinking things like that.

He realized as he watched her how much in love he was with this woman. He always had been. Thomas had honed himself into a pleasure master so that if he'd ever had another chance with Madison Rainey, he wouldn't screw it up. He understood the nuances now, how to fulfill a woman's innermost desires.

Thomas knew he'd learned those lessons because he wanted to fulfill *Madison's* desires. The women who came to the club weren't looking for love—they were looking to sate their bodily and emotional needs with someone like Thomas who could make it good for them. But Thomas, in his turn, was thinking of only one woman.

He entered the kitchen to watch Madison reach into a high cupboard and pull down a vase, then run water into it from the sink. She put the vase on the counter and started arranging the red roses and baby's breath, glancing at him over her shoulder.

"Glasses are in that cupboard. Corkscrew in the drawer under it."

Forget the wine. Thomas came to Madison, turned her around, and pulled her into his arms. He cradled her with the hand that held the wine bottle and opened her lips for a kiss.

She made a little noise in her throat before melting to him in sweet surrender. Madison's arms went around his neck, as Thomas met her tongue with his, sliding through her mouth, tasting her, licking her. He pulled back, kissed the corners of her mouth, and gently suckled her lower lip.

Madison's body flowed against his, pressing the length of his erection. He knew she felt his hard-on—how could she miss it? She held him tighter, and Thomas deepened the kiss, wanting more and more of her.

He became aware of someone else in the room—whether he heard a faint noise or simply sensed a presence, he didn't know. He broke the kiss and looked past Madison to the glassed-in porch.

A man sat in the shadows there, under the dark windows, where the lights weren't on. He was a big man with dark hair and eyes, the one called Alexi.

"What the hell is he doing here?"

Madison backed out of Thomas's embrace. "Sorry, I should have said. Alexi is joining us for dinner. I hope that's okay."

Chapter 6

Madison held her breath as she waited for Thomas's answer. Alexi had instructed her not to tell Thomas he'd be there, and Madison had humored him.

She didn't miss the look of disappointment in Thomas's eyes. He shrugged as he put the wine bottle on the counter and reached for the glasses, but his body was tight. "Sure, whatever."

"He says he wants to talk to us."

Thomas shrugged again, every line of him rigid with anger.

Alexi got out of his chair and came to the counter. "I'm not here to stand in your way, Thomas Dupree. I'm here to assist you. First, to tell you that the photos Keith Girard took of you and Madison have been destroyed. From his computer, from his server, from his camera."

Thomas already knew this, because that week he'd gotten in touch with the most talented computer hacker in the eastern half of the United States, a young man he and Marc used for jobs every so often. It had taken said hacker all of five minutes to get past the firewalls in Keith Girard's network and sift through his files. The photographs hadn't been there, though the hacker had turned up evidence that they *had* been there, but had been erased. Maybe this Alexi was just as good at hacking.

"Thank you for that," Thomas said.

"He says he did it with magic." The skeptical amusement in Madison's voice was evident.

"As long as it's done, I don't care how," Thomas answered. He poured the bloodred Merlot into the three glasses and handed them out.

Alexi raised his in toast. "To a magic-filled weekend."

The man did have magic in him, Thomas could feel that, but he wasn't certain what kind. Resigned, Thomas saluted Alexi and Madison with his glass.

"To a magic-filled weekend."

"Weekend?" Madison asked. Her lips hovered at the rim of her glass, and Thomas realized he was holding his breath, waiting to watch her drink.

Alexi nodded. "By the end of the weekend, you two will know each other very, very well. Intimately. I am here to see that this happens."

Madison cocked a brow at him. "If you mean Thomas and me going to bed together, we can make that decision on our own. And it's more likely to happen without you here."

Alexi set down his wineglass and leaned on the counter,

stretching his hands out along the countertop. "It is true that you could end up in bed together without my help. That is not what I meant by *intimate*. You wish to have sex with each other, yes, but you are both too inhibited to give in to what you truly desire."

"Inhibited?" Thomas drawled. Thomas Dupree, inhibited? The man was getting irritating.

"Thomas is a Dom," Madison said, grinning as though she found that funny. "That's what it's called, isn't it? At some kind of club."

"I am not referring to his sexual experience. I mean that Thomas is afraid to show you his innermost desires, what he most wants to do with you and your body. He fears frightening you away from his need and his true self. You, Madison, are interested in exploring the physical side of what Thomas wants, but you fear risking your heart and being hurt. You will try to keep physical intimacy from being tied to emotional intimacy, and you will hold back." Alexi gave them a dark smile. "I am here to make certain that neither of you holds back."

Thomas exchanged a look with Madison. She made a little shrug, as if to say, *I have no idea what he's talking about.*

"Dinner smells good, Maddie," Thomas said, pretending to ignore Alexi. "What did you make?"

Madison broke the tension by describing the fish chowder, chicken with peppers, and the cornbread. She flipped on the lights of the glassed-in porch to reveal a table set with old-fashioned china and silverware. She'd thought that the small kitchen table would be more, ah, intimate.

Three place settings, Thomas noticed. Alexi had been invited all along. Thomas hid his disappointment and murmured something about the food sounding good.

Dinner was fairly silent. Madison proved to be a damn good cook, and Thomas had been raised by a mother who could turn the most ordinary meal of rice and beans into a song. Madison credited her grandmother's cook, now retired, for the recipe, but Thomas gave Madison credit for the skill in preparing it. Some people, himself included, could follow a terrific recipe and end up with a mess.

Their conversation was stilted, Madison asking about his week, Thomas only able to tell her bits and pieces. Likewise, Madison made light of her day-to-day tasks. Alexi never spoke, only watched them.

This was *not* what Thomas had had in mind when he'd accepted her invitation. He'd pictured himself and Madison making a toast with the wine, him sitting next to her while they ate, maybe feeding her bits from his fork. Conversation would turn warm, involving a walk down memory lane, which would lead to kisses. Kisses would lead to more touching, and Thomas would then take her upstairs to her bedroom.

Those plans crumbled into nothing before Alexi's intense stare. Conversation faltered, and the three of them were reduced to the sound of silverware clicking on plates.

Once dinner was finished and the wineglasses nearly empty, Thomas pushed back his chair. "I'll help you clean up. Then Alexi and I will go and leave you alone."

Madison looked relieved, and that relief stung.

Alexi put a hand on Thomas's arm. "No, Thomas. You are not going anywhere, and neither is Madison. You will stay in this house this weekend and explore your need for one another." He gave them each a long look. "Put yourself into my hands, and I will see that all is well. Give me your trust."

"I'm supposed to be the one saying that." Thomas said. "To

Madison." His body was tense, both in uneasiness at Alexi's high-handedness and his raging desire to explore what he truly wanted with Madison. But Alexi was right—Thomas didn't want to hurt her.

"And you will say it," Alexi said. "Stay and tell her so."

"Only if Madison wants me to stay." Thomas rubbed the stem of his wineglass, his pulse throbbing in his fingertips. "It's her choice."

"No it isn't," Alexi said. "I've locked the doors. You both will stay in this house, with me, until you find what it is you seek."

Now Thomas's protective instincts raged, batting aside his lust. He shoved back his chair and went to the French door that led to the courtyard. He undid the locks and tried to open it, but the door wouldn't budge. He swung around, noting that Madison watched, worried, and made his way through the house to the front door. Same problem. He tried the nearest window and found that it, too, wouldn't open.

He strode back into the kitchen. "What the hell did you do?"

Alexi's dark eyes were relaxed, his arm resting on the back of his chair, an almost insolent posture. "By the end of the weekend, you two will be one. Trust me."

"Sorry, I don't."

Madison sat rigidly, her eyes wide. "This wasn't my idea, Thomas."

"I didn't think it was."

Thomas sat down again. Madison was worried, and Thomas wanted to wrap his arms around her and tell her everything would be all right.

"That's not all you want," Alexi said as though he'd read Thomas's mind. "Tell her what you do want. What is the one thing you want her to do most right now? Right this minute?"

Thomas squeezed Madison's hand where it lay on the table between them. The training he'd given himself for nine years, training for this moment, rose in him.

Madison wasn't a sub; she didn't understand that lifestyle. But he knew he could make her understand the beauty of the trust, of putting herself and her pleasure wholly into his hands.

Thomas gave her fingers a harder squeeze, withdrew, and sat back.

"I want Madison to strip out of her panties and give them to me," he said.

The panties in question grew wet. Madison squirmed as she met the warm and wicked gleam in Thomas's eyes. This was what he truly wanted, no games.

Madison had never understood why a woman would want to rush to a BDSM club and beg to be pleasured by the best master. There lay a world beyond her imagining. But now, picturing Thomas standing around in black leather in one of these clubs, waiting to discipline her—all right, maybe she could go for that.

Here in her kitchen, with Alexi watching, was a different story. She wet her lips.

"Why?" she asked Thomas.

Thomas leaned forward, never letting her look away. "So I can access you anytime I want, anytime I think you need me to."

Access her? Madison's pulse did a little jump, a hot point burning in her belly. "What exactly do you mean by 'access'?"

"I mean I want you open to my hands, my mouth, my cock, or anything else I might have brought with me to put inside you, any time I think you need it."

She hid her excitement by toying with her wineglass. "And how would you know if I needed it?"

Thomas's smile was Thomas's, but it also hinted of the dominant man beneath. "I'm letting you ask these questions for now, because I know you don't understand. You have to trust me to know. I *will* know."

"I think she shouldn't be allowed to put the panties back on until Monday morning," Alexi suggested.

"I agree," Thomas said.

Madison gave them a wild look. "Who died and gave you two authority over my underwear?"

"Do you want me to leave, Maddie?" Thomas caught and held her gaze again. "I'll make him unlock the doors, whether he likes it or not. I'll go, if you truly don't want this. It has to be your choice. I'd never force it on you."

A moment ago, Madison thought that Alexi controlled the room, locking the doors on them and telling Thomas what to do. But at this moment, she understood who truly controlled things. Thomas had decided to take over, and she had little doubt that he could force Alexi to do his bidding if he chose.

Thomas was asking her to trust him, to give herself into his protection.

Would she, or wouldn't she? Madison lifted her wineglass, finishing its contents in one long swallow. She thunked the glass back on the table, her mouth dry despite having just drunk.

"What the hell?" she said. "I don't have anywhere to be until ten o'clock Monday morning."

"Time enough," Alexi said softly.

Thomas held out his hand. "Panties."

Suppressing a shiver, Madison slid up her skirt without standing, inched off her panties, and drew them over her ankles. She'd been wearing a tiny black lace bikini, now nearly soaked from hot anticipation.

She held the underwear out to Thomas.

Thomas took the panties, briefly touched them to his nose, and tucked them into his pocket. Alexi's eyes darkened, and Madison shivered again. For some reason it no longer bothered her that the second man watched, desire in his eyes.

"Let's finish the meal," Thomas said. "You'll need your strength."

Madison's hands shook as she set her silverware across her plate. She'd made pecan pie for dessert, a nice sugary one, and Alexi had brought cognac for a finish.

It felt strange to walk to the kitchen to serve the pie sans underwear. She'd gone braless plenty of times, when the top or dress called for it, but never bottomless. It was just not something Madison Rainey would think to do. And anyway, who would she do it for?

She had to admit that the feel of her linen dress teasing the curls between her thighs and brushing over her buttocks was erotic. She wanted to stop and rub herself against the corner of the counter.

"Don't hold back," Thomas said, watching her. "Anything you want to do, it's all right to do."

Could he read her mind? Unnerving thought. Madison

carried two plates to the table, sidestepping Alexi, who'd risen to bring the third plate and the bottle of cognac.

"I can smell your pheromones," Thomas said. "You had a desire over there, and you walked away without fulfilling it."

Smell her pheromones? She'd never heard of anyone being able to do that, but then, she hadn't really believed in magic before tonight, either.

"It's silly," she said.

Thomas held her gaze, mastering her. "Nothing that brings you pleasure is silly. Do it."

Madison flushed. She'd never been shy about sex, but under Thomas's stare, she found herself nervous. At the same time, she wanted to be sexy for him. She was tired of being an oddity and wanted to be a woman.

She walked to the corner of the kitchen counter and placed her hands on the countertop. "I wanted to do this."

Madison parted her legs and rubbed her aching clit against the corner of the counter. It tingled and felt good. The hard corner put just enough pressure on her to stimulate her, and the absence of panties enhanced the feeling.

"Um," she murmured.

She heard a chair scrape. Madison closed her eyes as Thomas's large, hard body covered her back, his strong arms coming around her waist. One hand slid beneath her breasts.

"Keep rubbing," he said in her ear.

His voice trickled heat down her skin. He rocked his hips, pressing the ridge of his erection between her buttocks, and helped move her clit against the corner—not so hard so that the pleasure would evaporate to pain, but just enough to make her hum with contentment.

When she opened her eyes, she saw Alexi leaning on the counter from the other side. His eyes were so black they were like voids of midnight. He reached out and touched her face, his fingertip blunt against her cheekbone.

Two men were watching her get off against a counter, and Madison didn't mind at all.

"Do you like it, Maddie?" Thomas whispered. "Do you feel good?"

"Yes." The word was a moan. If she'd done this all alone, she might have allowed herself one embarrassed swipe then rushed to turn on the TV and make herself forget her crazy whim. But with Thomas's warm weight behind her, Alexi caressing her face, her legs parted, her core hot and relaxed, she loved it.

She felt the zipper at her back slide down, her dress part. Thomas's hands cupped her shoulders, fingers sliding under the straps of her bra. While he kept moving with her, her bra loosened and dress and bra slid down her arms, baring her to Alexi's scrutiny.

Alexi's gaze moved to her breasts, the man taking his time studying them, as though he wanted to miss nothing.

Thomas whispered to Madison, "Let him touch you."

"Yes." It was a moan. Madison's body was like hot wax, Thomas's voice in her ear completing the meltdown inside her.

Alexi reached out and gently tugged one nipple. The point was already hard, and his fingers on the sensitive skin had her crying out.

"Very pretty," Thomas said to her. "Your breasts are begging to be suckled. Would you like us to do that?"

Both of them? Holy God. Her fantasies of Thomas had never

included a second man. She'd barely thought she'd be able to handle *him*.

"I think you would," Thomas said. "It would make you feel so good."

Nothing would come out of Madison's mouth. Alexi cupped her breasts in his large, warm hands, thumbs flicking at the nipples while he studied them with reverence.

Madison had never done anything like this before. She had one man behind her, his body almost engulfing hers, while another man lightly caressed her breasts. It was like the best erotic dream she'd ever had.

The tingling pressure on her clit built and built and finally came tumbling from her mouth. She heard herself crying out, *"Yes, oh, yes, Tommy, yes, please!"*

Alexi's grin grew broad. He squeezed the points of her nipples, just hard enough to make her scream in pleasure. Thomas tilted her head back, and their mouths met.

Madison was going crazy. Her mouth banged Thomas's in her desperation to take him, and she sucked and sucked at his tongue. He held her with strong hands while she dimly felt Alexi push her dress and bra all the way down and off.

She was naked now, except for her high-heeled sandals; she hadn't put on stockings in the June heat. They'd taken her clothes away, and she didn't mind. She pressed against Thomas, the prickle of his suit erotic against her burning skin.

"Please, Thomas," she babbled. "Please, Thomas, now. *Now.*"

"Demanding, aren't you?" Thomas suppressed a chuckle. He was supposed to be in charge, but with Madison squirming all over him as she orgasmed, naked beneath his hands, he could barely hold himself back.

Alexi's presence helped him maintain control. Thomas knew that if Alexi hadn't been there, he'd have swept the dishes off the table, spread Madison across it, and taken her hard. She wanted it, he wanted it, he *needed* it.

The table was too far away. Thomas lifted Madison to the counter, laying her carefully back against the tiles. Alexi rolled up his coat and put it beneath her head.

"Lovely," Thomas said, tracing the length of her arm. "A Madison feast."

Madison gazed up at him, her face flushed, her brown eyes half closed, lips swollen from her frantic kisses. Her nipples were dark points, her skin slightly tanned as though she sometimes went out in the sun topless but didn't make a habit of it. At the join of her legs, coy curls of dark hair hid the entrance to her pleasures.

Alexi copied Thomas's movement on her other side, drawing his finger down her arm then over her hips the same time Thomas did. Thomas's fingers, with Alexi's matching, moved down her legs, touched her toes, came back up her body. As one, both men glided a finger into her cleft, Thomas nearly groaning when he found her wet and hot and open.

He withdrew his finger and lifted it to his lips. "You taste sweet, Maddie. So wet and ready for us."

"Yes," she rasped.

Thomas kissed her shoulder then trailed his lips down her arm. Alexi mimicked him on the other side. They moved their mouths down her legs again, bypassing her sweet pussy on the way up, but kissing her abdomen and the sides of her breasts.

Madison couldn't believe this was happening. Her body moved without her permission, rocking a little, hands clenching, back arching to put her closer to them. Thomas and Alexi kissed the cushion of her breasts, lips warm and soft, breaths hot.

She gasped out loud when both men drew her nipples into their mouths. After that, they stopped mirroring each other's actions. Alexi suckled her hard, drawing the entire areola into his mouth. Thomas used his teeth to tease her past endurance. Madison stroked her fingers through both men's hair, Thomas's thick and a little coarse, Alexi's black strands smooth as silk.

Madison looked down at the two heads bent to feast on her, lashes curling on skin, mouths working. It made her hips rock, her pussy very wet, and she wanted to come again.

"Please," she whispered.

She had no idea what she begged for. She only knew that she was coming apart with pleasure, feeling the contrast between the cool tiles under her back and buttocks and the men's hot mouths and hands on her. She was naked; they were clothed. She was laid out for their delectation; they were standing up, in control. They could do whatever they wanted to her.

"Thomas," she said.

Thomas lifted his head, his eyes nearly as dark as Alexi's. Something wild flickered inside them, but his gaze was steady, whatever predator within him tamed for now. "Do you like it, Madison? The surrender?"

She nodded, too far gone for words.

Alexi's mouth continued to torture her, the man drawing in more and more of her breast. Her skin would be swollen, marked, and Madison didn't care.

Keeping his gaze tangled with hers, Thomas skimmed his hand down her body and parted her legs. "Spread for me, Maddie."

Madison let her legs drape on either side of the counter, opening herself wider than she ever had. Thomas smiled as his gaze followed his fingers down to her wide-open cleft.

She nearly jumped when his fingertip found the burning point of her clit. Alexi softened his suckling, kissing her breast now, murmuring something in what she took to be Greek.

"You don't shave," Thomas said, running his fingers on either side of her entrance. "Or wax?"

"It never occurs to me." There was no one to see, no one to care what she did with her body, so why bother?

"It's no matter." Thomas ran his fingers through the curls. "You're silky. Very nice."

His hand stroking her felt ten times better than the corner of the counter had. Thomas spread her between his fingers, still looking, still admiring. Alexi lifted his head and looked, too, before he kissed her abdomen below her navel.

"She smells good," Alexi said.

Thomas nodded. "Beautiful." He leaned down and pressed a long kiss to her clit.

Madison's hips left the counter. Alexi pushed her back down, placed a gentle hand on her stomach. "Shh, love."

Thomas started to lick her. Madison moaned, heat rippling through her, her heart pounding like a jackhammer. She watched as Thomas placed his hands on her thighs and sucked the hot clit into his mouth.

As he had with her nipple, he used teeth and lips to suckle and nip, to tease her clit into standing high and hard. Madison couldn't stop herself lifting to him. She found her arms held in place by Alexi, and Thomas went on and on, kissing, nibbling, sucking, licking.

She was coming again. Alexi kissed her breasts, his tongue

a slow, gentle counterpoint to the madness of Thomas's mouth. She went crazy, rolling and screaming, any inhibition she'd ever had fleeing her as she cried Thomas's name.

The peak of the orgasm flooded her, and for a few moments, Madison saw and heard nothing. The only thing that existed was the feeling welling up in her mouth and breasts and pussy, spilling over. She knew she was wetter than she'd ever been before, knew Tommy was between her legs lapping her clean.

And then she was on the hard counter again, sobbing, Alexi soothing her with hands and voice, while Thomas kept licking.

"What does she taste like?" Alexi asked him.

Thomas raised his head. His lips were swollen, his chin gleaming with her moisture. He dipped one finger straight into her, making Madison cry out. Thomas held his finger out to Alexi. Closing his eyes, Alexi wrapped his mouth around Thomas's finger and sucked it.

The sight of the big man suckling Thomas's finger, while Thomas's eyes were dark and hot, made Madison orgasm a second time.

"Mmm." Alexi drew away. He touched his lips. "Thank you. Sweet spice and everything nice, Madison."

"Did you like that, sweetheart?" Thomas asked.

Madison fell limply against the counter, her breath in gasps like she'd been running, but a jog down a trail had never been as good as *this*. "What a question."

"I asked it. Did you like that?"

Thomas wanted her to answer, to obey. Madison nodded. "I loved it." She hesitated. "Will you do it again?"

"This is all about your pleasure. So yes. But I think we'll move someplace more comfortable."

Before she could sit up, Thomas slid his arms behind her

shoulders and knees and lifted her from the counter. "Your bed-room is upstairs, I take it?"

Madison drooped against him, loving his strength, his warmth, the mastery in his voice. She pointed into the hall with a languid hand. "That way."

Thomas lifted her closer, kissing her lips. He carried her out of the room with Alexi following, leaving the uneaten pecan pie to soften to goo on the table.

Chapter 7

Madison's bedroom was feminine but not frilly and flowery. She had simple tastes, from the carved Queen Anne four-poster with a handmade quilt, to the tall, stand-alone armoire, to the elegant cheval mirror beside the bed, to the honeysuckle trailing outside the window. The room wasn't the largest one upstairs, Thomas realized as they passed doors, but it looked to be the most comfortable.

Alexi followed as Thomas laid Madison on the bed. She looked sated already, her eyes half closed, her body open and pliant.

Thomas had taken women in a threesome before, but those women had sought nothing but sexual pleasure. Any two men would do for them.

With Madison it was different, personal. Thomas wondered why he didn't mind Alexi here. Madison belonged to him—Thomas—or at least, he planned for her to belong to him. But Thomas thought of Madison's reaction when they'd both touched her while she lay on the counter, both suckling her, both pleasuring her. She'd screamed in joy. He'd tolerate the second man if it brought Madison pleasure, if that's what she wanted.

Alexi sat on the bed, smoothing Madison's hair. "Do you feel good, Madison?"

Madison smiled, but at Thomas. "I'm not hating this. Is it the kind of thing you do at your club?"

"Not exactly." Thomas shoved his hands in his pockets. "I don't want to talk about the club tonight. Tonight, I'm with you."

In fact, Thomas never wanted to go back to the club. He wanted Madison, not for simple bodily satisfaction, but to hold in his arms through the night. The women he met at the club had become little more than fuck buddies, people he cared about, yes, but not true lovers. Always, always, his mind strayed to Madison, dreaming of a night she would sleep in his arms. He wanted to wake up and know that being with her wasn't a dream.

He was grateful to Alexi for forcing this situation. Then again, Thomas hadn't been prepared for tonight. He'd come over for dinner, expecting her to want to talk about Girard, and all his accoutrements were at home.

"What are we going to do now?" Madison asked.

She was thinking of this as a game. As play. Thomas sat on the side of the bed opposite Alexi and trailed the backs of his fingers across her face. "If I had you at my house, I'd bind your wrists, fasten you down. Then I'd ready you to take me, and him." He leaned closer, his lips brushing what his fingers had touched. "Have you ever had a man in your ass, Maddie?"

"Anal sex?" She flushed. "Yes. Once."

"Did you like it?"

Her flush deepened. "Yes."

"Then why only the once?"

Madison shrugged, her embarrassment so cute while she lay naked on a bed letting two men touch her. "The guy in question and I didn't stay together. It was a mutual breakup, nothing tragic. After that, I just never had an opportunity."

She meant that she'd not gone seeking sex. Thomas thought he understood. Madison liked sex, but she wouldn't deliberately go after it, wouldn't turn to a stranger to fulfill her. She and the other man hadn't stayed together, even though they'd enjoyed the sexual part of the relationship enough to experiment. Which meant that the emotional part of a relationship meant something to her. She wouldn't seek out or stay in a relationship solely for the sex.

Thomas kept the glee he felt out of his voice as he said, "I'm glad to hear you learned to take it. You'll know what to do then."

"I *sort of* know what to do. It's been a while."

Thomas touched her cheek. "Pretty Maddie. If I had my things, I'd open you with a plug, maybe a wand, make you relaxed and ready." He smiled as she squirmed, wriggling her hips as though she felt the butt plug already. "As it is, I'll have to make do with my fingers. And my cock."

Madison shivered again, her chest rising with her quickened breath. Her skin had an even pink tone, Madison flushing all over.

Alexi never took his eyes from her face. "But I brought my things."

Thomas's decided that Alexi was now his best friend. He kept his voice calm when he said, "Did you? Good. Get them."

Alexi gave a nod and left the room. Madison twined her legs

together, as though she wanted to squeeze her thighs and relieve the buildup of pressure between them.

"Are you always this bossy?" she asked Thomas.

Thomas leaned down until he lay partially across her, his face an inch from hers. "I am. I waited nine long years to get you here, *cher*. Nine years. I will make everyone in this house do my bidding if it lets me be here with you, doing what I've dreamed of doing."

She looked startled, eyes widening. "Nine years? Really? Well, damn, Thomas, what took you so long?"

So many things. Fear that she'd push away the Cajun boy, her high school crush behind her. Would elegant Madison want to be seen with a man from the back swamps of Fontaine? Then he'd been busy building up his business with Marc. Such things took time, though he wondered whether he'd let work absorb his full attention so that his social life could go to hell. The sex club took the place of that social life—the club where he dealt out pleasure and refused himself true connection with anyone.

Madison's brown eyes watched him, waiting.

"Things," Thomas said, shrugging.

"Not even a phone call?" Madison asked. "Not even a Christmas card? Barely a nod and a 'How are you?' if we happened to meet? And now you want to have a threesome with me. All for my pleasure? I'm not such a fool, Tommy. What do you really want?"

Thomas captured her wrists, lifted them over her head, held them in place with one hand. He heard water running in the bathroom, Alexi preparing whatever he'd brought with him. "Subs don't talk back."

"I'm not your sub."

Why did her defiant glare arouse him more than did his true subs begging him to use them?

"You are tonight," Thomas growled. "And disobedient subs get punished."

"They do, do they?"

"Yes." Thomas gave her a light slap across her pussy. "They get spanked."

Madison jumped, her eyes flaring with heat. "Spankings are done on the backside."

"Not necessarily."

Alexi entered the room at that moment, a box in his hands. "Discipline already?"

Thomas's cock was hard behind his zipper, the throbbing thing wanting to break free of the barrier. "She needs to be taught who exactly is in charge."

"Excellent." Alexi set the box on the nightstand and turned to the bed again. He patted her pussy where Thomas had, a little harder.

Madison gasped, not in pain, her eyes flooding with desire. Her hips lifted a little, as though seeking the sensation. Thomas and Alexi continued giving her pussy little spanks, coaxing her legs apart to get to her fully. She let out little cries of delight that pushed Thomas to the edge.

"Who do you obey, Maddie?" he asked, his voice dark.

She gave him a big, beautiful smile. "I obey no one."

Thomas's pounding cock gave a jolt. Then he laughed. "Oh, Madison, you'll pay for looking so adorable."

Before she could ask what he meant, he and Alexi increased their spanks until Madison was rising off the bed, squealing and moaning in ecstasy.

"Thomas," Madison heard herself screaming. *Please.*

"Do you want to come, Maddie?"

Thomas's voice was dark, his smile sinful, and Madison thought she'd come before she could answer him. Alexi was lazily watching her, resting his fist on the bed, his dark head bent to her. Alexi was a sensual man, dark-skinned, black-haired, eyes like midnight. But it was Thomas who Madison responded to, Thomas with his wicked smile and warm eyes.

"Yes," she moaned. "Yes, I'm going to come."

Abruptly the light spanks ceased. "Not yet," Thomas said.

Madison let out a frustrated scream. "Damn you."

For answer, Thomas laughed. Then he started to shed his clothes.

Madison stopped protesting to watch. Dear God, he was a beautiful man. His suit coat came off, then his tie, then his shirt. His chest was hard muscles dusted with dark hair, his tanned torso a sexy contrast to the formal slacks hugging his hips. He got rid of his shoes and socks, then opened his pants and dropped them. Black satin boxers hid his large cock until he pulled those off as well.

Naked, Thomas faced her, his cock as long and thick as she remembered it from last weekend. She felt even more heady watching it lift from his naked thighs, the balls beneath it tight and hard.

"Is this what you want?" Thomas asked in a soft voice. He ran his fingers up the underside of his cock. "This?"

"Yes." Madison could barely force out the word.

"Like you had it last weekend? Swallowing it down your throat?"

"Yes," she whispered. *Please, please, please.*

Thomas took a step back, putting himself out of reach. His smile made her heart turn over. Alexi leaned against the bedpost, watching, dark eyes glittering. He remained dressed, as though happy just to watch.

Thomas climbed onto the bed, on his knees between her legs. "This is what you want, Madison. Me inside you. Me fucking you."

"*Yes.*"

He spread her legs. "You're ready for me. So wet. So swollen."

Madison couldn't speak anymore. She wanted him inside her, on her, in her bed, in her life. She wanted him.

"Thomas, please."

He reached over her into Alexi's box and extracted a foil packet he'd seen there. Alexi caught the wrapping, and Madison watched Thomas unroll the condom over his hard length.

Thomas spread her legs wider, lifted her hips with his hands on her buttocks. "This is what you want."

"Yes. I want you. Please."

She begged some more, the words incoherent, while Thomas watched and smiled. Just when she thought she'd explode with longing, Thomas positioned himself at her entrance and slid straight inside.

Chapter 8

Madison cried out in pure pleasure. Yes, this was what she wanted, she needed. Oh, *yes*.

Thomas moved into her slowly, helping her take him inch by inch. Her vaginal lips stretched to fit him, and the feeling inside was hot, hard, as she pulsed around him.

"Look in the mirror, Madison." Thomas jerked his chin to the cheval mirror next to them. "Look at my cock invading your pussy. Watch it go in."

Madison looked, her body hot, a dark feeling swamping her. She saw the huge length of him, long and hard, being swallowed into her depths. Then it disappeared from view, Thomas leaning over her so she could take him as deep as she could.

"Is she tight?" Alexi asked, watching them with intense eyes. "Is it good to fuck her?"

Thomas knew what the man wanted to hear. He was used

to voyeurs who came to watch him, never participating, getting off by watching others. "She's so damn tight. She's squeezing me hard, and she's so fucking hot and wet."

"Good," Alexi breathed. "Good."

Madison did feel damn good, no exaggeration. Her hands grappled his buttocks, fingers clamping down. Thomas had planned to tie her wrists so she couldn't touch him, but he'd lost control too soon. Seeing her open and ready for him had made him want to plant himself inside her *right now*.

And Madison was beautiful. Her sheath squeezed him like hot silk, pulling him in, making him want to pump into her hard until he was breathless and coming. With effort, Thomas made himself slow down, let her get used to him. He was big, he knew that. He vowed to take her in her ass, too, but he wanted to show her how big he really was first. He'd let her change her mind if she truly thought she couldn't take him.

Alexi undid his belt and opened his pants, showing that, apparently, he didn't want to only watch. He stepped to the bed, his dark cock lifting with his need.

"Take him," Thomas instructed. "Take him in your mouth. Suck him and show him how much pleasure you're feeling."

Madison studied the cock hanging next to her. Alexi was different from Thomas: longer, leaner, the crown round and full. She couldn't believe that she was in this room with two men, one hard inside her, the other wanting her to suck him.

She shivered in pure pleasure as she licked the head of Alexi's penis and then drew it into her mouth.

Thomas watched the cock disappear between Madison's lips and couldn't suppress his groan. Alexi threaded his hand through Madison's hair, a smile on his face.

Watching Madison's mouth work, remembering how she'd sucked off Thomas's cock last weekend, made Thomas want to come. He felt the urge begin inside his balls, dying to work its way up. He tried to suppress it, tried to focus on Madison greedily licking and sucking Alexi.

"You're beautiful, baby," he whispered. "You like a long dick, don't you, sweetheart?"

Madison didn't answer, caught up in what she was doing. Too caught up. She'd forgotten about him, had she?

Alexi gave a vast sigh of pleasure, and his hips began to move. Good, he was almost done.

When Alexi finished and withdrew from her, Thomas lowered himself to Madison as she dreamily wiped droplets of Alexi's come from her lips.

Thomas backed most of the way out and drove hard into her again. Madison's legs came up to wrap around his hips, and now Thomas was the sole focus of her brown eyes. They rocked and grunted and gasped, sounds of loving filling the room.

"You love it," he said. "You love me fucking you. You love squeezing my cock in your pussy, don't you, *cher*?"

"Mmm." Madison was beyond words, her face beautiful as she began to really feel it. Her soft, feminine cries drove him to further frenzy, and Thomas pumped, giving up on holding back.

"Madison!" he shouted. "Madison, Maddie, sweetheart." He said her name over and over as his come shot out to be trapped by the barrier of the condom. *No.* He wanted so much to be bare inside her, naked inside his Madison.

But the careful habits he'd acquired over the years, knowing he participated in risky sex, wouldn't let him simply pour himself into Madison. He'd have to wait. If Madison wanted him, he'd quit the club, stay home with her, embrace monogamy, if monogamy meant being with Madison Rainey. Forever.

Forever. The idea of finishing this weekend and not having Madison in his life afterward suddenly terrified him.

Madison fell back against the pillows, panting, laughing. Thomas withdrew, not wanting to, but knowing he'd have bothered with the condom for nothing if he didn't.

Not being inside her hot, snug sheath was hell. He felt suddenly cold, bereft. Alexi, that peach of a man, handed him a towel.

"Are you all right, sweetheart?" Thomas wrapped the towel around himself, the prickle of the terrycloth both stimulating and irritating.

"Yes." Madison's eyes glinted from under half-closed lids. "I want more."

"You'll get it. Lie back and rest right now. I need you loose and relaxed."

Madison stretched her arms overhead, spreading her legs, wriggling her toes. "I'm relaxed."

"Good." Thomas leaned down and kissed her. He meant to make the kiss brief, but his lips lingered on hers, their tongues swept together, and the kiss turned serious. Her lips were soft and hot, mouth so warm, Madison kissing with the kisses of the sated. No more nervous anticipation, just sweet afterglow.

Thomas made himself lift away. Alexi sat down on the bed, softly stroking Madison's skin while Thomas went into the bathroom, discarded the condom, and washed himself as quickly as he could. He got back while Alexi was still touching, hands circling her breasts.

Thomas breathed hard, already stiff and aching again, wanting to be back inside her. But this weekend was about her pleasure, not his.

He rummaged in Alexi's carefully arranged box and smiled as he drew out a pair of leather handcuffs. *Perfect.*

While Madison hummed at Alexi's touch, Thomas lifted her wrist and wrapped a cuff around it. Madison's eyes widened as Thomas hooked it to the bedpost, then leaned across the bed and captured her other wrist.

She pulled experimentally at the bonds, and Thomas stopped. The sight of her, naked and tethered, her body moving in languid contemplation as she tugged the straps, made him hard and ready. She made a beautiful, sexy captive.

Alexi pulled a black satin blindfold out of the box and gently eased it over her eyes.

"Hey, that's not fair," Madison protested. "I want to look at you."

Thomas kissed her lips, then brushed a kiss to the blindfold. "Sensory deprivation. You can't see, you can't touch, but you can hear our words and feel us touching you."

"I know. That's why it's not fair."

"Listen and feel," Thomas said. "Concentrate only on that. Trust us, Madison."

"Trust?" She smiled, not afraid, that was his Madison. "I'm the one tied up."

"That is exactly why you need to trust," Thomas said. "Trust that we will make you feel the best you've ever felt. Trust us to know what's right for you."

"Well, I don't have a choice, do I?"

But she'd made her choice. She was trusting them already.

"Lie back and enjoy, baby."

Her smile widened. "Or you'll spank me?"

"Probably."

"In that case, I *might* lie back and enjoy. You never know what I'll do."

Thomas's cock pounded until it made him crazy. He leaned down and whispered in her ear. "You're a damned naughty little thing. I like that about you."

Madison tried to kiss him, but Thomas moved out of reach, and she made a noise of frustration.

"Enjoy," Thomas said. "Enjoy it all."

Madison was quivering with excitement already, and she felt open, hot, like she could take both their cocks into her pussy right now. She shivered at the mental picture. She wasn't quite certain how that would work, but imagination was a wonderful thing.

Then she felt their hands. Four hands, running over her body, each doing identical things on either side of her. Thomas had been standing on her right, Alexi on her left, but they could have switched places while she was busy imagining them fucking her together. She didn't think so—Thomas's presence tingled in a way different from Alexi's, but it was fun to pretend she didn't know. Four hands touching her, smoothing her skin, fingers swirling across her breasts, tugging at her nipples.

At first they copied each other's movements, but then they began moving randomly. One would massage her belly while the other pulled her clit in a quick pinch. One trailed fingertips down her thighs, one tickled her toes, one cupped his palm over her pussy.

All over, from head and face, neck, shoulders, breasts, belly, pussy, legs. Hands went under her back, gently massaging, under her buttocks, tickling, smoothing.

Her legs were raised by two hands circling her ankles. Whoever it was spread her legs, holding them up by the ankles, while the second man began exploring her pussy. He outlined it with two fingers before sliding one of those fingers inside.

The fingers came out, and then his lips, tongue, mouth, covered her entrance and began to play. Madison wriggled her hips, moaning, wishing she knew whose mouth invaded her. He ate her for a long time, until she was crying out and begging to be fucked. The man lifted away, and then *he* took hold of her ankles while the second man moved between her legs and began to feast.

Sensations rippled through her, enhanced by Madison only being able to feel the hot mouth on her, the hands holding her ankles. She pulled at the tethers, but while the cuffs were velvet-lined and held her gently, neither did they yield. The grip on her ankles was strong, too, male fingers hard on her flesh.

Madison arched her body, lifting her hips to the wonderful feel of his tongue. It was Thomas, she thought, aggressive and gentle at the same time. She couldn't tell for certain, because he made sure not to touch her in any way but with his mouth.

Whoever it was, he made her come. Madison cried out and pulled at the straps, wanting to gather Thomas to her, hold him tight. She couldn't wrap her legs around him, either, her feet held up and apart in the other man's firm grip. She squirmed and squealed. She'd never felt climax like this before, a solid point of sensation that she couldn't curl herself around.

At last, at long last, the mouth lifted away. The other man lowered her feet and let her rest on the bed, Madison nearly weeping with pleasure.

She felt lips on her face, smelled the ripe juices of her come, heard Thomas's whisper, "Hush, baby. You rest now." She'd been right; it had been him.

Madison took long, shuddering breaths, trying to wind herself down. Her body was hot, pounding, needy. She felt hands again, soothing this time on her sweating skin. The two men calmed her, let her take her heartbeat back down.

The men got onto the bed with her, one on either side, lips and hands still soothing. Madison pooled into warm happiness. Thomas was giving her this as a gift, to show her what pure pleasure was like. Alexi was making sure her crazy wishes at the fountain came true—for a night with Thomas and to be ravished by a sex god. Both of them were doing this for her.

Well, maybe not *just* for her. They sure seemed to be enjoying themselves.

"Thank you," she whispered.

"You're welcome," Alexi murmured.

"Ready for more, love?" Thomas asked.

"Hmm, let me think." Madison's smile moved the blindfold on her cheeks. "Am I ready for more sexual ecstasy?"

Thomas's warm hand rested on her abdomen. "She's ready."

Madison laughed out loud. Then she gasped as hands encircled her ankles once more. She felt breath on her pussy, then a hand, and then the cool slide of a lubricated finger against her anus.

The finger touched the entrance between her buttocks, softly pressing it until she felt herself relax and open. She groaned as one finger slid inside her.

She hadn't felt this in a long time, a man wanting in her ass. She'd been slightly drunk the first time she'd had anal sex with her boyfriend in college. She remembered liking the act, though, and him being astonished by it. It had been the first time for both of them. Whether said boyfriend had turned to a lifelong passion of ass-fucking, Madison didn't know, because after they'd broken up, they'd drifted apart and she'd not seen him again.

Drifting, that's what she seemed to be doing in life. Until now, in this bedroom, with Alexi's hands around her ankles, her hands bound above her, and Thomas's fingers warming and opening her ass.

"Can you take two fingers?" he asked.

"I think so."

The second finger stretched her wonderfully.

"The instant it hurts, you tell me," Thomas said. "It's more sensitive back here. More potential for pleasure, but also for pain if it's too much, too fast."

"Okay." Madison felt her body become heavy, so relaxed, Thomas's fingers loosening something inside her. There was no pain at all. "More?" she asked hopefully.

"All right, *cher*. You can have more."

A third finger slid inside, Thomas's hand cupping her buttocks. Good, so good. Madison moved her hips, trying to take him deep.

"I think she might be ready for a cock," Alexi said.

"That will go deep. Let's try something first." Thomas slid his fingers carefully out of her, and Madison whimpered with loss. "It's all right, love," Thomas said. "I'm not going anywhere."

She felt lube again, and then something cool and not exactly hard, but not exactly soft. "What is that?" she asked.

"Beads. It's a string, made of soft plastic, tapering from the smallest bead to the largest. I'm going to put it in you, and it will open you up, get you ready for us."

Us?

Madison shivered as a bead went inside, then another, then another. Her hips were off the bed, her legs held up by Alexi at her ankles. She could feel his breath on the sole of her right foot.

More beads, each stretching her wider than the last. She felt full, hot, like she wanted to squeeze. Finally they nestled completely inside her, a round stopper snug against her backside.

"How does that feel?" Thomas asked.

"Good. It feels good." She groped for adjectives to describe it. Tight, full, beautiful, fucking fine.

"Alexi wants to put his cock there," Thomas said. "While I fuck you in front. We won't let it hurt you. I promise."

"Yes," Madison breathed. *"Yes."*

Two men at the same time. This had to be a dream.

Thomas grasped the ring on the beaded string and took it out of her, slowly, one sphere at a time. He rubbed her gently when it came free, and she thought she'd melt from pure joy.

The bed listed as Thomas climbed down from it, and then the hands around the ankles switched again.

Madison made a disappointed sound. "I thought it would be both of you."

"Alexi's going to get you used to him first. While I watch."

"Oh."

Thomas rubbed her ankles with his slick hands, not wanting her to lose circulation. She looked so incredibly sexy lying there, the solid black mask hiding her eyes, her hands overhead in their bonds, her breasts high and tight, nipples dark with desire. Her legs pushed open, her pussy and ass exposed, ready for them do anything they wanted to her.

Brave Madison, up for any adventure. In his younger days, he'd never have been able to even imagine this moment. All right, so Madison naked and tied down had always been a fantasy of his, but he'd never in his wildest dreams thought it would come true.

Alexi was naked now. He climbed onto the bed, lifting her hips higher while he positioned his cock at her back opening. Thomas watched, his own cock harder than it had ever been, as Alexi slowly pushed into her ass.

Madison started squealing. Her head moved, her mouth opened in pleasure, her nipples squeezed until they were tight and dark. Thomas wanted to suck one. He needed to suck one.

Thomas lowered her legs carefully, letting her wrap them around Alexi. He held them in position as Alexi continued his slide inside. While Alexi rested there, getting her used to him, Thomas leaned over Madison and took one taut peak into his mouth.

She tasted like salt and honey. Thomas sucked, wanting so bad to drive into her, fucking until he couldn't see straight. His cock ached. He contented himself with suckling her, feeling her writhe with frustration that she couldn't touch him.

Soon, he promised her silently. *Very soon.*

"Oh, she's so ready," Alexi said. The man had closed his eyes, started moving, taking her a little bit now that he'd sunk inside to his balls. "She's tight and so damn hot. And wet. Her pussy is dripping all over me."

"Don't come yet," Thomas told him.

"Damn." Alexi's head tilted back. "This was worth five thousand years of exile."

Thomas had no idea what he meant by that, but he was past caring. He continued suckling Madison, liking how she arched up, craving his mouth.

He licked the areola one last time. "Now," he said.

Madison felt her bonds loosen. She almost protested, because the wildness of being tethered turned her on. Thomas didn't remove the blindfold, and when she reached for it, he pulled her hands away.

"Not yet, *cher*. You look too sexy like that."

Madison stuck her tongue out at him and then gasped when Thomas took her mouth in a hard kiss.

"Don't stick it out unless you intend to use it," he said in a mocking tone, mimicking what they used to say as kids.

Madison stuck it out again, and this time, Thomas sucked it, hard. At the same time, Alexi groaned softly as he slid himself out of her. "Hurry. I want back in," he said.

Thomas helped Madison to her knees, lying down under her and moving her to straddle him. His cock bumped her abdomen, and her breath caught at the hardness of it. Goose bumps rose on her body in excited anticipation.

Thomas held her back from him, however. "Swat her behind for being so coy and cute."

Before Madison could move, Alexi gave her a few spanks, which tingled rather than hurt, the sensations widening her already wide and needy body.

Alexi spanked her a few more times, making her want to raise her hips to him. Instead, Thomas positioned her on him and slid her down until he impaled himself inside her pussy all the way. He drew her forward against his chest, and she felt his heart beating swiftly beneath muscle and bone.

Just as she sighed her pleasure at him so far inside her, Alexi moved in. He lifted her hips a little, tilted her at the right angle, and lowered his entire body onto her. Her back opening widened without protest, and Alexi's cock glided inside, sandwiching her between two hard-bodied, beautiful men.

Chapter 9

Intense feeling poured through Madison. She couldn't see, she couldn't breathe. No, she *could* breathe, gulp after gulp of air as both men eased inside her.

After a few moments of simply filling her, they began to move. Gently at first, each man thrusting just enough to send her spiraling toward white-hot frenzy.

She heard her own voice, her incoherent cries. Thomas's hand tangled in her hair, his lips tender. Alexi's weight warmed her back, his arms protectively on either side of her. Both men wrapped around her, their scents and heat flowing over her body.

Thomas's fingers loosened the blindfold and lifted it away. His eyes were dark, fixed on her. It was like looking into his heart, a mixture of desire, tenderness, excitement. She thought she loved him more at that moment than ever before.

Alexi, now. He nibbled her ear, whispered words she didn't understand. He was pure excitement, pure sex, while Thomas was love and warmth.

Back and forth, they traded thrusts, Madison open and wet, the lube making things wild and slippery. Alexi was hard, but he glided in and out without impediment, encased in a condom, and so did Thomas. It felt so good, so good, so *fucking* good.

Madison started to come. She screamed with it, her heart in her voice, but they didn't stop. They held her while she writhed in joy, let her settle, and then they brought her to climax again.

The second time, Alexi's voice broke. "Gods, I'm coming." He sped his thrusts, his chest rubbing her back, his breath hoarse in her ear. He pulsed, growling low in his throat, and then he slowed, making noises of pleasure as he kissed her hair.

"You want her alone?" Alexi asked, voice subdued. He lifted the weight of Madison's hair, and air touched her damp skin.

"Yes," Thomas said. His voice was soft, mouth warm on Madison's. "I would. Very much."

Alexi withdrew. Madison cried out at the absence of his heat, but the next thing she knew, Thomas had hooked his foot around hers and rolled with her until he was on top of her. He slid out in the process, but he went right back in again.

Thomas raised up on his arms, face-to-face with her, a conventional position, but Thomas made it unbelievably exciting. Madison wrapped herself around him, welcoming him in, letting herself move to climax once more. Thomas's thrusts came faster and faster, the old bed creaking.

And then they were both shouting their pleasure, the bed thumping as they held each other and sought more. Madison was dimly aware of Alexi standing next to the bed, naked, hands on hips as he watched, but then her climax took over, and she saw and felt nothing but Thomas. She collapsed in his arms, him laughing and kissing her hair, and then she closed her eyes and dropped into profound sleep.

Madison opened her eyes to sunshine pouring through the windows. Her body felt pleasantly tired, heavy, and for a moment, she couldn't remember why. The warm weight at her back shifted, and Thomas's hand came around to rest on her abdomen.

Everything flooded back to her, the dinner with Thomas and Alexi, the beginnings of pleasure in the kitchen, Thomas carrying her upstairs, the incredible sex sandwiched between him and Alexi.

It hadn't stopped after the double. She'd awakened after a nap that had taken the edge from her sexual exhaustion, and Thomas had made love to her again, quietly and gently. When they'd finished, their bodies had been coated with sweat, both of them gasping for breath. They'd cuddled together after that, kissing and touching.

She'd been aware of Alexi pulling on his pants and moving out to the honeysuckle-covered balcony that ran across the back of the house, felt the cool air waft in from the door. Alexi had watched them from there as Thomas had touched and kissed and loved her again.

After that, she and Thomas had slept for good, spooned against each other on the tumbled bed. Thomas had pulled sheets over them to cut the draft, and they'd fallen into slumber.

Now in the bright morning, Thomas drew his fingers up

her body, around her breast, the nipple tightening at his touch. "Good morning, Maddie."

"Morning." Madison yawned. "What time is it?"

"I don't much care."

"Neither do I, really. Where's Alexi?"

"Around somewhere." His tone said he didn't much care about that either. Madison had the feeling that Alexi hadn't gone, however. The air felt thick and heavy, slightly spicy, as it had last night, and she tied this to his presence.

Thomas caressed her breast then his touch drifted to her hip. "I need to tell you something, Maddie. Before this goes further."

"Mmm?" she asked sleepily. "What?"

"It's about me. About my family. And what I have to tell you can't go beyond this room."

Madison drowsed again, leaning into his warmth. "About how you and your brothers can shape-shift into animals?"

Thomas went so still that Madison turned to look at him. His eyes were fixed, pupils dilated in shock.

"Marc told me," she said. "A long time ago."

"Marc. Told you."

Madison nodded. "He was in the same grade as me, remember? I sat next to him all through the fifth grade, had lot of classes with him after that. He told me, because he knew I liked you." She snuggled back into him again.

"You believed him?"

"Not at first. But he kept insisting, so I dared him to show me. He did. Freaked me out at first, but I've gotten used to the idea."

"Hell," Thomas said. "I'll kill him. He never bothered to tell me that you knew."

Madison shrugged, liking the feel of his bare chest against her shoulder. "It didn't work out between you and me, and then we all lost touch. I guess he thought it didn't matter."

Thomas resumed his caresses, though his breathing came faster. "You never told anyone."

"Of course not. It was your secret. I figured if you and your brothers wanted other people to know, you'd tell them yourselves."

His strong hand rolled her onto her back. "Madison." His voice was soft, thick with longing.

She smiled. "Yes?"

Thomas kissed her. It was a slow kiss, leisurely, a kiss because he wanted to savor her for a long time. He was hard already—his cock pressed her thigh then slid between her legs as he got on top of her.

"Thank you," he whispered.

Madison opened to his touch, and he made sweet love to her in a pool of sunshine.

Alexi watched from the balcony he'd strolled onto from the bedroom next to Madison's, honeysuckle screening him from the neighbors. Clad only in his pants, he lounged on the chair Madison had placed there so she could enjoy the shade on hot summer days, and propped his bare feet on the railing. He watched, growing hard, as Madison took Thomas deep inside her once again.

She loved him. The fact screamed itself to Alexi, but Thomas, the dickhead, had no idea.

They were so beautiful together, Thomas's long, brown body

entwined with Madison's more pale limbs, both of them a contrast to the crisp white sheets on the bed. Madison's dark hair flowed across the pillow, and Thomas's tight backside moved up and down as he loved his lady. They didn't need a third, didn't really need Alexi as their catalyst to find deep passion.

Alexi's thoughts moved involuntarily to the loving couple he'd destroyed, so long ago that no man alive remembered it. They hadn't been famous; no records existed of them. They'd simply been a man and woman destined to be together, and Alexi had ruined their lives.

Alexi had wanted the mortal woman, Sophia, lusted after her as only a god could lust. She'd been beautiful, his Sophia, her black hair flowing, her eyes dark like onyx. The man who'd loved her had been called Thanos, a young man from a decent, if dull, family. In Alexi's opinion, no way good enough for Sophia.

Alexi had used his god magic to turn Sophia from Thanos. Alexi had tricked and coerced her into his own arms, where he'd made certain she found the greatest pleasure she ever could.

After weeks together, where she lived only to serve his every need, Alexi had been certain she'd love him without compulsion, and he'd removed the spell. But Sophia had looked at Alexi in fear, loathing, and hatred. She begged to be returned to her family, to Thanos, though by the culture of her people she was now ruined, having let Alexi take her virginity. Thanos, by rights, could shun her, and so could her own family.

In desperation, Alexi had tried to spell her again, to erase that horror on her face. But his magic wouldn't work now that Sophia knew the truth. Sophia fled him, back to her family, where she killed herself in front of her father and Thanos to retain her honor.

Alexi hadn't been able to save her. Alexi's father, Eros, had explained to young Alexi that he'd violated the most sacred of laws, that the gods of love didn't use their power for personal gain, especially when the mortal in question belonged to another. Eros had been charged to punish Alexi for his transgression, and Eros had cried as he'd explained. Alexi must either be killed or sent into exile until he did five thousand good deeds, one per year, in the name of love.

Alexi had chosen exile, being too afraid of to face a death meted out by the gods. After five thousand years, however, his loneliness was almost unbearable. He'd made friends of other demigods who made their home on this plane—Demitri, Nico, and Andreas—but they each had their own problems to solve, had found their own ladies to love.

Alexi lived doggedly century after century, each year bringing together a couple who, without his help, would have spent their lives in lonely solitude. Alexi was not allowed to manipulate their thoughts with magic; he had to rely on mundane means, though he could use minor spells, as he had locking the doors to Madison's house so Thomas wouldn't leave.

Some of the people he'd helped had been royalty, some peasants; some so rich they could purchase cities, some so poor they could barely afford to eat. Alexi had learned, as his father had wanted him to, that love cared nothing for wealth and class, race and rank. It was Alexi's job to see that couples at risk worked through their problems and stayed together, else the deed would not count toward ending his exile.

Madison and Thomas were job number five thousand. If Alexi successfully brought these two together, his sentence would be lifted, and he could return home to his father and mother, his friends, his lonely exile over. If he muffed it, he'd be trapped on this plane of existence forever, stripped of his magic, made mortal.

Madison and Thomas.

Alexi hid a smile. In spite of his task being punishment, he liked his work. Nothing tasted more satisfying than watching two people finally open up and admit their love, the more vulnerable they had to make themselves, the better.

Thomas and Madison had been dancing around each other for years. And now . . .

Madison softly cried Thomas's name. Her hips lifted, her breasts pressed his chest. Thomas's head rocked back, his eyes closed, and he groaned as he released his seed.

Thomas was bare inside her. They'd been so engrossed in each other, neither one had given a thought to condoms, to protection.

They didn't need it. Alexi could see with his magic that they were both clean, and if a child resulted of this day, it would bind them with an even stronger love.

Alexi also knew how to help Madison's financial dilemma. The magic of this house had hidden what she needed, almost as though it—or Madison's grandmother, a magic woman of some repute—had been waiting for Alexi to come and reveal its gift.

Thomas's movements slowed, but he was still inside Madison, smiling at her, while she ran gentle fingers along his back. It was a beautiful moment. If they declared their love right now, Alexi could go home.

But they didn't. Alexi had known it wouldn't be that easy. These two had too much fear, held themselves too tightly to trust. They had to reveal their true selves before each could accept the other, before their love could catch hold and last.

Alexi might not be able to use coercive magic on them, as he had with Sophia, but he had a few non-magical tricks up his sleeve. He knew now what pushed Thomas's buttons, and Madison's.

Alexi rose from his chair and padded into the room and to the bed. Neither Thomas nor Madison looked at him, absorbed in each other.

"Well, my friends," he said, touching Madison's soft hair. "Ready for one of my famous breakfasts?"

Alexi could cook, Madison gave him that. By the time she and Thomas had showered and descended to her kitchen, he'd made omelets stuffed with spinach and feta cheese, fried some sausage, brought out pita bread with hummus, and brewed rich-tasting coffee. Madison didn't remember purchasing pita, hummus, and feta on her last grocery trip, but she no longer was terribly surprised at anything that happened around Alexi.

"So," she said brightly as she sipped the coffee. They sat around the kitchen table, comfortably eating, talking a little, but mostly enjoying the languid quietness of this warm summer Sunday. "What shall we do today?"

Alexi smiled his dark, sultry smile. He really was a good-looking man and should have a woman to gaze at him adoringly. He seemed lonely, despite his sex-god looks, and Madison's heart went out to him.

"I have many ideas," he said.

Madison quirked her brows. "Do they involve sandwiches?"

Thomas nearly choked on his coffee. He'd worried that

Madison would be ashamed of what they'd done last night, maybe demand that Alexi open the doors and let her out. But she sat haloed in sunlight, sipping her coffee, giving Alexi a teasing smile. She hadn't even flinched when Thomas confessed that he was a shape-shifter. She'd known, accepted, and kept the secret. What a woman.

"They could," Alexi said.

Thomas finished eating, deliberately keeping his imagination in check until he could swallow his food. He sipped coffee, savoring the smooth, almost malt taste.

He loved this. Sitting here comfortably with Madison, she in jeans and a tight top, he in his suit pants and white shirt from yesterday. He wanted with everything he had to live here with her, to eat breakfast in this sunny kitchen, to watch her sweet ass move as she got up to pour more coffee.

No wonder she loved this house. It spoke of warmth and family, of comfort, the happiness of generations soaked into its bones. Babies had been born here, couples had married, grandparents had watched grandchildren grow up, and the cycle had gone on. Madison was the last, and Thomas suddenly didn't want her to be the last.

He set his silverware on his empty plate. "By the way, Maddie. I meant to tell you something last night before we got . . . distracted."

Madison refilled his cup, the aroma of the coffee curling pleasantly in his nose. "Tell me what?"

"The real reason Keith Girard wants to get his hands on this house. Apart from the fact that it's on prime real estate."

Madison filled her cup and Alexi's and returned the pot to the counter. "Do we have to talk about him right now?"

"You'll want to hear this. It's funny."

"Tell us," Alexi said in mild tones. "It will be important."

Thomas wasn't sure what Alexi meant or whether the man also knew the truth. Thomas fixed his gaze on Madison as she sat down again and reached for her cup.

"Girard thinks there's buried treasure in this house," he said. "Legend says that Jean Lafitte was a close friend of your great-great-great-et-cetera-grandfather, Jacques Bouvier—some say the lover of your great-whatever-grandmother. Lafitte gave her a gift, the story goes, worth a hell of a lot, his personal possession, not pirate plunder. After the War of 1812 ended, Lafitte sailed off, never to be seen again. But the Bouviers kept the gift, handing it down through the women of the family, and the last to have her hands on it was your grandmother, Felice. People suppose that she brought it here when she married your grandfather. Not that people talk about it much anymore. Mostly the story's been forgotten. But I found evidence that Girard has been looking up the legend, trying to find out everything he can about your family's connection with Jean Lafitte, and where anything could be hidden in your house."

Madison listened as Thomas talked, her cup hovering at her lips. When he finished, she set down her cup, tilted her head back, and laughed. "Keith believes *that*? What an idiot."

"Story's not true then?" Thomas asked.

"Oh, who knows? There's a legend about Jean Lafitte in every old family—people swear their ancestors were best friends with him or that they know where he's really buried or where he hid some of his booty." She shook her head. "I always knew Keith was a moron. I should marry him and let him get his hands on the house just to make him look stupid."

"No," Thomas said abruptly.

"I was joking."

"Damn right, you were."

Madison gave him a look of surprise. "You're high-handed this morning."

"We're not finished here," Thomas said. "For another day and a night, you belong to me."

Heat flared inside Madison, but she pretended his words didn't affect her. "I only meant that Keith is stupid. My grandmother told me about Jean Lafitte's 'gift' when I was a kid. I went all over this house looking for it. Other kids went to summer camp; I tapped on walls looking for secret compartments. The treasure doesn't exist."

Alexi smiled to himself. Yes, the old house hid its secrets well. He'd tell them all about it, in the fullness of time.

"Thomas is right," Alexi said. "For this weekend, you're ours, and I have many ideas about what to do with you." He watched her eyes darken, desire stirring her blood. "Are you up to them, Madison?"

"After last night? Let's see, you two tethered me to the bed, felt me up, ate me out, put a toy up my ass, and topped it off by fucking me together. I'm surprised I can walk this morning, but I feel pretty good."

Alexi knew she did. His magic could do more than lock doors.

Madison made a wry face as she sipped her coffee. "But if any of your ideas involve a French maid's uniform, count me out. Even worse, a cheerleader."

Thomas laughed. Alexi pinned her with a black stare. "I have nothing like that in mind," he said. "However, Thomas and I agreed that having you as our captive slave for the day might be fun."

Madison ran her finger along the rim of her coffee cup, her

pussy clenching in a pleasant way. "And what kind of things would that entail?"

"Anything we wanted," Thomas said, letting his voice go dark. "Like you sucking us off, right now, while we sit here at the table."

Madison shivered at his words, pleasantness giving way to hard excitement. "Lucky me," she said faintly. "I've just had the floor cleaned."

Alexi gave her a wicked look. "Then do it, slave. First him, then me."

Madison went hot all over. She slid out of her chair and crawled under the table to where Thomas sat. He moved his chair back a little bit and spread his thighs. Madison worked his button and zipper open—liking that his cock tumbled free, unobstructed by underwear—and took him fully into her mouth.

Thomas groaned, pressing his palm to her head. She leaned in, loving the taste of him, smelling the soap from his shower, liking that nothing existed under this table but her and his penis.

Two penises. Thomas eased her off him and made her turn to see that Alexi had also opened his pants and was as hard as Thomas. Two cocks, one happy woman. She licked and sucked, loving her power, until both of them were coming. She drank them down, and laughed.

Madison had always been of independent spirit, but she decided she liked Alexi's game of captive slave. They made her do all kinds of things, like go down on them wherever and whenever they wanted her to. At one point Thomas demanded she strip down to everything but a pair of red satin panties, the only thing she was allowed to wear for several hours. They ate lunch like this, Madison mostly naked while they remained clothed, and then Thomas had Madison straddle him on his chair, making love so deep she screamed.

Later Thomas commanded that she put on one of her dresses with no underwear at all, and Madison again enjoyed the feel of cool linen against her skin without a barrier. That way, Thomas explained, when he wanted to taste her, all he had to do was lift her skirt and have at it, which he and Alexi proceeded to do—in the living room, the dining room, the kitchen, the back courtyard.

At times they didn't do anything at all, and simply lounged in the living room, reading newspapers or books. In the warm afternoon, Madison gave them a tour of the house.

As Madison took them around, Thomas understood how much she loved the place. Pride and happiness flowed from her as she showed them the nursery where she'd spent her summers, the photos of her grandparents when they were young and madly in love. Madison greatly resembled her grandmother in the photos—put Madison in flapper clothing and an old-fashioned hat, and she would be the spitting image. Her grandmother had favored elegant and distinctive hats throughout the years, he saw, which was probably where Madison had developed her interest in them.

Thomas loved Madison's willingness to play along with their sex games. She was having as much fun as they were, if the wicked glint in her eyes was anything to go by.

I want to tell her I love her. But not now. Not with Alexi and

during these games. When it's the two of us alone, no ménage,
no play, I'll tell her. If she doesn't love me back . . . I'll have to
live with that.

Thomas knew he'd never simply "live with it." He wanted
Madison for the rest of his life.

But for now, he enjoyed making a slave of her. The best game
was when they tied her to a porch post in the back courtyard
after they stripped her of the dress. They tethered her facing
them, hands over her head, and then he and Alexi licked her
all over, trading places between her legs. They had her coming
three times before they finally let her loose.

Alexi was good at this. He became the master, ordering
Madison to perform various acts of pleasure on Thomas, prom-
ising punishment if she didn't do it to his exact specifications.
Thomas got to be the recipient of her sucking him off, her bending over the back of the couch so he could have access to her
pussy and ass. Screwing her with a wand, then with his cock, in
both entrances, made him crazy with excitement.

Madison did everything Alexi told her, though once, with a
sly smile, she disobeyed, and squealed with joy when she had to
be turned over Thomas's knee for a spanking.

After that, Thomas took her on the floor, both of them desperate for release.

Later, after dinner, they went upstairs and prepared Madison for another double. She was enjoying this so much that
Thomas wondered if she'd ever be satisfied with Thomas alone,
when playtime was over. Thomas didn't like that thought.
Although Alexi was making life very sweet for Thomas this
weekend, Thomas didn't want this ménage to be a permanent
thing. Madison was his. When the weekend was over, he wanted
her with him. Alone.

But for now, sex was wild, wicked, and crazy, and they reveled in the freedom of it. Thomas tried to stay awake as long as he could that night, making love to her again and again, but in the small hours of the morning, he finally dropped off, spooned against Madison, where he should be forever.

When he woke in the morning, Alexi was gone, the air felt light, and he knew that the weekend was over.

Chapter 10

When Madison opened her eyes, the room was already bathed in sunshine. Something felt different, and it took her a moment to realize what. The thick, sultry feel to the air had gone, leaving it cool and ordinary. Everything felt, well, *normal*, again.

A warm weight depressed the bed behind her, a long wall of man against her back. Thomas, she knew it was him. She recognized his warmth, his scent, the way he cupped his hand casually on her hip. Of Alexi, there was no sign. He wasn't in the room or sitting on the balcony.

Madison knew without checking that the doors and windows would be unlocked now, and she'd no longer be trapped inside the house with Thomas.

No, *trapped* was the wrong word. Not once in the preceding night and day had she wanted to leave. Even when Alexi had allowed them out in the courtyard, running away had been the furthest thing from her mind. Besides, she'd been stark naked, and letting herself be tied up for their pleasure had been much more fun.

Thomas lay behind her protectively, his head resting between her shoulder blades, warm breath brushing her back. He'd stayed, even when Alexi hadn't. That thought warmed her heart. They could have both abandoned her, let her wake alone.

But Thomas was still there.

She teased herself even more by imagining waking like this with him every morning, his arm around her. He'd grunt when she woke him up, then give her his sleepy smile, the one that warmed his eyes.

Madison sighed as she scooted over to look at the clock on her bedside table. It was just nine.

Damn. Her heart sank. She had an appointment downtown at ten. She had to shower, put together her portfolio, and get the hell out of here, or she'd lose a commission she desperately needed.

She started to slide out from under the covers, trying not to wake Thomas. Thomas's big hand clamped on her wrist, and in one swift move, he'd pulled her down onto the mattress and rose over her, bracing his weight on his big arms. His knee parted her thighs, and he nuzzled her neck as though taking in her scent.

"Where you going, *cher*?"

"Work. I have an appointment in an hour."

"Mmm. Time enough."

"Tommy." She pressed her hands against his chest but didn't push. His heart beat evenly beneath his muscles, blood warming that fine, tall body. "I can't afford to miss this appointment. I need the orders."

"You won't miss it. I'll drive you."

"I have my own car."

"Too bad." Thomas lowered himself to her again, brushing warm lips across hers. "One more time?" he whispered.

Madison twined her arms around him, his dark eyes and tousled hair breaking her heart. "Yes," she said. "One more time."

Afterward, they showered, Madison pushing Thomas away when he tried to slow it down. Giving him her big Madison smile, she told him she had to get downtown, and snapped off the water before he was finished rinsing.

Thomas turned the water back on as she danced out of the shower, her wet ass gleaming in the sunlight. She was the most beautiful thing he'd ever seen.

By the time Thomas finished rinsing off and got out to dry himself, Madison was in the bedroom, dressed. She pinned earrings into her ears, leaning over the dresser to peer at the mirror.

She wore another sheath dress, this one black, her black high-heeled sandals already on. She reached for a hat with a white crown and black brim, which was shaped a little bit like a boat, but when Madison slid it over her dark hair, it looked cool and elegant. He knew that as soon as she appeared in it, every wealthy woman in New Orleans would want one for themselves.

Thomas dried himself slowly, not bothering to hide his hard-on. She was as luscious dressed as naked, and now his body knew the feel of her.

"Got to go." Madison flashed Thomas her sweet smile and

breezed out of the room. She'd noticed his obvious need, which was probably why she'd smiled. Thomas might have played the Dom all weekend, but he'd known damn well who'd had the upper hand. It hadn't been him or Alexi.

Thomas followed her out, tucking the towel around his waist. "Wait twenty seconds, and I'll drive you."

"Can't. I'm late already." Madison flowed down the stairs, grabbing her purse from a table at the bottom. She blew him a kiss. "Thanks for the lovely weekend. Really, Tommy, it was fantastic, something to remember for always." She smiled again, and his heart heated and turned over. She was beautiful, sensual. And leaving.

Madison stopped at the front door and called back to him, "Please don't let my neighbors see you go, if you can help it. They'll tell everyone in town that Thomas Dupree spent the weekend here."

The warmth in Thomas's chest turned to a burn. *Sneak out the back way; don't let anyone know you were here making love to me.*

Madison was going back to her everyday life, which didn't include her weekend lover.

"Sure thing," he made himself say.

Madison gave him one last smile, opened the door, and waltzed out.

Thomas sat down on the stairs, the towel cushioning his butt as the door swung shut. He opened his hand, looking down at the ID bracelet he'd brought with him, the one Madison had given him nine years ago. Sunlight from the windows above him winked on it, touching the fine grooves that formed his name. He'd planned to pull it out, wrap it around her wrist, and let her laugh at him for keeping it all this time.

Fuck.

Waking in her bed the last two mornings had been the closest thing to heaven. Madison had finally been his.

Illusion. She'd been in charge the entire weekend, allowing him to assume the dominant role and show her what he liked. Because she asked it, because she wanted it. He would have backed off if she'd been truly afraid or upset. He also wouldn't have let Alexi touch her if Madison hadn't wished it.

His brother Marc had long held the theory that the subs were truly in control, because they knew that a good Dom would never hurt them. Thomas had thought Marc's theory crazy, but now he agreed that Marc was probably right.

Madison wasn't about to give Thomas control over her life or whatever relationship this was. She wasn't the surrendering kind.

And damn, didn't Thomas love her for that?

Thomas climbed to his feet, went back upstairs, dressed, and left the house. He'd parked his black BMW convertible at the end of the alley, out of sight behind her garage. He started it up and drove away, making damn sure none of the neighbors saw him.

Two weeks later, as Thomas walked into his office, Marc and Angela abruptly ceased their conversation and stared at him.

"What?" he growled.

"Touchy," Marc said. "You have been, bro, since you spent that weekend with Madison Rainey."

"You want to drop it?" Thomas sat down in his leather office chair. "It was a weekend. It's done."

Thomas had called Madison once, the Monday night after he'd left. She'd sounded surprised to hear from him. She'd told him that her appointment had been so successful that she was going to Houston for a week to meet with a new couture house. She promised to call Thomas again when she got back.

She never had.

Thomas had met Alexi once at the Les Bon Temps bar for an after-work drink. When Thomas had told Alexi that Madison hadn't called him, Alexi had smiled wisely and told him to give her time. He'd been quietly confident that Thomas and Madison would end up as a couple.

Dream on, Greek boy.

"You'd better tell him," Angela said, breaking Thomas's thoughts.

Marc shot her a look, one that said he'd been shoved toward a place he didn't want to go.

"Tell me what?" Thomas logged on to his computer and started going through his e-mails. He tried not to be annoyed that none were from Madison.

Marc heaved a sigh as he got to his feet and came to Thomas's desk. "You'd hear it sooner or later, I guess. Madison's getting married."

Thomas's fingers froze on the keyboard. He felt his heart turn to ice and glacial blood sweep through his veins. "*What?*"

"Yep. Mom told me."

"*Mom* told you?" Thomas sprang to his feet.

Marc nodded, unhappy. "Mom brought Val to New Orleans to shop, and they ran into Madison. Madison showed them her engagement ring. She, um . . . She looked happy, Mom said."

Thomas sank to his chair again, so dizzy he thought he'd be sick. Madison? Marrying? What the fuck?

"Who? Who is the dickhead she's going to marry? The *dead* dickhead."

Marc hesitated, glancing around the room as though making certain no lethal weapons were in reach.

Angela broke in while Marc was still dithering. "It's Keith Girard, Thomas," she said.

Thomas stood, very slowly this time, like a lion rising from the veldt to make a kill. "That can't be right. Madison hates the asshole."

"I don't know the details," Marc said. "Something must have happened to make her desperate enough to marry him."

What? "Then why the hell didn't she ask me for help?"

Angela gave him a pitying look. "She's a proud woman, Thomas. I understand—I wouldn't want to turn to my friends and beg them for a loan, probably a huge one."

"But you'd marry Keith Girard to get it?" Thomas glared at them both. "This is bullshit." He grabbed his keys and made for the door.

"Where are you going?" Marc asked in alarm. As though he couldn't guess.

"To spank Madison's sweet little ass."

He sensed Angela and Marc exchange helpless glances as Thomas slammed out of the office.

He drove in rage to Madison's house and parked right in front of her gate, damn what her neighbors thought. His rage increased when, in answer to his hard jabs at the bell, the model-handsome Alexi opened the door.

"What the fuck are you doing here?" Thomas demanded.

"I invited him." Madison's cool tones floated from the house, and she stepped out onto the porch. "This is my house. I can invite whomever I wish."

Thomas glared at Alexi. "Did you know?"

Alexi gave him a brief, silent nod.

"And you didn't tell me. Neither of you told me?" He switched his hard stare to Madison. "I had to find out that Girard bagged you from my *mother*?"

Madison fixed him with an irritated look. Oh, God, she was going to send him off in front of the gossip-loving neighbors she'd warned him about. All of New Orleans would talk about how Thomas Dupree had slunk away from the Lefevre heiress with his tail between his legs. How Madison Rainey had put him in his place.

His anger took over. He grasped Madison's elbow and steered her into the house.

Madison glared at him, but she didn't fight him. As Alexi shut the heavy front door, Madison shook off Thomas's grip and went to the back of the house and the kitchen. There, Madison busied herself pouring a glass of tea, making a show of dropping four perfect ice cubes into it. She put the pitcher back into the refrigerator and took a sip, pointedly not offering any to Thomas.

Rage curled inside him, the predator in him wanting to break free. *I want to take care of you, Madison. Let me.*

"Well?" Madison asked. "Did you come over here just to yell at me? Or were you hoping for another easy fuck?"

Thomas burned at the anger in her eyes, and his own rage tangled in his throat. Damn Girard to hell. "Is that what you think I want?"

She shrugged, her body tight. "It's what you wanted two weekends ago. I didn't see you for nine years, and suddenly you're here, screwing my brains out. What am I supposed to think?"

"I came here to ask you why the *hell* you're marrying Girard."

"That's my business."

"Shit, Madison, you hate him. He tried to blackmail you, you said. Marc and I are having him watched—if he puts another foot wrong, our cop friends have him." Thomas sucked in a breath. "I can't believe you'd do this. Without telling me."

Madison slammed down her glass, and tea sloshed to the counter. "I didn't hear you proposing any solutions, Thomas. You never once offered to help or at least help me figure out what I could do. With Keith, I'll be able to stay here, in my family home, the only place I've ever been happy."

"Did you give me a chance? You ran off to Houston, in a hurry to go. You promised to call me when you came home, and you didn't. So I convinced myself to give you space, to not push myself on you. But that was sure stupid. How long did it take Girard to snatch you up?"

"Thomas." Madison's face softened, and now she looked almost worried. "I didn't call you when I got back, because . . ." She wet her lips. "Because Alexi told me not to."

Thomas froze, disbelief breaking through his anger. He slowly turned to Alexi, who was leaning against the doorframe, hands in pockets. "Alexi told you not to?"

Alexi didn't even look ashamed. "I thought it best."

"What the fuck?" Thomas asked him, his voice deadly quiet.

"I had my reasons."

Thomas's rage blazed again. "You're an asshole, Alexi. 'Trust me,' you said. Well, fuck you. Like hell I'm going to let Madison marry Keith Girard."

"It's my life, Thomas," Madison said coolly. "I get to marry whomever I want."

Thomas swung back to her. "Not *him*, for God's sake. Marry me instead."

The words echoed around the kitchen, bounced off the glass walls of the eating area. Madison blinked. "I beg your pardon?"

"I said, marry me."

The words came out of Thomas's mouth before he could stop them, but he knew he didn't want to stop them. He needed to say this to her, needed to pour out his heart. "I love you, Madison Rainey. I've always loved you. Everything I've done, everything I've become in the last nine years has been for you. All for you."

Madison's eyes widened. "What do you mean, 'all for me'?"

"Everything I tried to be—successful businessman, bad-ass adventurer, skilled lover—was so I'd be worthy of you. Look, I even kept that damned ID bracelet you gave me, to remind me what I was living for."

He lifted it out of his pocket. A beam of sunlight caught the gold, the chain throwing spangles against the walls and Madison's face.

"Thomas," she whispered.

Thomas's throat ached. "For God's sake, Madison, throw away that damned ring and marry me, not that waste of space."

Her breath catching on a sob, Madison pulled off the ring and flung it to the floor. It rang on the tiles until Alexi picked it up.

Madison ran at Thomas and threw her arms around his neck. "I'll marry you, Tommy." Her voice was beautiful in his ear. "Of course, I'll marry you. I love you. I always have."

Thomas closed his arms around her, holding her against his body, where she belonged. "Madison Rainey, I love you so much."

She drew back, and he cupped her face. As he bent to kiss her lips, he caught sight of Alexi out of the corner of his eye. The man gave Thomas a broad smile, shook his head, and walked away, leaving them alone.

Alexi just happened to have brought champagne. After Thomas had kissed Madison until their lips were swollen, they broke apart to find Alexi pouring out three glasses of frothing champagne. Madison caught up her glass, clinking it against Thomas's and Alexi's.

"There's so many people we have to tell," she gushed. "Your mother, first—your whole family. My girlfriends in Fontaine . . ."

"What about Girard?" Thomas broke in. "You should tell him first. Can I watch? Please?"

"Girard?" Madison looked puzzled, then she laughed. "Oh, I was never engaged to Keith, Tommy. I made that up."

"*What?*" Thomas choked on his champagne. He coughed and wiped his mouth. "Then why the hell did you tell my mom you were? Where did you get the ring?"

"It's my grandmother's. Your mom was in on this, too. It was all Alexi's idea."

Thomas swung on Alexi, who was holding the ring in question between his thumb and forefinger. Thomas realized then that of course, Madison couldn't have really been engaged to Girard. Gossip would have spread like wildfire if she had— Girard would have made sure everyone in town knew he'd landed the last Lefevre. The fact that Thomas hadn't heard a thing gave it the lie.

"Alexi, man, you have a lot of explaining to do," he said.

Again, Alexi didn't look ashamed. He lounged against the counter, holding his champagne negligently. But he looked different somehow, as though a glow of pure light shone beneath his skin.

"You still needed a little push," he said. "Telling you she was marrying Girard was just the right catalyst."

"Catalyst?" Thomas walked the edge of dangerous anger. "You were goading me to confront Madison? What if it hadn't worked?"

Alexi took a sip of champagne. "But I knew it would."

"You *used* her. And me."

Alexi didn't look worried. In fact, he looked triumphant.

"I shouldn't have told you that," Madison said. "I had serious doubts, but for some reason, I wanted to believe Alexi." She turned her brilliant smile on Thomas. "And I wanted you to get your ass over here and ask me."

Thomas thunked down his glass. "You devious, naughty little . . ." His voice went low as his fantasies stirred. "I should punish you for that, *cher*."

"That sounds like fun." Madison's smile suddenly faded. "But make sure, Thomas. You'd be marrying a woman in a hell of a lot of financial straits. That won't be fair to you."

"You let me worry about that."

"Neither of you has to worry about it," Alexi said. "Your grandmother did have Jean Lafitte's treasure, Madison. She kept it for you, so that you would reap the benefit of it when you needed it most."

Madison looked at him in disbelief. "I told you, I searched all over this house. It's not here."

"She used her magic to hide it. She was a pretty good witch, your grandmother."

"If she hid it so well, how do you know it's still here?"

"Because the magic of a mortal witch is nothing to my magic," Alexi said. "It's in the wall between your bedroom and the balcony. It's a silver service, sterling and quite fine, made in Paris. It not only has intrinsic value but also the provenance of the maker, plus the fact that it was owned by Jean Lafitte. Owned, not stolen. It will fetch a good price for you, plus make you *very* popular."

"Why didn't she just give it to Madison?" Thomas asked. "Or put it in a safe-deposit box? It would have made Madison's life much easier."

"Because the wrong people might have gotten hold of it," Alexi said. He smiled a knowing smile. "Felice, she knew it would be revealed at the right time."

Madison's eyes lit up. Thomas loved seeing her like this—happy, excited, full of joy. "Let's go look for it," she said.

Thomas pulled her back. "Later. I still think you need your punishment."

Madison's eyes darkened. "I guess it could wait. It has all these years." She came to him, resting her body the length of his. "Now about that punishment."

Thomas closed his hands around her wrists. His cock was hard and pounding with need, and he wanted to consummate their engagement right here, right now.

"*Cher.* You are going to pay for looking so fucking adorable when you say that."

"Am I?" She gave him a coy smile.

Thomas put his lips to her ear. "Panties. Off."

"Yes, Thomas. I love you."

"Love you too, Maddie."

Madison wriggled out of her bikini panties and spent the next several hours laughing with happiness.

Epilogue

Alexi stepped onto the slopes of the magic realm within Mount Olympus, barely able to contain his joy. After all this time, all these years, he was home.

He'd left Thomas and Madison drowsing in each other's arms. He'd whispered a good-bye, but they hadn't heard him. It didn't matter. They didn't need him anymore.

Alexi didn't worry that no one was in sight. The fact that he was allowed to step on this hallowed ground meant that Eros had kept his side of the bargain. Alexi had served his sentence, learned about the truth of love, and was now free.

He shed his human clothes and walked naked, feeling the sacred sun kiss his backside. He started running for the enjoyment of it.

"Alexi. I heard you were back."

A female voice stopped him. She stepped out from behind a

tree, a lovely thing with flowing black hair and a compact body in gauzy robes.

"Chloe?" Alexi asked. The daughter of a lesser god and a mortal woman, Chloe had been accepted here, been kind of a pain in the ass to the young Alexi thousands of years ago. "You've grown up."

"I hope so." She sauntered away from him, her thin garment clinging to every curve. Did she deliberately sway her hips, enticing him to follow?

"Well?" she asked over her shoulder, when Alexi remained rooted in place. "Are you coming?"

Alexi laughed. He shouted his laughter to the sky, and he ran through the soft grass to catch her.

Dungeon Dreams

SHERI WHITEFEATHER

Chapter 1

Kendra Madden battled an erotic chill.

This, of course, made no sense. But nothing in her head constituted logic, not since the dreams had started.

Dreams of a dark, gothic place with brick walls, iron shackles, and rough-hewn devices with leather restraints. A place that made her dangerously aroused. A place vastly different from where she was now.

Confirming her soft, fanciful whereabouts, she stopped to study the mansion in front of her. Nothing could be more whimsical, more gingerbread, more Queen Anne Victorian than the Bonswa Inn, an extravagant bed-and-breakfast located in New Orleans's Garden District. The pink, lavender, and white structure boasted curlicue details and frosting-style scrollwork.

So why did she have goose bumps? Why did this fairy-tale structure create a sex dungeon sensation?

Because she was losing her mind, damn it. Because those dreams were interfering with her sanity. Whenever she awakened from one of those episodes, all she thought about was kinky sex: bondage fantasies, acts of debauchery, things she'd never craved or even considered before.

She took one last look at the fancy exterior of the building. Then, determined to behave as normally as possible, she proceeded to the entrance. The wheels on her basic black suitcase bumped up and over the porch steps, making a soft thudding sound.

Summers in New Orleans were hot and humid, or so she'd been told. But today the weather was warm and pleasant.

She went inside and entered an impressive foyer that served as a reception area. Decorated with rose-motif armchairs and painted side tables, it presented a colorful invitation. Seated at a carved writing desk was a middle-aged woman with fluffy auburn hair and sparkling jewelry. Flamboyant in her own right, she fit the environment.

She stood up, showcasing her full figure, and said, "You must be Kendra Madden. I'm Claire, the innkeeper's assistant."

Kendra smiled and said hello. She wasn't surprised that Claire presumed who she was. Her arrival time had been prearranged. Kendra was a bridesmaid at a wedding that would take place at the inn. She'd booked her reservation a day early because she was anxious to get out of Los Angeles. The rest of the wedding party would be filtering in tomorrow and were only scheduled for a short stay. Kendra had decided to combine this trip with a much-needed two-week vacation.

Claire said, "I'll let the innkeeper know you're here. He'll get you situated."

While the assistant called her boss, Kendra noticed that the reception area led to a parlor. She caught glimpses of crushed velvet settees and marble-topped tables.

A few minutes later, a man emerged from that direction, and Kendra could do little more than stare. He owned this place? She'd been expecting an older gentleman, but he was about her age.

Mercy me, she thought.

Although he sported casual business attire and carried himself in a professional manner, he was tall, dark, and hot. Stylishly mussed straight black hair, caramel-colored skin, and strong-boned features illustrated a wildly ethnic quality.

Was it any wonder? She'd read on the inn's website that this was a Creole-owned establishment, and from what she understood, the Louisiana Creole hailed from French, Spanish, African, and Native American roots. Or at least some sort of combination thereof.

Kendra had a fair complexion, blue eyes, and natural blonde hair, but she'd always been intrigued by exotic men. Not that she'd ever been with anyone who looked like him. Her ex was blond and blue-eyed, too.

Their gazes met from across the room, and she sensed that the attraction was mutual. He glanced away first, but the male-female ritual had already begun, creating an awkward moment.

He apparently did his best to recover. As he moved closer, he played the perfect host and smiled. But that only made things worse. His smile was slow and naturally sexy.

He closed the gap between them, and she waited for him to speak, wondering if he would greet her in a local accent.

"Hello, Kendra," he said, making polite use of her name. "Welcome to the Bonswa. I'm James Rideau."

He didn't speak in the "Nawlins" way. In fact, aside from reciting *Bonswa* and *Rideau* with a gentle French inflection, he sounded as West Coast as she did.

Even more intrigued, she extended her hand. "It's nice to meet you."

He reached out, too. "The pleasure is mine."

Oh, no, she thought. *No. Pleasure* was the wrong thing for him to say. The very instant they touched, the tie-me-up hunger associated with her dreams slammed straight into her.

She wanted to pull away, but she followed through with the handshake, pretending that her heart wasn't sticking to her throat.

"Would you like a tour of the inn?" he asked. "Or would you prefer to go to your room first?"

"I'd like to see the inn." She was too nervous to enter a bedroom with him. She needed time to get a grip on reality, to clear her mind of forbidden fantasies.

"You can leave your bag with me," Claire said.

Kendra started. She'd actually forgotten the other woman was there. Pasting a smile on her face, she handed over her suitcase.

James gestured toward the parlor. "Ready?"

She nodded, and they passed a sweeping staircase that most likely led to the room she was avoiding.

Soon they were alone in the parlor, and she struggled to focus on what he was saying: something about guests gathering for afternoon tea.

From there, they entered a formal dining room, and he explained the breakfast routine. She nodded as if she were paying attention. But at least she'd caught enough to know that the buffet-style morning meal was served between eight and ten.

The tour continued to the library, and he pointed out tapes, books, and tourist brochures about New Orleans, along with whatever else the floor-to-ceiling shelves contained.

Once they reached the opulent ballroom where the wedding reception would be held, he engaged her in small talk, forcing her to use her bumbling brain.

"Is this your first trip to New Orleans?" he asked.

"Yes. My first time as a bridesmaid, too. But weddings aren't really my thing."

He flashed a playful smile. "And here I thought weddings were every woman's thing."

"Not me. But maybe it's because I'm divorced."

His smile fell. "Oh, I'm sorry."

Kendra could have kicked herself for revealing something so personal. In fact, she had no idea why she'd said it, other than because the dreams had started after the divorce.

She tried for a little damage control. "It's okay. The divorce was my choice. And it's been over a year. Plenty of time to move on."

He didn't respond, and in the silence, the air seemed to thicken, intensifying the body heat between them.

"I've never been married," he finally said.

To keep herself from moving closer, from breathing him in, she remarked, "A bachelor who hosts weddings."

"It goes with the territory." He made a wide gesture, indicating their surroundings. "But I enjoy making other people's dreams comes true."

She didn't want to discuss other people's dreams, not when all she wanted was for hers to disappear.

She cleared her mind. "The inn seems quiet today."

"It is. Aside from you, we only have a few guests tonight. But they'll be checking out tomorrow before the rest of your party arrives."

"Then you'll be full."

He nodded. "And busy with the wedding preparations." He opened a set of stained-glass doors. "The ceremony will be out here."

Together, they stepped onto a courtyard surrounded by ancient oaks and thriving magnolias. Scores of potted plants and flowers lined the way to a majestic gazebo.

"No wonder Cathy picked this place," she said.

"Ah, yes, the bride. She and Ken have stayed at the inn before. They're a great couple."

"Yes, they are." And this was getting awkward again. She and James had walked onto the wedding aisle and were standing much too close.

Several beats of silence passed. She couldn't think of anything else to say, and apparently neither could he.

Not until he asked, "Do you want to see your room now?"

"Yes, please." It was better than being trapped on a wedding aisle.

They returned to the foyer and got her bag from Claire, who remained at the desk.

Kendra and James ascended the stairs to the second floor. Her room was located near the stairwell.

"Do you live here?" she asked, curious about how close he would be at night.

"My apartment is on the third floor." His voice went a little rough. "And above me is the attic."

She frowned at his reaction. "It's not creepy, is it? Or haunted or something?"

"The attic? No. There's just a bunch of junk up there. Typical stuff."

None of this seemed typical to her. When James unlocked her door, she braced herself for the intimacy of being in a bedroom with him.

They stepped inside, and he showed her around.

The room was decorated with antiques, and the bathroom offered modern conveniences with antique-style fixtures. There was a balcony, too, with a lovely view.

But it was the bed that attracted her attention. She kept glancing at it, wondering if she would dream there tonight and wishing that she wouldn't.

She looked up at him. "When I was little, my parents used to say that if you wished hard enough, you could make anything happen." Of course, in her case, she was trying to make something *un*-happen. "Do you think that's true?"

"I believe in magic, voodoo, and whatnot. But I suppose it's in my blood." He made a serious expression. "If there's a wish you need fulfilled, you can visit Marie Laveau's tomb. She's considered the queen of voodoo, and they say that you can call upon her spirit to grant your wish. I can give you the spell. Lots of tourists do it."

Kendra made a face. She didn't want to create hocus-pocus at a gravesite, no matter how commercialized it was. "How about something simpler, like a good old-fashioned wishing well?"

"You could toss a coin into the *Jaillissement de Plaisir* fountain." He cleared his throat. "But then your wish will probably turn sexual."

Kendra blinked. Had she heard him right? "I'm sorry. What?"

"The fountain was favored by Marie Laveau's daughter. She was a voodoo practitioner in the eighteen hundreds, too. They say that she used to cast erotic spells there. So now if you wish upon it, it's supposed to grant sexual fulfillment. *Jaillissement de Plaisir* means Spurt of Pleasure."

She went silent. Her wish was already sexual, wasn't it? If her dreams went away, she would stop having kinky fantasies, and her sex drive would return to normal. To her, that would be fulfillment.

"I didn't mean to embarrass you," he said.

She met his gaze, and his dark eyes nearly penetrated her soul. He'd mistaken her silence for shyness.

Kendra took a step back and bumped into the bed. Bad move. Bad girl. Bad everything. "I'm not embarrassed."

"That's good." He cleared his throat again. "If there's anything you need, just let me know."

She released a shaky breath. "I will."

He gave her the key to her room, along with the combination to a lockbox at the front door, which would give her access to the inn after hours.

She tried for a casual tone and failed miserably. "Thank you, James."

He seemed just as rattled. "It's my pleasure."

There went that word again. Only this time, she associated it with Spurt of Pleasure. And, heaven forbid, she could totally imagine him spurting into her.

When he turned to leave, she caught his attention.

"Where is it?" she asked, desperate to make a wish.

He didn't stop to question what "it" was. He quickly responded, "In the French Quarter." He reached for a pen and paper on the nightstand and wrote the directions for her. "You can take the St. Charles Avenue streetcar to get there."

He handed her the paper, and their fingers brushed in the process. Every cell in her body reacted, sending little shock waves straight to the V between her thighs.

Luckily, he ended the madness, saying good-bye and making his retreat.

After he left the room, she sat on the edge of the bed, gearing up for the fountain.

Damn, James thought. *Damn.* He knew better than to get hot for a guest. It was wrong; it was unprofessional; it was his worst nightmare.

Could Kendra look any more innocent? Could she drive him any crazier? Such soft skin and pretty blonde hair, such sparkling blue eyes. So different from the darkness twisting and turning inside him.

Worse yet was her interest in the fountain. He had no idea what her wish entailed, but he sure as hell could make a few of his own. He wouldn't, though. His libido was already bursting at the seams.

He'd told Kendra that he had magic in his blood. But the only thing he could feel right now were hard, hammering jolts of testosterone.

How was he going to survive the next two weeks? How was he going to sleep under the same roof with her? He should have built a cottage out back. He should have separated himself from his guests.

For all the good that did now. Besides, he'd chosen to live in the mansion so he could be near the attic.

His obsession. His sin.

He glanced at the stairwell, cursing its winding path. He wanted so badly to go up there and release the tension.

But he knew it wouldn't cure what ailed him. His lotion-slicked hand wasn't going to take the place of a woman. Nor would it quell the salacious things he hungered to do to her.

Maintaining what was left of his sanity, he expelled the air in his pent-up lungs and went downstairs to immerse himself in the upcoming wedding preparations.

But before he headed to his office, he decided to check in with Claire. She was his girl Friday, and her husband, Leon, was the chef who made taste buds come alive at the inn.

James entered the foyer, and Claire glanced up from her desk, where she was typing away at her laptop.

"Hey," she said in her usual upbeat way. "I just e-mailed you the rehearsal dinner schedule."

"Thanks. Will you send over a copy of the menu, too?"

"No problem." She leaned in and lowered her voice. "So, what do you think of Kendra? If I'm not mistaken, I detected some chemistry between you two."

Please, Lord. The last thing he needed was a happily married matchmaker watching his every move. "She's a guest, Claire."

"Yes, but she's also an attractive young woman who was checking you out. And you"—she wagged a finger at him—"were trying way too hard not to look back."

He scoffed at her observation. "I was not."

"You were, too, and I'll bet you could have a nice little affair with her if you quit being such a stick-in-the-mud and enjoyed yourself once in a while."

A nice little affair? If he wasn't so stressed, he would have laughed. "I don't do flings, and I certainly don't do them with guests."

Claire rolled her eyes. "You don't do anything, James. When's the last time you had a girlfriend?"

"I'm too busy for a relationship."

"You know what they say about all work and no play."

Yeah, and if she knew the type of play that consumed him, she would probably fall over and die. "It wouldn't be proper to pursue her."

Claire rolled her eyes again, and he turned away, hoping his stick-in-the-mud manner would get him off the hook.

Anxious to take refuge in his office, he exited the foyer. But he get didn't far.

Proper be damned.

Kendra was descending the stairs, and he stopped to look up at her, even though he should've kept right on going.

She wore the same slightly wrinkled summer dress, and the hem fluttered as she moved. She was the kind of apparition a man hoped to see at the foot of his bed.

As she reached the bottom step, he wondered what type of bra and panties she was wearing. Practical, delicate, cotton, lace . . . ?

He imagined stripping her where she stood and taking a long, lustful look at her lingerie.

Then what would he do? Sweep her into his protective arms and carry her to the gates of hell?

As uncomfortable as ever in his presence, she stared at him, and he grappled for something appropriate to say.

"Are you on your way to the streetcar?" he asked.

"Yes. To explore the Quarter."

He avoided direct mention of the fountain, and so did she. But it lingered between them, as thick as steam from a swamp.

"Then you'd better go," he said.

His cock was pressing painfully against his fly, and her nipples had become visible beneath whatever sweet little bra she was wearing.

With a whispered good-bye, she flitted past him, like a butterfly about to be pinned to a wheel.

His wheel, he thought. Which was exactly where he longed for her to be.

Chapter 2

The fountain was surrounded by a passionately overgrown garden, and Kendra imagined it as it was in the nineteenth century when Marie Laveau's daughter had cast her erotic spells.

She moved closer. The large stone pool brimmed with coin-speckled water, and around its circular base was the *Jaillissement de Plaisir* name, along with another French inscription.

But she suspected that the centerpiece, with its three topless muses, was what contained the most magic.

Each delicate female had been created from the same image, and the flowing fabric carved around their hips gave them a Romanesque quality.

Regardless of the fountain's origin, the alluring trio looked like goddesses, with water trickling from the basin above them.

Kendra removed her wallet from her shoulder bag, mulling

over what type of coin to use. Would it make a difference? Probably not, considering the pennies, nickels, dimes, and quarters that had already been tossed.

She settled on a nickel from the year she was born. That seemed like a good omen, or so she hoped. Clearly, she was out of her element and probably out of her mind, too.

Still, she wanted to believe that the fountain had the power to help her.

She clutched the nickel until it warmed in her hand, then wished for her dreams to stop and tossed the coin. It pinged off one of the muses and plunked into the pool.

Rather than turn and walk away, she remained at the fountain, inhaling the garden-scented air.

The moment itself seemed magical, and she was certain that her dreams would stop and she would find satisfaction in fantasies that didn't involve restraints.

But she was wrong.

Late that night, she dreamed the same chilling dream, only it was even more vivid, more real. She saw a wider view of the dungeon, where lanterns flickered, and an X-shaped cross, designed for human bondage, was hinged to the wall.

She awakened the next morning feeling insanely sexual. With her nightgown sticking to her skin, she sat up and pushed the covers away, cursing the fountain.

Had it backfired? All she could think about was being strapped to the cross while it turned in an upside down motion.

Naked and spinning.

But who was turning the strange device? Who was her lover? James popped into her mind, and her flesh burned from the wicked want of him.

She squeezed her thighs together to keep from touching herself. No way was she going to strum her clit and fantasize about the innkeeper. She was already a nervous wreck around him.

Yes, but he wouldn't know that she was making her fingers sticky for him, and it would feel so good, so naughty.

She squeezed harder, warning herself to behave.

Before she gave in, she climbed out of bed and stumbled to the bathroom, where a cold, cold shower awaited.

Kendra went downstairs with a raging appetite. Luckily she hadn't missed the two-hour breakfast window, although she was at the tail end of it.

As she entered the dining room, several other guests were leaving. They passed her with chipper hellos, and she returned their friendly greetings.

So far, so good. No sign of James. She was hoping that she didn't run into him.

She headed for the buffet table and reached for a plate, a napkin, and silverware. A selection of breads, sweet muffins, eggs, and fresh fruit was available, along with a variety of cereals. She noticed bread pudding, too.

Kendra put a hodgepodge of food on her plate, including a generous helping of the pudding.

She turned around and sucked in her breath. The object of her lust had just walked into the room.

As always, their gazes met and held.

He spoke first. "Morning, Kendra."

"Hi." She clutched her plate a little tighter and glanced at the big, empty dining table.

He followed her line of sight. "You can eat on the veranda if you prefer."

"Oh, that sounds nice. Thank you." She could have left it at that, but she added, "Would you like to join me?"

Plain and simple, she couldn't handle tiptoeing around their attraction anymore. At least this way, they could try to have a casual conversation.

He seemed surprised by the offer, but he said, "Sure. You go ahead and choose a table, and I'll get you something to drink." He indicated the beverages at the buffet. "Coffee, tea, or orange juice?"

"Juice, please." The door to the veranda was already open, where a grouping of wrought-iron tables topped with fresh-cut flowers made a picturesque presentation.

She went outside and sat down. As she waited for James, she hoped she was doing the right thing.

He appeared with her juice and coffee for himself.

"You're not eating?" she asked, as he settled in across from her.

"I had breakfast earlier."

She glanced down at her plate. "I took more pudding than anything. But it's my favorite dessert."

"Mine, too. The Creole recipe is with bourbon sauce. But we don't serve it that way. It wouldn't be kid friendly."

"I'll have to try it that way sometime."

"I'm sure you'd like it. The sauce is creamy and smooth."

Her skin went as warm as the weather. Creamy and smooth sounded luxuriously erotic. "I'm always game for something sweet."

"So am I." He snared her gaze, and silence sizzled between them.

This wasn't good, she thought. This was exactly what they shouldn't be doing.

Before things turned too intimate, she asked, "Where are you from?"

He kept looking at her. "The city."

She made a puzzled expression. "What city?"

He snapped to attention. "San Francisco."

At least they'd gotten past the staring jag. "Do you have family in New Orleans?"

"My father is from here, but I don't remember him. He died when I was a baby. He was a party boy. Drinking, carousing, womanizing. He got himself killed over another man's wife."

"That must have been difficult on your mom."

"It was. But you know what? That didn't stop her from missing him." He frowned. "I don't understand why women always seem to be attracted to the wrong men."

Was James the wrong the man, too? Was that why he'd mentioned it? Or was she reading too much into their attraction? "Is your mom still in San Francisco?"

He shook his head. "She passed away when I was in college."

"I'm sorry." Both of her parents were alive and well and still married.

A butterfly landed on the floral centerpiece, drawing his attention.

"It's a viceroy," he said.

She assumed he meant the butterfly. "I see that type around all the time, but I thought they were called monarchs."

"People often mistake them for monarchs. They look the same, except the viceroy is smaller, and it has a black line that goes across its wings."

Kendra tried to see the distinguishing mark, but she wasn't quite sure what she was looking for. The orange and black butterfly had lots of lines.

He continued the lesson. "In earlier studies, they used to say that viceroys mimicked monarchs because the monarch is toxic. But now they say that they're both toxic and they mimic each other. Either way, it keeps them safe from predators."

"Wow. Who knew?"

"You remind me of a butterfly."

Taken aback, she said, "After your description of them, it makes me sound like a femme fatale."

"I didn't mean it like that."

Then how did he mean it? "I'm not toxic, but I'm not fragile, either."

"In most cultures, butterflies represent transformation. But they can symbolize innocence, too. You seem innocent to me."

She sighed. "I suppose in some ways, I am. My ex is the only guy I've ever been with. We dated a long time before we got married."

"What ended it?"

"Predictability. Incompatibility. We just weren't right for each other. He didn't fight me on the divorce. He was feeling trapped, too."

"And now you're free."

Not in her mind. Not in the bondage fantasies that aroused her. Twisted innocence, she thought.

The viceroy flew away, and James watched it depart.

"How do you know so much about butterflies?" she asked.

"My mom taught me about the symbolism. She also worked at a science museum, so she was practical, too. When I was a kid, I used to hang out there a lot."

A practical mother and a wild-spirited father. She couldn't quite fathom it. "So what brought you to New Orleans? Was it your father's family?"

"In a roundabout way. I inherited this house from my great-uncle. He made a fortune in commercial fishing. After he retired and sold his company, he bought this place, then holed up in it like a hermit."

"He sounds like a Howard Hughes type."

"He was. When I was around ten, Mom brought me here to see him because he wanted to meet me. He was odd and reclusive, but he taught me a little about my Creole side."

"Did you ever see him again?"

"No. That was it. I grew up, and he kept his distance. Can you imagine my surprise when the executor of his estate notified me that my uncle had passed away and I was the heir to his house?"

"What made you turn it into a B and B?"

"My degree is in hospitality management. I worked for a five-star hotel chain in San Francisco, so this was a natural transition. Something that just seemed right."

"I think you did the house proud."

"I hope so." He glanced at the flowers. "Hey, look who's back."

She smiled. The mimic. "He must like us."

"It's a she."

"You can tell?"

He shook his head. "I'm not that much of an expert." A small breeze fluttered the front of his hair, spilling strands onto his forehead. "But if it reminds me of you, then it must be a she."

Intrigued by his rugged romanticism, she got caught up in

staring at him again. He looked at her, too. Intense eye contact. They couldn't seem to escape it.

Suddenly she wanted to tell him about her deepest, darkest, sexiest secret. Suddenly she wanted him to know about her dreams.

But when she tried to form the words, she couldn't quite piece them together.

Kendra chickened out, leaving it unsaid.

Chapter 3

For James, the next few days went by in a blur. Between tending to a full house and hosting a wedding, there was no time for anything else.

Or almost no time. Kendra continued to invade his mind, especially when he was alone at night, buck naked and tossing the covers aside.

And now, here he was, at the wedding reception, watching her dance with another man. An old friend? A coworker? Clearly he was someone Kendra knew fairly well. Their body language conveyed *relaxed* rather than *romantic*. Still, it was a slow dance, and James envied the other guy.

"She looks gorgeous," Claire said.

James turned toward his assistant. The bride and groom had invited both of them to the festivities. "Don't start."

"Start what?" She dug into the plate of food in front of her.

"Matchmaking."

"All I said was how good she looks."

"You said gorgeous." And it was true. Kendra wore a slim-fitting, silky pink dress that rode just above the knee. The jewels at the neckline matched the glittery comb in her toss-of-summer-waves hair. The classic silhouette and slightly tousled mane worked on her.

He could imagine her waking up beside him that way, minus the dress and glittery comb. Spent, he thought, from being wildly fucked and desperately bound.

Cripes almighty. Did he have to think of that now?

Claire cut into a crab cake her husband had prepared, then offered James a bite. He shook his head. The spicy remoulade sauce was the last thing he needed.

His blood was already hot.

Kendra and her partner left the dance floor. He headed for the buffet, and she returned to her table.

As James watched her, the rough-sex urge came back. But not too rough. He wanted it to be tender, too, if that made a lick of sense.

Steeped in the way she made him feel, he shifted in his chair. Maybe he should—

"You should ask her to dance," Claire said, beating him to the punch.

He made an exasperated face, and she laughed. "Oops, sorry. Am I am being a matchmaker again?"

"If you want me to have a nice little affair, then you need to let me do it on my own terms."

She quit laughing. "Does that mean you're going to go for it?"

He had no idea what he was going to do. "I might."

"You'd better." She leaned over to kiss him on the cheek.

"And to prove how non-meddlesome I can be, I'm going to head over to the kitchen and hang out with Leon."

She stood up, taking her plate with her, giving him a cute little finger wave as she departed.

Claire likened herself to being his surrogate mother, and he adored her for it. But her interest in his love life was a bit more than he could handle.

Why? Because he was feeling guilty about his nocturnal cravings? Thank goodness Claire and Leon didn't live in the mansion. At least James had the place to himself at night. Or mostly to himself. He still had his guests to consider.

He gazed at the guest consuming his mind. The music remained soft and slow, and he was hankering to hold her.

He crossed the ballroom and approached her table. As he got closer, Kendra turned and saw him. She reacted by sitting a bit more forward. He suspected that she sensed what was coming.

He reached his destination and asked, "Would you like to dance?"

Perched on the edge of her chair, she readily agreed. "Yes, thank you."

They found a spot on the crowded dance floor. He reached for her, and they went body-to-body. He couldn't begin to describe how good it felt. She followed his every lead.

Would she follow him into destruction, too?

Captivated, he inhaled the scent of her skin. She smelled like flowers mingled with fruits and spices. Unable to help himself, he slid his hand down her back.

She made a soft, sweet sound. Was she affected by the hunger in his touch?

With his hand poised expectantly on her tailbone, he said, "Tell me about your *Jaillissement de Plaisir* wish."

She lifted her gaze to his. Big blue eyes. "I've been thinking about telling you."

"So do it. Share it with me."

"Not here." Her breath hitched. "Not with so many other people around."

"You can whisper it in my ear."

She shook her head. "That would be too . . ."

Intimate? Erotic? Embarrassing? He had no idea what she was going to say, and she didn't fill in the blank.

"We can go outside after this song is over," he said. "We can find a private place to talk."

She agreed, and when it ended, he led her onto the courtyard. Party lights lit their way, some of which were strung in trees, creating a fairy-tale setting.

Moving away from other guests who'd also stepped outside, they found an isolated spot.

James turned to face her. "We can talk now."

"All right. But you're probably going to think I'm strange or perverted or something."

"You?" He noticed her skin was flushed. "Somehow I doubt that." Especially with the lewd and lascivious thoughts that tore through his mind.

"I've been having these dark dreams, and I wished for them to go away. But they haven't stopped."

"What do you mean by dark?"

"Gothic. There's this place I keep seeing." She winced. "A sex dungeon."

James just stared at her. That was the last thing he'd expected to hear. "Describe it."

She tried for a joke. "You know, the usual."

"No, really, Kendra, tell me what it looks like."

She glanced up at the sky, as if she needed a moment to collect herself. "Brick walls, sconce lanterns, chains and manacles, an X-shaped cross, a stockade, a long wooden table with leather restraints."

His heart nearly pole-vaulted out his chest. Could this be happening? Was this real?

She continued, "Ever since the dreams started, all I do is imagine having kinky sex." She made a tortured expression. "I told you it would make me sound perverted."

Was she kidding? He thought she was amazing, the most glorious creature on earth. He could barely concentrate, barely breathe. "I think the place you've been dreaming about is in my attic."

She gaped at him. "You have a sex dungeon in your attic?"

"It was already there when I inherited the house." He paused, trying to still his rocky emotions. "No one knows about it except me. I doubt my uncle was even aware of it. I discovered it by accident. It's behind a hidden door, and it's been there for ages. Probably since the house was built. The original owner must have been a Marquis de Sade type." He gave her a moment to process everything before he added, "Will you come with me? I want you to see it."

Kendra hesitated. Should she go with him? Was his dungeon an omen of some kind? And if it was, what did it mean? Omens could be good or bad.

He waited for her to make a decision, and she nervously agreed, if only to see if it was the same place she'd been dreaming about. She left the reception with him, and they went upstairs and stopped on the landing of the third floor. The door to James's apartment was on the right, and a set of narrow stairs was on the left.

"Ready?" he asked.

She nodded, all too aware of the intensity brewing between them. Anxious, she followed him up the cramped stairwell. They reached the attic door, and he removed his keys from his pocket and unlocked it.

They went inside, and he flipped a light switch. The room was larger than she'd expected and cluttered with boxes, old trunks, and battered furniture. Two small windows were trimmed with lace curtains.

"Some of this stuff is mine, and some of it was already here," he said.

"It's spooky."

"There's nothing to be afraid of. I promise it isn't haunted."

Maybe not by ghosts, but she was getting chilled just the same.

He took her hand and led her to a tight space behind the furniture, where a wall was covered in wood panels.

"I was moving some stuff around in here, when a stack of boxes tipped over and hit the wall. That's how I discovered the door." He pushed on a panel and it moved, creating an opening.

Kendra's stomach flip-flopped. "It's like something out of an old movie."

"I know. Isn't it great?"

He flashed that sloe gin smile of his, and she felt downright faint, like a silly Victorian miss.

He offered to let her go first. "After you."

She hesitated. "Will it be dark?"

He shook his head. "When I turned on the lights in the attic, it turned on the lights in there, too. It's the same switch."

Taking the lead, she crossed the mysterious threshold and walked straight into the dungeon that had been living in her mind.

"Is it from your dreams?" James asked from behind her.

"Yes." She released the air in her lungs. "But it looks newer and prettier." Softly illuminated, the gothic scene all but glittered. The manacles were bright and shiny, the cross was sleek and smooth, even the floors were polished to perfection. She turned to look at him. "It was rougher in my dreams."

"Then you must have been seeing it the way it was before." He moved closer. "I spent months restoring everything."

She could little more than ask, "Why?"

"Because from the moment I discovered this room, it consumed me, and I wanted to bring it back to life." He glanced around. "I've never been the fetish type, so it was a bit weird, getting attached to a dungeon. But the more I worked on it, the more I wanted to become part of it. I started having these hot, wild thoughts. Bondage and discipline. Dominance and submission. I even researched it online."

She stood there in her bridesmaid's dress, surrounded by the ambience he'd created. She was both aroused and afraid, her pulse skittering beneath her skin.

"It's supposed to be perfectly normal to have these types of fantasies," he said. "But it makes me feel dark inside."

Me, too, she thought.

"See that cabinet?" He pointed to an armoire near the wood panels and the door.

She shifted her gaze. It was the only section of the dungeon that hadn't appeared in her subconscious.

He continued by saying, "It's filled with bondage gear and sex toys and all sorts of crazy stuff. Things I ordered from the Net. Things that intrigue me."

Kendra sucked in her breath. Should she drop down and kneel at his feet? Or run away and never come back? "I was afraid to get too into it. I didn't look anything up online."

"So you've been having dreams about a culture you don't know anything about?"

"I know what I feel."

"Which is what?"

"That I want someone to restrain me. In all sorts of ways."

He made the ultimate offer. "I could do that for you. We could experiment together."

Oh, God. She wanted him desperately. But that didn't lessen her fear. She glanced at the cross and imagined the spinning sensation.

"We could come back here later tonight," he said.

Her pulse went haywire. "What time?" She needed structure, a schedule to follow.

"How about one o'clock?"

After the bewitching hour. "That's good."

"Yes, good." He leaned forward to kiss her, but he didn't use his tongue. He simply skimmed her lips with his, teasing her, taunting himself.

She nearly creamed her panties.

He drew back. "We should go before your friends start wondering what happened to you."

She nodded, and they returned to the normal part of the attic. On their way out, he turned out the lights, leaving the room in shadows.

After he locked the door, he removed the key from his key ring and extended it to her.

She was still reeling from her near-damp undies. "Don't you need it?"

"I have a spare in my apartment."

She accepted the key and closed her hand around it.

From there, they rejoined the wedding reception and made a point of going their separate ways, preparing in their minds to meet again.

Chapter 4

Kendra stood in front of the vanity mirror in her room, gazing at her reflection. She'd changed her clothes at least three times, then decided that she should wear a nightgown.

It wasn't a sexy garment, but it was soft and pretty. Adorned with lace, embroidery, and ribbons, it flowed to her ankles. The color was almost the same shade as her skin, but with a hint of shimmer. She even had a robe to match.

Anxious, she glanced over her shoulder at the clock on the nightstand: 12:22 a.m. She still had time to kill.

She turned back to the mirror. She was braless, of course. Who wore a bra with a nightgown? As for panties, that was another matter. Kendra always wore underwear to bed.

Yes, but she wasn't going to bed. She was going to a medieval-style dungeon in a Victorian attic.

Oh, goodness.

Shaking her head, she lifted the hem of her gown and exposed her panties. They were as soft and pretty as the nightgown. She suspected that James would like them.

She thought about the barely there kiss he'd given her earlier and how easily it had threatened to make her wet.

Her sex life would never be the same. After tonight, she would be forever changed.

But it was fate, wasn't it? Why else would she have dreamed about the dungeon James had been compelled to restore? Between the two of them, this was meant to happen. A tie-me-up rendezvous on someone else's wedding night. It didn't get any hotter than that.

Kendra sat on the edge of the bed and waited until it was time to go. Finally, at twelve forty-five, she donned her robe and a pair of ladylike slippers.

Instead of dealing with a cumbersome purse, she placed the key to the attic, along with the key to her room, in a delicate little satchel she'd received as a bridesmaid's gift.

She opened her door and peered out. There was no one in the hallway, but she hadn't expected to run into another guest at this hour. Still, she quickly headed for the stairwell and ascended to the third floor.

After glancing in the direction of James's apartment, she made her way to the attic and unlocked the door, hoping he was already there. But she found herself in a darkened room.

She flipped the light switch and crept over to the paneled wall. At first she couldn't get the door to work, but then she realized she was pushing on the wrong panel.

When it finally moved, she took a deep breath and slipped inside, closing the passageway behind her.

Alone in the softly lit dungeon, she gave herself a moment

of acclimation, then placed her satchel on the floor beside the sex-toys cabinet.

Curious, she reached for the handle, wondering if it was unlocked. It was. Unable to resist, she opened it and scanned the shelves.

Holy mother.

Fancy handcuffs, silky blindfolds, gags, dildos, vibrators, lubricants, massage oils, body paint, condoms . . .

She reached for a jar of strawberry something or other that was supposed to enhance the flavor of oral sex. Just as she twisted the cap and dipped into it, a voice came out of nowhere.

"Having fun?"

She spun around. She'd been so engrossed in the toys that she hadn't heard James come in.

He looked gorgeous as ever, but he hadn't fussed over his appearance. He was wearing the same suit he'd worn to the wedding, but without the jacket or tie. That left him in black trousers and a pale blue shirt, the first two buttons undone.

"Go ahead and taste it," he said.

"What?"

"The flavor you put on your finger."

Oh, right. The strawberry stuff. "No, that's okay."

"Taste it, Kendra."

Her heart hit her rib cage. Apparently the dominance had already begun. Oddly exhilarated, she stuck her finger in her mouth and sucked on the tip like a good little girl.

"Now take off your slippers and robe."

Once again, she obeyed him.

He stepped back to study her, scanning the length of her body. "You look pretty."

"Thank you."

"I like that you wore a nightgown. But I want you to take it off, too."

Before a major dose of shyness set in, she peeled the gossamer garment over her head. Then she stood quietly, allowing him to look at her, wearing nothing but lace-trimmed panties.

He gazed at her for what seemed like an endless amount of time, and she could tell that he appreciated what he saw.

"Are you nervous?" he asked.

"Yes. But in a good way." Hot, hungry fear. She'd never experienced anything like it.

"In this type of play, we're supposed to use a safe word."

Confused, she merely looked at him.

He explained, "A code word that will either stop the activity if you want it to end or decrease the level of intensity if you want to keep going."

"What if I don't want to use a safe word?"

"Then we don't have to." James came forward and pressed against her. "But it's considered risky not to."

She lustfully pressed back. She could feel his hard-on through his pants. "I want it to be risky." She wanted to put her faith in a man she barely knew.

He finally kissed her, *really* kissed her, his tongue making wild contact with hers. She moaned her pleasure, and he reached down and slid his hand along the waistband of her panties.

"Take those off," he ordered in the gruffest of whispers.

Kendra tugged them down. Already she felt as if she belonged to him. His naked toy. His innocent prize. His fuck-me possession.

He gazed hungrily at her. "Put the strawberry gel down there."

While he watched, she reached for the jar and dipped into the slick substance. She applied it generously, all the way inside, then around her clit.

"I'm going to restrain the hell out of you." James motioned with his chin, indicating the direction of the cross. "On that."

Kendra's knees turned to putty, and he led her to what was about to become her bondage christening.

He positioned her so that she was facing him in a spread-eagle stance. After securing her wrists to the wood, he knelt to cuff her ankles in the same manner. He stood up and finished the process by pulling a strap around her waist.

He studied his handiwork. "Now you really are a butterfly on a wheel."

Her pulse pounded at her pussy. Was that how he'd been thinking of her? With pins through her wings?

She waited for him to maul her. But he was excruciatingly gentle, nuzzling her neck and nipping at her collarbone.

Kendra's instinct was to slide her hands through his hair and return his affection. But she couldn't. She was helpless to his ministrations.

He moved lower, teasing her nipples with tongue-flicking licks. Back and forth he went, making her areolas crinkle around each rising bud.

When he got on his knees and blew air across her navel, she sucked in her stomach.

Soon he was headed toward the flavor she'd slathered between her legs. Her pussy swelled, the folds going naturally damp.

He looked up at her. "Do you want me to taste you? Do you want me to eat your sweet little cunt?"

Kendra moaned. "Yes."

"Then say please."

"Please." *Pretty, pretty please.*

He parted her with his fingers, spreading her labia for his entertainment. "Saint Andrew was martyred on a cross like this. That's why it's called a Saint Andrew's cross."

Martyrs, butterflies, and a powerful man on his knees. Her head swam with it.

He put his mouth against her, and she fixated on how primal he looked, sipping from her swollen sex. She tried to press closer, but the restraints hindered her.

He took his time, pleasuring her with probing stabs and long, lethal strokes. Slow, hard, soft, deep, fast, shallow. He used a maddening rhythm.

When he sucked on her clit, all she wanted was to come. But apparently he had other ideas.

He actually stood up and wiped his mouth while unrequited wetness drizzled down her thighs.

She cursed him in her mind. "Why did you stop?"

"Because it isn't time."

He moved to stand beside the cross, and she realized he was going to rotate her.

Preparing for the upcoming motion, for the swirling, twirling fantasy of her dreams, she prayed to Saint Andrew.

Slowly the cross began to move, creaking like a demented carnival ride. He kept turning it until it made a complete circle. Before she could catch her breath, he repeated the full rotation, only faster. The dungeon tilted before her eyes, the room going topsy-turvy.

Finally, when he stopped it, she was in an upside-down

position. He came around to stand in front of her, and all she could see were his pant legs.

He said, "Now I'm going to make you come."

She could feel him leaning forward. Eager, she braced herself, silently chanting his name.

He placed his hands on her wide-open thighs and buried his face between them. She focused on the crease in his pant legs, thinking this was the strangest, sexiest, most thrilling moment of her life.

He used his tongue, his teeth, his entire mouth. While he played with her clit, she struggled not to scream. If she cried out, she feared that James would gag her.

Not that she wouldn't let him.

He continued his oral foray. He fingered her, too, stroking her with cream-coated digits.

Desire, thick and hot, burned through her body. She was at her lover's mercy. Totally. Completely. He was doing whatever he wanted, using the free rein she'd given him.

Kendra moaned and balled up her fists, her nails digging into her palms. Pain, pleasure, bondage.

The climax started at her clit and worked its way through every pore, every crevice, every inch of her flesh.

Slick and wet, she sped into a mind-bending, heart-rocking spasm, convulsing against his oh-so-perfect mouth.

James waited until she stopped shaking, then turned the cross and brought her face-side up.

She blinked at him in a post-orgasmic haze.

"You okay, baby?"

Was she? "I don't know." She couldn't think beyond the floating, melting sensation. But she liked that he'd called her baby.

"Here. Let me get you down." He undid her restraints and took her in his arms.

She put her head on his shoulder, thinking how easy it would be to fall in love with him.

Of course that was probably just the fountain voodoo talking. Surely, she'd been zapped with a spell.

Spurt of Pleasure.

"Are you going to fuck me now?" she asked.

"Not tonight."

She bumped her hand against his fly. He was big and hard. "But I want your cock."

His voice turned rough. "It's a tempting offer, believe me. But you've had enough."

"Will you do it if I beg? If I say please?"

"Oh, Christ, Kendra. Let me at least try to be a gentleman."

"What for?"

"Because you can't even stand on your own." To prove his point, he let go, and she swayed like a nymphomaniac in the wind.

"I guess I do feel a little funny. Like I did a really sexy, scary drug."

He brought her back into his arms. "It's your nervous system kicking in. That sometimes happens in this kind of play, especially when someone is new to the scene."

"You're new to it, too."

"I wasn't the one being dominated or turned on a wheel." He stroked a hand down her hair. "As soon as you're steady on your feet, I'll help you get dressed and take you to your room."

"I don't want to be alone."

"You won't be. I'll stay until you fall asleep."

"Okay." She relished being close to him. "Can we play again tomorrow night?"

"If you're up for it."

"I will be." She was certain of it. There was nothing Kendra wanted more than another night in the attic.

Chapter 5

James squinted at the clock. He'd overslept, and in Kendra's room, no less.

Dragging himself into a stronger state of awareness, he sat up and looked over at her. She was still asleep.

He hadn't meant to stay the entire night. But sometime while keeping her company and making sure she was all right, he'd conked out beside her.

Aside from his shoes, he remained fully dressed. But that didn't change the fact that he'd bunked down with a guest.

Yeah, and he'd bound her to a bondage wheel, too. He'd had his very wicked, wicked way with her.

She stirred in her sleep, and he gazed intently at her. She looked so pretty, so soft, like a butterfly fairy. He couldn't help feeling protective.

Strange to want to dominate a woman so badly yet be obsessed with the delicate side of her.

At this point, there was no reason to rush out of her room. Besides, if he wanted to sleep until noon, that was his business. He rarely took a day off, and, by damn, he needed one today. But, still, he'd better call Claire.

He patted himself down and found his cell phone crammed in his pocket, where it had been since the wedding. He hadn't purposely taken it to the dungeon, but now he was glad it was available.

To keep from disturbing Kendra, he went out on the balcony to make his call.

He speed dialed Claire and told her that he was going to chill out for the day. She didn't question him further, but she probably suspected that he'd hooked up with Kendra. Claire had good instincts. Not so good that she would suspect him of kinky misdeeds, though.

After ending the call, he returned to the room and noticed that his new lover was awakening.

Blinking into the light, she sat up and leaned against the headboard, the covers draped around her waist.

She started when she saw him. "I didn't know you were still here."

He shoved his phone back in his pocket. "I fell asleep beside you." He'd held her exceptionally close, too. "How do you feel?"

"Fine." She fussed with the straps on her nightgown, making sure they were in place. Then she smiled, as if her modesty made no sense.

It didn't, he supposed, but he didn't mind. To him, it only reinforced her innocence.

He returned her smile. "I could use some coffee. How about you?"

"Totally. New Orleans has the best coffee."

"It's the chicory. Stay put, and I'll make it."

The coffeemaker was on the counter outside the bathroom. He scooped the Café Du Monde blend into the filter and stayed there while it brewed, waiting for the liquid to drip into the carafe.

Upon completion, he called out to her, "How do you take it?"

"More sugar than cream," she called back.

James doctored hers first, then took care of his. He carried both cups and handed her the sweeter of the two.

She took a sip. "It's perfect. Thank you." She drew her knees up, and the covers fell partially away. "I didn't dream last night."

"Maybe being in the dungeon made the difference."

"That's what I'm thinking." She looked across the rim of her cup at him. "Do you think the fountain had anything to do with it?"

He turned the question around. "Why? Do you?"

She nodded. "I feel like I'm under a spell."

"So do I, and I didn't even make a wish."

"Maybe the magic that got me rubbed off on you."

"With voodoo I suppose anything is possible. It's funny, too, because I've walked past the *Jaillissement de Plaisir* a zillion times, but I've never actually gone into the courtyard or looked at the fountain."

She seemed surprised. "Why not?"

"I never had any reason to."

"You should see it up close, James. The muses in the center-piece are beautiful."

"That's what I've heard. I'll have to check it out sometime." He shifted in his chair. "I should have told you this when I first sent you there, but the fountain is next to a *maison*. That's slang in the Quarter for bordello. Or house of ill repute or whatever."

She widened her eyes. "I didn't see anything like that."

He couldn't help but grin. She looked properly shocked. "It's a high-end place, disguised as a boutique hotel."

Kendra put her coffee on the nightstand. "Have you been there?"

"To the *maison*? Me? Not likely."

"Oh, right." She half teased, half reprimanded him. "Says the man with a dungeon in his attic and a cabinet crammed with sex toys. Who did you plan on using all that stuff on?"

"No one. At least not consciously."

"You bought condoms. That's conscious."

"What responsible man doesn't have a supply of protection these days?"

"You have just about every type imaginable."

"So I like variety. Besides, what are you complaining about? I'm going to be trying them out on you."

"So you are." A quick smile, followed by a pout. "I wish we didn't have to wait until tonight to go back to the dungeon."

Damn. He put his cup down, his mind spinning in an illicit direction. "Maybe we could sneak up there this afternoon, unless you already made other plans for the day."

Her gaze locked onto his. "I didn't. I haven't. I'm completely free. But don't you have to work?"

"Normally I would, but I decided to take the day off. So, do you want to meet me up there?"

"Just tell me when."

"As soon as we're both ready."

"It might take me longer to get ready than you."

"That's okay. I'll wait for you in the dungeon. But bring your key. I don't like leaving the attic unlocked."

She smiled. "And understandably so."

He got out of his chair and crawled onto the bed. He gave her a chicory-laced kiss and whispered, "I'm going to chain you up and fuck you good and hard."

"Promise?" she whispered back.

"Absolutely." Enthralled, he kissed her again, then left her room and headed to his apartment to prepare for their liaison, anxious to keep his promise.

As expected, James was the first to arrive in the dungeon. But that gave him time to decide on what method of restraints to use and how he wanted the scene to unfold.

A short while later Kendra showed up. Bright and afternoon fresh, her hair gleamed and her skin was rosy from her shower or bath. Clothes-wise, she'd chosen a sleeveless yellow top, pleated shorts, and sandals.

After he'd gotten cleaned up, he'd donned a casual T-shirt and jeans. Between the two of them, they looked as if they were going on a sun-kissed outing, maybe to the aquarium or the zoo, when, in fact, they were messing around in a windowless dungeon.

"Ready?" he asked.

"I'm more than ready."

He pointed to the wall shackles. "Then go over there and strip down to your underwear."

She obeyed, giving James the desperate makings of a hard-on. Away went her top and shorts. She discarded her sandals, too.

She was wearing simple lingerie: a basic white bra and matching bikini panties. He appreciated the simplicity. He admired her body, too: gentle curves and small, round breasts.

He approached her, and she watched him through veiled lashes. Taking the liberty of getting her naked, he removed her bra and panties.

"Pretty sub," he said.

"Sub?"

"Submissive." One by one, he lifted her arms and cuffed her wrists so she was shackled to the wall. "You look like a virgin sacrifice."

"I feel like one."

Yeah, and she liked it, he thought. Anxious, he turned away, walked over to the cabinet, and rifled through the toys.

After putting a couple of the much-talked-about condoms in his pocket, he chose a flesh-colored, anatomically designed dildo with a long, thick shaft, a flared head, and veined texture. It had a hefty set of balls attached, too.

He returned to his lover and showed her the lifelike cock. She gazed at it, and his pulse pounded in anticipation.

"Do you like it?" he asked.

Her voice went breathy. "Yes."

He brought it up to her face and skimmed it against her cheek. "You're a bad girl, Kendra." A beautiful girl. His sexual ideal.

"I can't help it," she responded.

Neither could he. He brushed the dildo across her lips. "I'm going to make you suck it." He paused for effect. "But not yet."

He moved it down her chin, along her neck, and over her breasts, where he took his time, rolling the head around her nipples.

"Feels good," she said.

She looked longingly at him, and he suspected that she was thinking about his cock. Nothing could have excited him more.

He slid the dildo to her stomach and poked her navel. Finally he rubbed it between her legs without putting it inside.

When he penetrated her for the first time, it wasn't going to be with a rubber likeness. He wanted to reserve that glorious rite of passage for himself.

But that didn't mean her clit was off limits. James went ahead and used the phallus on her most sensitive spot, utilizing the tip to stimulate her.

Kendra made a sensual sound, and he kissed her. Their mouths came together quickly, creating a flurry of tongue-thrusting sensations.

He kept the dildo pressed against her, rubbing until her hips flexed and she rattled the chains on the manacles. On the edge of an orgasm, she started to close her eyes, but he wanted her focused on him.

"Look at me."

Her eyes flew open, and while she gazed directly at him, he watched her come.

James reacted like the hungry male he was. Not only was he painfully erect, he was leaking pre-cum.

After she had recovered from her climax, he removed a

vanilla-flavored condom from his pocket, opened the packet, and sheathed the dildo. Giving himself a thrill, he brought it to her lips.

She stuck out her tongue and licked it. "It tastes like pudding."

Ah, yes, he thought, like her favorite dessert. "Do you want more?"

She nodded, and he pushed it gently into her mouth and moved it back and forth, creating a blow job rhythm. While she sucked, he imagined that she was doing it to him.

By now, he was leaking like crazy.

She had a slow, sultry technique, and he watched and watched, mesmerized by her.

When he couldn't take it anymore, he got rid of the dildo and dug around in his pocket for the other condom, preparing to use it on himself. Kendra looked so damn sweet standing there with her arms above her head, waiting to be fucked.

He ditched his shirt and shoved down his jeans, and once he was properly protected, he moved in for the kill, clutching her ass and pulling her against him.

The air in her lungs whooshed out, and he maneuvered her hips so he could thrust into her.

Just like that, he was inside. She was tight and wet and moaning his name. She couldn't move her arms, but she was doing her damnedest to sling one of her legs around him.

Not that he was complaining. He grabbed the leg she was trying to hoist and helped her get into the position she craved. It worked mighty fine for him, too, enhancing the frenzied friction.

James loved the mindless pace. He loved listening to the jangle of chains as he pumped into her. Steeped in aggression, he kissed her hard and fast.

He'd never been addicted to anything before, but he feared this would be his downfall, his drug of choice.

More of the dungeon. More of her.

Embroiled in lust, he sucked on the side of her neck, leaving marks on her skin. She reacted by bowing her body and inviting him to thrust deeper, to use her for his pleasure.

Experimentation. Bondage and domination.

Sex in the darkest of ways.

Chapter 6

Now that it was over, Kendra felt as if she'd been in a train wreck. Her entire body ached. Yet nothing could have aroused her more.

James took care of the condom, then removed her manacles. She went straight into his arms. All she wanted was to stay close to him.

He nuzzled her hair. "Are you okay?"

"I'm fine. I'm not spacey like last time." Did that mean she was getting used to being a sub? That it was part of her nature?

He ran a hand up and down her naked spine. "Are you hungry? We could go to my apartment and fix something."

Food, she thought. Sustenance. It was the middle of the afternoon, and neither of them had eaten. "That's probably a good idea."

They nuzzled a moment longer, then got dressed, closed up the attic, and made their way to his apartment.

In keeping with the rest of the house, he'd filled it with Victorian antiques. The living room furniture consisted of a large sofa with a button-tuft back, matching side chairs, and an ornately carved table. Converted oil lamps and area rugs were scattered throughout. So was a bit of clutter. As nice as his place was, he was still a bachelor who left things sitting around.

He gave her a tour, and they lingered in his bedroom.

He said, "Bedsteads from this era weren't very big, so I had it extended so it would fit a king."

She imagined being tied to the iron posts. But she envisioned sleeping in his arms, too. "It looks comfortable."

"It's a feather mattress. If you want to stay with me for the rest of your vacation, you can."

Oh, wow. Was he a mind reader? Or just feeling the same way she did? "I'd like that very much."

"Once Claire finds out that you temporarily moved in, she'll probably take some of the credit. She's been encouraging me to be with you."

"If I tell Cathy and Ken about us, they'll probably think it's cool, too." She laughed a little. "I guess I better tell them before they realize I'm not in my room anymore."

He grinned. "Yeah, I suppose so. But they'll be leaving soon."

She nodded. Most of the wedding party would be gone by the end of the week, including the bride and groom.

"I'm glad you'll be here a little longer," he said.

"So am I." She wondered what it would be like to stay with him forever. He was everything a girl could wish for.

Wish? Like at the fountain?

Last night she'd considered how easy it would be to fall in love with him, and today she was daydreaming about being his life partner. Damn that voodoo.

"Are po'boys okay?" he asked. "I've gotten pretty good at making them."

It took her a moment to realize he was referring to their food. Obviously her mind was somewhere else. Love and forever. She had to quit thinking about it.

She focused on his question. She knew that po'boys were New Orleans–style submarine sandwiches. "Sure."

"How about sausage? Fully dressed?"

Once again, she agreed. Fully dressed, she assumed, meant lettuce and tomato and whatever else went on the sandwiches.

They headed to the kitchen and got started. While the sausage cooked in a heavy skillet, he showed her how to make Creole mustard.

"You're quite the New Orleans boy," she said.

"I like it here."

"You certainly look the part." She studied his features. "What combination of Creole are you?"

"A fair amount of French, a touch of Spanish, and whole lot of Native American. I've got Choctaw blood on my mother's side, too."

Which, she surmised, accounted for his straight black hair and bold features.

"What about you?" he asked.

"Me?" She shrugged. "I'm white bread."

"White bread means plain, Kendra." He roamed his dark gaze over her. "And there's nothing plain about you."

Her skin went warm. He had such a sexy way of making her feel beautiful. "I'm English, French, and Scandinavian."

"So there you go." He was still gazing at her. "We've got French roots in common."

"I don't know the language."

"I'm not fluent, either. I only know enough to get by. Besides, French isn't spoken much here anymore, except among the Cajuns, and they have their own dialect."

"Isn't Creole a French dialect, too?"

"It's not a dialect. It's a language, and in Louisiana it was derived from French with traces of Spanish, Native, and African influences."

"Like the people?"

He nodded. "*Bonswa* means good evening or good night in Creole. So this is the Good Night Inn."

"That works." She imagined having plenty of good nights here.

They finished making the po'boys, then sat across from each other at the kitchen table and dived in. It was just about the messiest sandwich Kendra had ever eaten. But it was wonderfully spicy, too.

"So what do you do?" he asked.

She blotted her mouth. "Do?"

"Your job."

"I work for a charity that helps the homeless."

"Really? That's great. New Orleans could sure use a girl like you. Parts of this city are still suffering."

"Were you here during the storm?"

He shook his head. "I inherited the house after it happened. But I'm happy to be involved in the regrowth."

"The organization I work for has an office here. I could probably get transferred if I set my mind to it."

"Would you want to live in the Big Easy?"

Good question. Would she?

Yes, she thought, if it meant making some sort of life with him. Once again, she cursed the fountain and its voodoo. Honestly, how mixed up could she be?

Unsure of how to respond, she skirted the issue. "So what's your favorite thing to do here?"

"Mostly I work. But I like going to blues clubs."

"I've been to some bigger blues venues in L.A., but I've never been to one of those smoky little retro clubs."

"I know of a place like that, and I'd be glad to take you." He looked directly across the table at her. "Maybe tonight?"

He was asking her on a date? Kendra's heart went pitter-pat. Foolish and girlish. "I'd love to go with you."

Tonight or any other night, she thought, unable to fight the spell she was under.

As James escorted his companion into the club, the singer moaned out a Skip James song and a harmonica wailed from one of the other players.

"Is this what you had in mind?" he asked her.

She nodded. "I feel like I'm in another world."

"You are." Smoke drifted in shadowed corners, clinging to scarred wood and purple velvet.

He glanced around and located a table in back, and they were forced to sit body-heat close.

Once they were settled, he put his hand on her knee, pleased that she'd worn a short skirt. He appreciated that women rarely wore stockings anymore. He loved the look and feel of bare flesh. Leaning forward, he kissed her, tongue and all. James wasn't prone to Frenching in public, but this place and this woman seemed to demand it.

They separated, and she looked about ready to climb into his lap. He still had his hand on her leg.

Her breath rushed out. "I want to order a Southern cocktail. Do you have any suggestions?"

"You could do a mint julep. Or if you want something that originated in New Orleans, you could try a Sazerac. It dates back to the eighteen hundreds. The original recipe was French brandy, a secret blend of bitters, a splash of water, and a bit of sugar."

"What's the recipe now?"

"It's pretty much the same except it calls for rye instead of brandy, and the bitters are no longer a secret." James let his hand creep up a bit more, moving toward her thigh. "You're supposed to sip it slowly so you can taste the layers. The rye is spicy with a touch of honey."

She looked into his eyes. "I'll get one of those."

"Good choice." He kissed her once again, savoring her much in the way he'd told her to savor the drink.

As soon as they came up for air, the cocktail waitress appeared at their table. With her dark skin, bright cotton dress, and thick accent, James suspected that she was a Creole of color. She smiled quite seductively. She'd obviously watched them kiss.

Kendra ordered a Sazerac. James gazed curiously at the waitress and went for a gin and tonic.

When she left he said, "She looks like Marie Laveau's daughter."

Kendra blinked. "That's not funny, James."

"I'm not trying to be funny. She reminds me of the paintings I've seen of her."

"What was the daughter's name? I don't think you ever told me."

"Her name was Marie, just like her mother.

"There were two Marie Laveaus?"

He nodded, and soon the waitress returned with their order, shooting him the same seductive smile. As she walked away, the band began to play "I Put a Spell on You."

Kendra shivered. "Okay, now this is getting creepy."

He latched on to his drink and took a quick belt. "It's nothing to worry about."

Clearly, she wasn't convinced. "A mystic fountain, a telling song, and a cocktail waitress who resembles a voodoo queen. How can that not be something to worry about?"

"The waitress isn't a ghost." To make his point, he added, "Everyone else at the club can see her, too." Or could they? Maybe her appearance looked different to the rest of the patrons.

"Whoever or whatever she is, I think it's proof that we're both under the same spell."

"Maybe so, but it doesn't matter, does it? The magic was already at work before you got here. You with your dreams, me restoring the dungeon. We were meant to have this affair."

"It was a predestined spell, and when I leave New Orleans, it'll be broken?" She searched his gaze. "Is that what you're saying?"

"Yes." Or so he hoped. "I should take the dungeon apart after you're gone, just to be sure." To stop the craving, he thought. To keep from missing her.

"So, when this is over between us, you're never going to do to anyone else what you've been doing to me?"

"No, I'm not." He couldn't imagine pinning another butterfly to his wheel. "What about you? Are you going to do it again?"

"No way. When I get home, the crazy sex is over."

"What about tonight?" He was already excruciatingly close to her, but he moved closer, putting his hand back on her thigh. "Do you want to go to the dungeon later? Do you want be crazy?"

"God, yes."

This time, she initiated the kiss, and as their mouths came together, the band rolled into "Hoodoo Party," a song about voodoo kings and queens and wild nights in New Orleans.

Chapter 7

Kendra entered the dungeon and glanced over at James. Maybe it was better that he'd been bewitched, too. At least it made her feel less alone.

But was it the same for him? Was it as powerful? Had falling in love entered the equation for him?

"What's wrong?" he asked, making her aware that she'd been frowning.

"I was thinking about the spell."

"I thought we already figured that out."

"We did, but I was just wondering if you . . ." She tried to think of a simple way to say it, but no matter how she fused the words together in her mind, it seemed complicated.

"If I what?"

She spoke quietly. "If you've been worried about falling in love, if the spell has affected you in that way."

He went statue still. Even the rise and fall of his chest stopped. Was he still breathing?

"James?"

He blinked, moved, visibly breathed. "Is that what it's been doing to you?"

Her stomach went tight. But worse was the pressure around her heart. "I've been telling myself how crazy it is." Crazy sex. Crazy love. She was overwhelmed by it.

He tugged a hand through his hair, scattering the stylishly messy layers. "What does falling in love feel like?"

She considered his question carefully. "I don't think I really know."

That gave him pause. "Didn't you love your ex?"

"Yes, but it wasn't the kind of love I've heard other people talk about. It wasn't consuming or obsessive. It didn't make me ache inside."

"And you're getting achy over me?"

She tried not to wince. "Yes."

"I feel that way about you, too." He made a troubled expression. "But what we're experiencing can't be love. That doesn't make sense."

"I know." But knowing didn't make it any less confusing. "It's probably just lust."

"I've been calling it an addiction."

"That's a good description." A logically tormented way to define it. "And since it's just part of a spell, it isn't real anyway. We're not going to feel this way forever."

"Can you imagine how that would mess with our lives? We'd never be able to think straight again." He glanced around. "This place would keep screwing with our minds."

"That's why you're going to dismantle it."

"Totally. Everything is going to go. I'm going to seal up the door, too."

She took a step closer. "We better hurry up and take advantage while we still can." Another step. "I want to touch you."

"Here?" He unzipped his fly.

"Yes."

He untucked his shirt and unbuttoned it, leaving the tails hanging open. Then he took her hand and guided it down the front of his pants.

She felt young and wild, groping him like a teenager and making him fully erect.

James kissed her, and they stripped off their clothes, deep in the throes of their addiction.

He asked, "Do you want to be restrained?"

"Always." She couldn't imagine it any other way.

He retrieved a pair of padded handcuffs and locked her wrists together in front of her.

He stepped back. "Get on your knees."

Anxious for what came next, she dropped down and inhaled the dungeon's aroma: new leather, restored wood, lemon-scented polish.

She knew how hard he'd worked to renovate it, and by next week, it would be gone. But so would she. New Orleans would be a memory.

James moved forward and stood directly in front of her, putting his cock closer to her face.

He slid his hands into her hair. "Do you know how badly I want this?"

"Bad enough to push it into my mouth?"

"Is that how you want it?"

"Yes." She liked that he was letting the fantasy play out in a way that kept him in control, creating the submissive feeling she craved.

He cupped the back of her head, and within the thrust of a heartbeat, she was giving him a blow job. He watched her, and she reveled in the power that being powerless gave her.

"Use your hands, too."

Oh, yes, her cuffed hands. She lifted them up, and the metal jangled. She sucked and stroked. She fondled his balls. She did everything an obedient lover should do.

He rocked his hips, and all she could think was that this wildly exotic man was fucking her mouth. With every movement, his abs tensed.

Drops of semen pearled from the tip. She wanted him to come full force, but he didn't.

He pulled away, leaving her reeling for more fellatio-driven madness.

"Stand up, Kendra."

She rose from her knees, and he orchestrated the scene so she was lying on the wooden bondage table, and he was straddling her face in a backward position.

Her pussy went warm and wet. She couldn't have imagined a hotter scenario, especially when he lowered his head and went sixty-nine.

As he licked her, she pleasured him. They laved and sucked and painted each other with their tongues.

A syrupy sensation flowed through her veins, tingling her heart, tantalizing her clit.

She came in a wave of emotion, her cuffed hands gripping the base of James's penis while he moved inside her mouth.

Her climax triggered his, and he tensed, then thrust deeper, finally spilling into her.

He waited a beat before he lifted his body from hers. He got off the table and stood beside it, looking down at her. With the salty taste of him on her lips, she returned his gaze, and the primal intimacy just about knocked her for a loop.

He leaned over and kissed her, and she felt as if she were part of an erotic fairy tale. A submissive princess locked in a dungeon tower with a dominant prince.

Talk about bewitchment.

"Do you know how truly beautiful you are?" he asked.

Not nearly as beautiful as he was, she thought.

Kendra sat up, but she didn't get off the table. She swung her legs around, and James stood between them.

He removed the restraints, and she wrapped her arms around him, putting her cheek against his chest.

"I'm going to bring some of the toys into my apartment," he said. "So we can play in bed, too. Is that okay with you?"

She responded with a definite, "Yes." All Kendra wanted was to be his lover—everywhere and anywhere.

Until the spell was broken and she would be able to survive without him.

James leaned on his elbow and gazed at Kendra. She looked warm and sultry in his bed, the sheet draped over her naked body.

"Tell me about where you live," he said.

She made a puzzled expression. "Haven't you ever been to L.A.?"

"Yes, but I'm curious about what part of the city you're in, if you have a house or apartment. You know, that sort of thing."

"I'm in Glendale. I live in a one-bedroom duplex with planter boxes on the windows. I put herbs in them in the summer and perennials the rest of the year."

"What about the interior? What's that like?"

"My kitchen is yellow with frilly curtains, and my living room is mostly beige, with bits of yellow and blue. Nothing too interesting."

It all sounded interesting to him. "How about the bedroom?"

"It's beige and blue, too."

"Do you have a backyard?"

"It's a little patio. I put a couple of chairs out there and a gas barbecue."

He imprinted her lifestyle on his mind. He wanted to envision her after she was gone.

Why? So he could remember her fondly? Or because he was going to miss her so badly?

He didn't want to think too deeply about what they'd discussed earlier, but it kept zinging through his mind.

Lust . . .

Love . . .

He knew better than to mix them up. But damn if it didn't make him feel strange inside. Carnal voodoo. Emotion-laced magic. He couldn't seem to get enough.

He stared at her. "I want to blindfold you."

She clutched the edge of the sheet. "Right now?"

He nodded. "Will you let me?"

Her voice quavered. "There's nothing I wouldn't let you do."

"Then why do you sound afraid?"

"It's overwhelming to want to give so much to someone."

He understood her reasoning. He was overwhelmed, too.

Anxious, he opened the nightstand drawer and dug through the toys he'd brought from the dungeon, removing a satin eye mask created for sensory play.

As Kendra sat forward, the sheet slid to her waist, revealing her breasts. Already her nipples were hard.

He slipped the mask around her eyes. "All dark?"

"Yes."

A pair of silk restraints came next. He tied her wrists to the iron bedposts and nudged her thighs open.

"How do you feel?" he asked.

She shifted her hips a bit shyly, a bit wantonly. "Exposed."

James admired his bound-and-blindfolded lover. Her wild innocence never failed to excite him.

He opened a bottle of lubricant and rubbed a dollop between her legs. "Describe the sensation."

"It's wet and silky."

He put a finger inside her and moved it in and out, stroking softly. Then he went for two fingers, just as gently, just as erotically. "What about this?"

"It feels warm and slippery. But it also feels like you're preparing me for something bigger."

Clever girl. He took two dildos from the drawer. He rubbed the first one over her nipples and down her stomach. "Do you like this one?" He repeated the same pattern with the second phallus. "Or this one?"

She shivered sexily. "Are they the same size?"

"Yes." He gazed at the toys. "Seven inches of insertable cock, with a nice thick circumference."

"Then I like them both."

How naughty could she be? "You have to choose a favorite."

"Touch me with them again."

He used the dildos at the same time, running them everywhere, along her outstretched arms, down the sides of her body, across the top of her pussy, and over each widespread leg.

Her breath caught. "I still can't decide. Will you tell me what they look like?"

"They're identical, except for the color. One is clear, and the other one is gold."

"Metallic gold?"

"Yes. Why? Does that intrigue you?"

She nodded. "I've never imagined having something shiny inside me."

"Then gold it is." He leaned over to kiss her, just once, before he made hot, slick love to her with an artificial penis.

She moaned softly under his mouth, and he cursed the spell. How was he ever going to touch another woman and not think about her?

James ended the kiss and readied the dildo, adding a thin layer of lubricant. He inserted it slowly, giving her an inch at a time.

The dominance of the act aroused him, and so did her reaction. She lifted her hips, offering him the pleasure of her excitement.

He went deeper, then studied her expression. She was sucking her bottom lip between her teeth.

The sweet sub.

He worked her with the dildo, fucking her with gilded warmth. By the time he increased the tempo, she was wild with need and making breathy sounds. He kept thrusting the phallus, but he rubbed her clit, too.

Teasing her. Arousing her.

She tugged on her bonds, and James played her until she came, until she shook and shivered and thrashed uncontrollably.

When he removed her blindfold, they stared achingly at each other. But it was just lust, he reminded himself.

Lust and only lust.

One week drifted into the next, and James and Kendra spent as much time together as they could. Of course, he still had a bed-and-breakfast to run.

He sat behind his office desk, organizing the summer schedule. Cathy and Ken had gone home, but two more weddings were pending.

Not that he cared. At the moment, all he wanted was to be with Kendra, and she was right upstairs in his apartment. Unable to concentrate, he ditched his work.

As he crossed the parlor, he ran into Claire.

"Where are you going in such a hurry?" she asked.

He tapped his antsy feet. "Nowhere."

"Nowhere, my butt. You're playing hooky to get some nooky."

Guilty as charged, he frowned at her. "Jesus, Claire."

She grinned. "I'm just saying." She stifled her grin. "Go on. Shoo. Be with your girl."

He did exactly that. He shook his head and continued on his way. But he didn't get far.

Claire said from behind him, "Be careful, James, or you just might fall in love."

He spun around. Love was the last thing he wanted to talk about or think about or get consumed with. "It isn't like that."

"It could be."

"But it isn't." Done with the conversation, he shot her a look that said not to mention it again. She didn't know about the magic, and he wasn't inclined to tell her.

Silent, she let him be. Grateful for the reprieve, he headed upstairs and entered his apartment.

Kendra was curled up on the sofa in front of the TV, and as she turned toward him, he was struck by how sweet and cozy she looked in his home. It made him feel married.

Married?

Christ, he thought. Marie's daughter was really doing a number on him. Claire's comment probably factored into it, too. He was getting it from all sides.

"I needed a break from work," he told Kendra, explaining why he'd shown up.

She patted the space next to her, and he sat down. They took a moment to kiss softly, chastely.

When they separated he asked, "What are you watching?"

"*The Wedding Planner.*" She frowned. "Me, the one who isn't into weddings."

James frowned, too. Another voodoo influence? "I was working on the upcoming wedding schedules. Maybe our minds were in sync."

She turned off the TV. "That must be it."

Determined to banish the wedding stuff, he reached for her again, kissing her deeply this time, letting her know exactly what he wanted.

More than compliant, she straddled his lap, and the foreplay began.

He unbuttoned her blouse and unhooked her bra. Once her breasts were bared, he caressed them, making her nipples peak beneath his touch.

She sighed, and James tugged off her jeans and divested her of her underwear. She undressed him, too, but before she tossed his pants aside, he snatched a condom from the pocket.

He handed her the packet and told her to do it.

Beautifully submissive, she tore it open. And while she fitted him with the rubber and made him desperate for her, he promised himself that when the week was over, he would be done with Kendra.

No matter how much it pained him to let her go.

Chapter 8

Kendra sat on a wrought-iron bench in the courtyard at the inn. Flowers bloomed all around her, bright and cheerful in hanging baskets.

But that didn't improve her mood. Her vacation was almost over. Tomorrow she would be going home.

While she stressed about leaving, James was off running errands. *Errands.* It sounded so trivial. She couldn't help feeling hurt that he hadn't taken the day off to be with her.

She closed her eyes, doing her best to relax. When something tickled her hand, she opened her eyes and saw that a butterfly had flitted past her fingers and landed on a nearby flower. A viceroy? A monarch? She couldn't tell. Either way, the symbolism struck her.

Innocence. Transformation.

Was this a sign? Was she supposed to emerge from her cocoon and admit that what she felt for James was real?

Yes, she thought, she was. Because no matter how much she blamed the fountain or the wish she'd made or Marie Laveau's daughter, Kendra was responsible for her own heart. No amount of voodoo could make a woman ache this badly.

Footsteps sounded, and she looked up. It was an elderly couple who'd checked in yesterday. They said hello and walked toward the gazebo.

Kendra returned her attention to the butterfly, but it was gone. Fleeting, like her time in New Orleans.

Before she got teary eyed, she left the courtyard and went into the library, finding a quiet spot to be completely alone.

At dusk, James entered the room, and she missed him already. He looked so tall, so dark, so elusive.

"I've been searching all over for you," he said.

She lifted the book in her hands. "I've been reading." Mostly she'd been staring blankly at the pages.

"I have a surprise for you, Kendra."

Excitement fluttered low in her belly. Had he been reanalyzing his feelings, too?

"A surprise?" she parroted.

He nodded. "I want our last night together to be special."

Their last night. Her heart deflated, but she refused to let it show. Whatever he had in store for her, she would rejoice in it.

He led her to the dungeon, where he'd draped the bondage table with red satin and wound silk roses around the stockade. He'd also created a cozy sitting area, using furniture from the attic. Heightening the ambience were red and white candles, flickering in tall brass candelabras.

"I wasn't running errands," he said. "I was doing this."

Her heart tripped and stumbled. "It's beautiful." She noticed a small table with two crystal bowls filled with bread pudding. "You made my favorite dessert."

"It's the Creole recipe, with bourbon sauce. It seemed like a good time for you to try it."

"It looks wonderful." So did the wine he'd provided to go with it.

"I have a gift for you, too." He reached into his pocket and handed her a jewelry-sized box.

She opened the top and discovered a pendant with a butterfly perched on a silver arrow. The necklace was adorned with seed pearls, garnets, and topaz.

She blinked back tears, and he said, "It's from the Victorian era."

"It's exquisite. Thank you." She lifted her gaze to his. "I saw our butterfly today. Or one that looked like it."

"Really? Maybe it's part of the magic. No matter what we do, we can't seem to escape it."

She ventured a romantic response. "Maybe we're not supposed to."

"I guess not. At least not yet." He took the pendant from her. "Let me help you put it on."

She turned and lifted her hair, and he placed it around her neck and closed the clasp. Afterward, he circled her waist, pressing the front of his body to the back of hers.

Warm in his embrace, she turned to face him, to look into his eyes. If only tomorrow would never come, if only she could stay with him forever.

"Do you think butterflies represented transformation in the Victorian era?" she asked. "Or innocence or any of the symbolism that applies today?"

"I don't know. Everything was supposed to be innocent then." He glanced around. "That's why it shocked me when I discovered this dungeon. It didn't fit the house."

"It does now. You glamorized it, James."

"Yes, but it's just for tonight."

He opened the wine, and they sat on a battered settee and enjoyed dessert. The flavor of late-harvest Riesling and Creole pudding melted on her tongue.

"After we eat, you're going to touch yourself for me," he said.

Kendra pulled the spoon out of her mouth. "I am?"

"Yes. Right over there." He indicated the satin-draped bondage table.

"I've never done that in front of anyone before."

"That makes it even better." He got up and went over to the toy cabinet and returned with a pink vibrator shaped like a penis with two prongs attached. "Have you ever used a rabbit vibrator?"

She shook her head. Her first experience with sex toys had been with him.

"The shaft goes inside and the little bunny ears stimulate the clit." He handed it to her.

She examined the pliable device and noticed separate controls for the shaft and the ears, with various speeds. She pressed the phallus switch, and the vibrator hummed in her hand. Another control made the head rotate.

She glanced up at James, and he smiled. The ache of missing him returned.

They finished the pudding, and he told her to undress. She stripped down, leaving nothing but the butterfly necklace.

Vibrator in hand, she climbed onto the table, the satin cool against her skin. James gave her a bottle of lubricant, then positioned the settee so he could watch.

He spoke softly. "Sit forward, draw up your knees, and open your legs."

She did what he asked of her, and in her mind's eye, she imagined how she looked, fully exposed and bathed in candlelight.

"Perfect," he said just as softly.

Feeling oddly romantic, she turned on the vibrator and rolled the shaft across her breasts, recalling how James had done that to her with the dildos he'd used.

She made the head rotate against one of her nipples. Knowing he was watching, she brought it to her labia and rolled it around there, too. She wanted to please him as much as he wanted her to please herself.

Taking it to the next level, she turned off the vibrator and coated it with lubricant, stroking it as if it were a real penis.

James scooted to the edge of the settee, and her breathing quickened. He had an obvious ridge beneath his fly.

She inserted the phallus, and when the ears were aligned with her clit, she turned on the vibrator, making all the parts move.

While the ears stimulated her clit, the shaft buzzed, the head rotating deep inside.

She keened out a moan, and James watched the entire time.

Steeped in her own juices, she widened her legs, giving him a sexier view. Then she lost all reason and increased the speed.

Inside and out . . .

Faster and faster . . .

Kendra came in a whirlwind, her heart spinning right along with her body.

When it ended, when she could think and breathe and move her limbs, James helped her to her feet.

Standing beside the table, they kissed, his mouth hot and hungry against hers.

"Are you ready for me?" he asked.

"Yes." *Oh, yes.* No matter how incredible the vibrator felt, nothing compared to him.

He led her to the stockade, bent her over the wood, and locked her wrists.

She heard him behind her, removing his clothes: the thud of his shoes, the rustle of his shirt, the rasp of his zipper, denim being dragged down his hips.

The tearing of a condom packet came next. Kendra suspected that it was ultrathin, that he'd chosen the sheerest protection possible. A moment later, the weight of his body bore down on hers.

One powerful thrust and he was inside.

He rode her hard and unmercifully fast. The copulating motion rocked her to the core, making the butterfly tap, tap, tap against her skin.

He didn't slow down, not for an instant, and she didn't want him to. She needed it this way.

Hot. Hammering. Unbridled.

Yet, with each lust-driven stroke, she agonized over loving him, torn between how good and how bad it felt.

He nipped the nape of her neck, scraping her with his teeth. More pain. More pleasure. Even the clamps on her wrists seemed too tight.

Beautiful bondage. Desperate domination.

She closed her eyes, and he clutched her waist and held her more possessively than he'd ever held her before.

Claiming her, she thought, for one last fractured time.

Chapter 9

James entered the bedroom while Kendra was packing. She glanced up at him, and their gazes locked. He'd offered to drive her to the airport, and he hoped and prayed that it wasn't going to be a long and painful good-bye. They were both already hurting.

He could see the ache in her eyes, the same miss-you pain churning inside of him. And on top of that was the phone call he'd made, the information that confused the hell out of him.

Should he tell her or keep it to himself?

He sat on the edge of the bed. A moment later, he got up and walked over to the window. A second after that, he plopped down on a chair and cursed his restlessness.

James decided to tell her. Otherwise it would be burning a hole in his mind, and he was already struggling with his sanity.

He said, "I called the antique store where I bought your

necklace. First I talked to the salesgirl who sold it to me, then I spoke to the owner."

"I don't understand." She clutched the pendant. "Do you think something is wrong with it?"

"No. I was curious about what butterflies meant in the Victorian era."

"And did they tell you?"

"The salesgirl didn't know, but the owner did. To the Victorians, the butterfly symbolized the soul." He frowned so hard he feared his forehead might crack. "In fact, the owner told me what that specific piece means."

Still clutching the necklace, she waited for him to expound.

He continued by saying, "The arrow is associated with Cupid, so, basically, the pendant means that love captured the giver's soul." His voice went shaky. He could hear it rattling from his chest. "*My soul*, since I'm the one who gave it to you."

Kendra didn't respond, but she gazed at him in a way that made him feel worse. His distress was obvious, and he suspected that she didn't know how she was supposed to react.

After a beat of uncomfortable silence, she asked, "Do you want the necklace back? Do you want to return it to the store?"

"No, of course not. I wouldn't take a gift away from you." Nor could he bear the thought of her not wearing it. "Do you think Marie's daughter did this?"

"Did what?"

"Drew me to the pendant and willed me to buy it for you." He dragged a hand through his hair. "What if dismantling the dungeon doesn't break the spell? What if the magic is too strong for that? Or what if I freak out after you're gone?"

She exhaled an audible breath, the sound soft and vulnerable. "Maybe you shouldn't let me go."

James resisted the urge to pace. "Don't tempt me to make this permanent, Kendra."

She lifted her chin. "Why not?"

Yes, a voice inside him asked . . . *why not?* "Because it scares me." He actually felt as if his soul had been captured. Taken hostage by a butterfly. He'd pinned her to his wheel, and now he was being pinned to hers.

"The way I feel scares me, too. But if you asked me to stay, I would. I'd transfer to New Orleans and be with you." She clutched a half-folded garment against her chest. "I love you, James."

Oh, God, he thought. Everlasting love. Everlasting voodoo. Everlasting everything.

"It's a spell," he said, still fighting the feeling.

"No, it isn't. What's happening is real. Marie's daughter just helped us along."

He imagined making her his lifelong lover. He even envisioned her being his wife, like the day she'd been watching the wedding movie. "Our life together would be crazy. We'd never stop touching each other."

"That would be okay with me. I'd let you touch me day and night."

He wanted to put his hands all over her now. But he wanted to give her his heart, too. To show her how hard it was beating.

He reached out, and she came toward him. When she fell into his embrace, he buried his face in her hair.

"Will you stay?" he asked, even if he already knew the answer.

"For an eternity," she responded, pressing closer to him.

"Will you come upstairs with me?" He wanted to seal their fate, and he wanted to do it in the dungeon, a place he was no longer going to dismantle.

She went willingly, and he knew he was making the right decision. This was his destiny. Her destiny. The world they were meant to share.

Once they were inside the secret room, he unbuttoned her blouse and slipped off her skirt until it pooled around her feet. He got rid of her bra and panties, making her beautifully bare.

Lost in the feeling, he led her to the bondage wheel and strapped her onto it. When she was secure, when he could look directly into her eyes, he said, "I love you, too."

Sweet and tender, she smiled, making him glad, so very glad, that they belonged to each other.

Later that day, Kendra and James went to a coin shop, then to the *Jaillissement de Plaisir*.

For Kendra, it was a poignant moment. They'd brought special coins to toss into the water, not to make a wish, but to thank Marie's daughter for bringing them together.

James said it was going to be a voodoo offering, as he seemed certain that the younger queen would appreciate the coins they'd chosen, one representing the year of her birth and another one that was minted in the year she'd died.

As they walked through the garden, Kendra inhaled the floral scent. They reached the base of the fountain, and she gazed at the three muses.

"They're beautiful, aren't they?" she said, aware that this was James's first time seeing them.

"They're more than beautiful." He steeped closer to the fountain. "They're mesmerizing."

She stood quietly, letting him absorb the feeling. Then she looked across the courtyard, where a brick wall stood. Beyond it were a series of balconies that lorded over the garden. "Is that the *maison*?"

He followed her line of sight. "Yes, that's it."

"It actually seems kind of sexy." Now that she knew what it was.

"Everything is sexy when we're together." He turned to look at her. "I'd make love to you right here, right now, if I could."

She melted inside. "I'll bet the muses would like that."

"Marie's daughter, too." He leaned forward to kiss her, to put his mouth against hers.

It was a light touch, a gentle kiss, but it was highly sensual, too. Their bodies brushed in the most provocative way.

A moment later, they faced the fountain once again, but the feeling of togetherness remained.

She gazed at the *Jaillissement de Plaisir*, then studied the inscription on it: *Tout quoi vous voulez*.

"What does that mean?" she asked.

"All that you wish."

She had all that she wished, all that she'd dreamed.

"Ready?" he asked, removing the coins from his pocket.

She nodded, and he gave her one of them. Although neither was rare, they held emotional value.

They tossed them at the same time, and the coins spun before hitting the water. As they plunked to the bottom, a small breeze blew. Proof, Kendra thought, that magic was in the air, and that it belonged to her and James.

Always and forever.